Double Indemnity

Maggie Kavanagh

Dreamspinner Press

Published by
DREAMSPINNER PRESS

5032 Capital Circle SW, Suite 2, PMB# 279, Tallahassee, FL 32305-7886 USA
http://www.dreamspinnerpress.com/

Double Indemnity
© 2015 Maggie Kavanagh.

Cover Art
© 2015 Maria Fanning.
Cover content is for illustrative purposes only and any person depicted on the cover is a model.

ISBN: 978-1-63216-377-6
Digital ISBN: 978-1-63216-378-3
Library of Congress Control Number: 2014951373
First Edition January 2015

Printed in the United States of America
∞
This paper meets the requirements of
ANSI/NISO Z39.48-1992 (Permanence of Paper).

To my partner in crime, always.

Acknowledgments

Writing does not occur in a vacuum, and I'm incredibly grateful to have the support of so many people. Thank you in particular to Olivia, Michela, and Asya, dear friends who have offered their insightful feedback and cheerleading at all stages of the drafting and editing process. This novel wouldn't exist without them.

Chapter 1

SAM HAD never believed in alien abduction stories, but the way he felt, he finally understood how those rumors got started. He squinted at the mildewing shower curtain and tried to recall the night before. His head hurt, though, and thinking was hard. His ass hurt too, but it didn't take a genius to figure out the reason. It sure as hell hadn't been the work of an anal probe. At least not an alien anal probe.

Honey, it was aliens. Aliens made me drink a ton of booze and then fucked my ass, I swear.

He tilted his head and let the spray wash away the taste of cock and beer. From the way his back and neck ached, it seemed like it had been a night to remember. How ironic.

"Ouch. Dammit." He cursed as the shower went from lukewarm to scorching hot, which meant the little talk he'd had with apartment 512 the week before about the shared water supply hadn't had the desired effect. Protecting his balls with one hand, he fought the showerhead with the other, forcing it toward the wall so he wouldn't cook himself. He needed to get a new place. The same thought occurred to him every time this happened, and yet he'd lived in the building for over five years. But doing the same thing over and over and expecting different results was pretty much his credo.

It would be a shame to change now.

When he stepped onto the shirt serving as a bath mat, he rubbed his hands over his face to determine whether he needed a shave. The stubble hadn't started to itch yet. Bloodshot hazel eyes stared back at

1

him in the mirror—a reminder he hadn't slept more than four hours. Still, with youth on his side, he didn't look too bad, in spite of the comical contrast between his tan neck and arms and his pale chest. He ran his hands through his damp, dirty blond hair and decided against applying product. It would only sweat down his face once he got to work.

It seemed primed to be another brutal New England summer day with 100 percent humidity. Even the air outside the bathroom felt mossy and wet. Sam grabbed a pair of not-too-dirty shorts from the laundry and pulled on a Manella's Landscaping tee, then pocketed his keys and headed for the door. Along the way he caught a glimpse of a discarded baseball hat. Yankees. *Yuri's.*

The answer to what had happened last night. Or rather, who.

He grabbed the hat, and his phone buzzed in his back pocket.

"What's up, Rach?"

"Oh my God, Sam. You will never believe what happened." A trace of alarm edged Rachel's usually smooth voice.

"Are you okay? What's going on?"

"Mark Feldman is dead."

Sam froze in his tracks. "What? How?"

"I don't know. It's breaking right now. Sounds like the cops found him at home, though. Do you have a minute before work? I'm at the Star."

Sam glanced at the time. "Yeah, I'll come down." He didn't technically have to be at the Walkers' place for another hour.

"See you in a few."

The Lucky Star pub tried a bit too hard to be Irish and wound up on just the wrong side of cheesy. Still, they had good burgers, better fries, and the best bartender in Stonebridge, Connecticut—if you asked Sam, though he'd admit to bias. Sam gave the window a tappity-tap-tap since the place wouldn't open until noon, and a few seconds later the door swung open. Rachel's full lips were set in a grim line. She gestured him inside before the neighborhood drunks got wind and descended en masse.

The room was empty. A spray bottle full of cleaner and some rags sat abandoned on one of the small round tables in the general seating area, evidence Rachel had been cleaning up from the night before.

2

Sam's boots stuck to the floor, making Velcro sounds with each step as he followed Rachel toward the bar, where one of the TVs was tuned into a morning newscast. He did a double take. Words flashed on the screen below a large picture of a smiling man he recognized as Mark Feldman. *Local Philanthropist Found Dead.*

"Hot damn. CNN?" Sam slid onto his favorite stool.

"Yep. And Fox News." Rachel rolled her eyes and smoothed her Afro away from her face. "It's practically a national story."

"Glory comes to Stonebridge in strange ways." Sam snorted. "Hell, I think I need a beer."

"After how drunk you were last night? I don't think so."

"Haven't you ever heard of hair of the dog?"

Rachel smacked his arm with a bar towel. "Just shut up and listen."

They both turned their attention to the TV as the male reporter introduced a local news briefing. The screen changed to the pressroom at the courthouse, one Sam was familiar with from the few times the local newspaper had called him in to cover a story. Chief Sheldon stood at the podium wearing his grandpa reading glasses, perfectly poised. His bushy gray eyebrows were drawn together, a telltale sign he was serious.

Sam grinned. "The old man's on TV. Would you look at that?"

"At six fifteen this morning, we received a call from a family member who found Mr. Feldman unresponsive. Police and medics reported to the scene, but all attempts to revive the deceased were unsuccessful. We will keep you updated with the latest as the case develops. Right now I ask that reporters give the family the respect and privacy they deserve during this terrible time. Thank you." Sheldon began to back away, but not before being hit by a barrage of questions.

One reporter, a guy from the *Gazette*, yelled the loudest. "Is it true you found him in the bathtub?"

Sheldon frowned, and he glanced over his shoulder at someone else before turning back to the crowd of reporters. "Yes."

"Was it a suicide?"

"I have no further comments at this point."

"Did you find a note?"

"Again, no further details are available at this time. Thank you."

To put a definitive end to the conference, Sheldon strode away, a couple of deputies trailing behind him. The news cut back to the main studio. "That was Chief of Police Dan Sheldon with a short briefing of what we already knew, that local financier and philanthropist, Mark Feldman, has been found dead in his home. Cause of death is under investigation."

Rachel sighed and crossed her arms. "You think it was a suicide?"

"No idea. It seemed like he had everything going for him."

In the last several years, Mark Feldman had gained popularity for restoring some of Stonebridge's crumbling, turn-of-the-century buildings with personal funds. He'd planned to save even more with the help of his eponymous nonprofit foundation. Sam suspected he was gearing up to run as the democratic candidate for mayor, which would have pitted him against Mayor White, a recently re-elected Republican with a twenty-year history in the city. Though White's policies continued to ignore the ongoing poverty and drug crisis downtown in favor of courting wealthier suburban inhabitants, he'd won a landslide victory over his latest opponent. People were afraid of change. In a few years, however, Feldman would have been the perfect challenger. Well, not anymore, Sam thought morosely. Though he hadn't personally known Feldman, he'd respected what the guy had tried to do for the city.

Sam sighed as another pundit joined the first for more conjecture. Maybe the *Gazette* would give him a call for Feldman's obit, unless they already had one written and ready to go. Feldman was as close to famous as you got in Stonebridge. He hoped he'd get to write it. He could use the money, and lately his assignments from the paper had been few and far between. Damn budget cuts.

"So what does this mean for Stonebridge?" Rachel asked.

"Well, with any luck, this won't put an end to the restoration projects. Come to think of it, I wouldn't be surprised if White had Feldman killed 'cause he was making him look bad."

Rachel rubbed her hands up and down her smooth arms, as though she were fighting a chill. "You don't really mean that. I mean, granted, White is a douchebag, but that's taking it a little far."

"Maybe. Maybe not." Sam eyed the taps. Just a half-pint would clear his headache right up. "I'm only saying it smells fishy to me."

"That's the breeze coming in from the docks. Anyway, if you're so convinced something is going on, why don't you write about it for your blog? You talk enough, but I don't see you doing shit. When's the last time you wrote something really good?"

"I'm busy." Sam's schedule with Manella's and occasional pieces for the *Gazette* left him little time for his pet project. He barely had time to sleep, let alone write.

"I know you are, baby." Rachel gave his hand a pat, and her dark eyes grew soft. "You going to see Tim today?"

"Yeah. Later on." Sam looked away. "Speaking of which, I better head out."

"To tend the yuppie lawns."

He grinned at her and leaned over the bar to kiss her cheek. "Touché."

THE DRIVE from downtown to the suburbs of West Stonebridge took around twenty minutes. Houses turned into estates and then grew fewer and farther apart, and eventually gave way to farmland and wilderness. The contrast never failed to make him a little sorry for Stonebridge, which, despite the pretty name, was a huge dump of a port city. Most of it, anyway. Out here the air got fresher, the colors brighter, the people richer.

Sam cranked up the A/C in his truck and stopped for a coffee to wash down a couple of aspirin to kill his hangover. His first stop was the Walkers' place, an old converted farmhouse on acres of land, most of which was covered with trees. Sam had often wondered what it would be like to live with nothing but bears and bunnies for neighbors. It might get lonely, but at least the water temperature would always be just right. He parked his Ford flatbed on the gravel driveway and hopped out. Because the job was only a weekly mow and maintain, Sam hadn't bothered to ask any of the other workers to join him. And

Yuri had taken the day off, Sam remembered, so he wouldn't see his partner until the next day. At least it would avoid another awkward morning after.

Emma Walker's cruiser was still parked in the drive when he pulled in, and next to it, her husband Nathan's sleek black Mercedes. Sam's pulse quickened like it always did, but the butterflies in his stomach reached swarm proportions when he noticed Nathan getting out of the driver's side.

With his black sunglasses and trendy suit, the cut of which showed off his powerful shoulders and trim waist, Nathan couldn't have looked less rustic in front of his country home. His dark hair gleamed in the morning sun.

He had a few inches on Sam, and Sam had often admired his swimmer's build on the occasions Nathan was home while Sam worked the yard. The guy could do laps for hours as Sam mowed and raked and tried not to marvel at the way he cut through the water like a hot knife through butter. An attractive man, but a very heterosexual, very married, man, Sam reminded himself as he returned Nathan's wave. He pulled something out of his trunk—a suitcase—and vanished into the house. Sam often wondered where Nathan disappeared to on all of those long trips. He could have been a government agent or some kind of contractor. Even a hit man.

"Heya, Sam." Emma Walker appeared at the front door wearing her uniform, her red hair frizzing out around her head. She was a petite woman with pale skin and wide blue eyes. On more than one occasion, Sam had wondered if the whole country-living thing had been her idea in the first place.

"Emma," he greeted her, slamming the door to his truck. He didn't need to unload. The Walkers had a riding mower in their barn and plenty of tools, most of them left over from the previous owners. The former occupants had maintained a functioning apple orchard, and an unpaved, winding road led from the side of the barn, past the house, and up to the groves. One of these days, Sam would get up there and see about pruning the trees.

"It's a scorcher," said Emma. "You be sure to come in and have a drink if you need one. Nathan just got back from a trip, so he'll be working from home."

"Thanks. I appreciate it." Today would probably be one of those swimming days, then. His pulse spiked at the thought.

"Well, I'm off." She blew out a breath. "I really can't believe Mark Feldman is dead. Mess of paperwork today, and I'm sure things will be crazy down at the station. I'd rather stay home and help you in the yard, to be honest."

"You hear anything else about it? I saw the chief's briefing."

"Nothing until we get the autopsy results, but we won't rule anything out until then. I feel so awful for his family."

"Yeah," Sam agreed. He knew more than a little about loss, but he wasn't going to bring it up right then. "Hey, I'm thinking of doing something for my blog. Maybe we can chat once the results are in?" He gave her his most winning smile.

Emma smiled back. "Yes. That would be fine. It'll be at least a few days, though." She glanced at her watch. "I've got to go, but I meant what I said about asking Nathan if you need anything. The last thing we want is for you to pass out from heatstroke. Don't you have a hat?"

Sam watched her slim figure retreat and then grabbed Yuri's stupid Yankees cap from the cab of his truck. Better to wear it than burn to a crisp.

Mark Feldman was dead, and he couldn't have been more than fifty. Sam had met him a couple of times around town, and in each instance the man had been gracious, if a bit frayed around the edges. He'd apparently lost a lot of money in the market crash. Maybe that drove him to draw his last bath. Or maybe he'd slipped and fallen. In cases like this, sometimes you never found out.

The sweltering morning drew on, filled with smells of gasoline and freshly cut grass. At least his noise-canceling headphones muffled the sound of the riding mower. He put his foot on the brake and whipped his shirt off, then used it to mop the sweat off his brow. He couldn't imagine Nathan objecting, and no one else was around for miles.

The thought appealed to him a little more than it probably should.

He'd just finished the front yard when he looked up and was startled to find he wasn't alone. Nathan stood not ten feet away, watching him and holding what appeared to be a glass of iced tea. The towel slung over his shoulder indicated his intent to swim. Sam cut the mower engine and stood up. He hoped his sweat wasn't visible through his shorts.

"Emma told me to make sure you didn't keel over out here." Nathan extended his tan, muscled arm. No visible tattoos. He could have been a swimsuit model.

"Thanks. I appreciate it." A long sip of the strong and lemony tea soothed Sam's throat, though Nathan's proximity was disarming. His dark eyes focused on Sam and seemed to assess him.

"So you're a Yankees fan?"

An uncomfortable moment passed, during which Sam tried to figure out what the hell Nathan meant. "Pardon my French, but fuck no."

"It's just… your hat."

Sam blushed and tugged the thing off his head. "This isn't mine, it's a friend's. I was wearing it because of the sun."

"Ah, I see." Nathan's mouth curved in a half smile as he watched Sam drain the rest of the tea. "Sox, then."

"Of course."

"Do you want some more?"

Sam shook his head and passed back the glass. "Nah, thanks. I'm good." He knew he should probably get back to work, but his legs refused to move. "So what do you think about this whole Feldman thing? You think he killed himself?"

"I don't know. Maybe. What do you think?"

"It's strange. People loved him, and he was really making an impact on the city. Didn't seem like a guy on the verge of killing himself, but who knows."

"You're a reporter, right?"

"I wouldn't exactly call myself a reporter. I write piecemeal for the *Gazette*. Oh, and I have a blog." Sam cringed at how stupid he sounded, but Nathan cocked his head, his expression curious.

"What's it called?"

"*Under the Bridge*." He immediately regretted saying it, and prayed Nathan would forget. He hadn't posted in months.

"Like the song."

"Yeah. Like the song."

"So what do you write about?"

Sam shrugged. "About things that piss me off. Mostly about what's going on around here, you know. There's been a lot of drug-related arrests lately, mostly of minorities. But no one wants to talk about racial profiling. No one wants to talk about inequality. They say there's no money to fill the potholes in Stonebridge, but yet the city builds a new road out to the goddamn mall so people can go waste their paychecks on hand soap. Meanwhile all the shops downtown close." Sam realized he'd started a rant and, moreover, that Nathan himself was one of the people he was railing against. "Sorry. I'll shut up now and get back to work."

"No. Don't be sorry. I agree with what you're saying."

Sam stared back at the guy, not sure if he was joking or not. Even though Sam knew Emma well enough—she was one of the few cops who didn't seem to mind his occasional presence at the station—Nathan remained an enigma. He didn't strike Sam as someone who'd be into liberal politics, for one. But you learned something new every day. "Oh."

Nathan's eyes crinkled a little at the edges as he shielded his face from the sun. "You're a smart guy, Sam. I think you're wasting your talent out here."

"There's nothing wrong with what I do."

"Of course not. I don't mean to offend. It seems from what you've said, like your interests lie elsewhere."

"I've gotta pay the bills. And, I'll have you know, I have many talents." Sam waggled an eyebrow, unable to stop himself. If Nathan noticed the flirting, he didn't seem to mind.

"How old are you, anyway?"

"Twenty-seven."

Nathan nodded. "You've got time."

Sam scrubbed a hand through his sweat-damp hair. Time. Time was one thing Sam knew a lot about. The blazing sun made his head feel like a skillet hot enough to fry an egg. Dammit. He was going to have to put the stupid Yankees hat back on.

"I don't mean to pry, but why not move to a bigger city?"

"Can't. I've got… obligations." And no way was he getting into some feelings show-and-tell with Nathan Walker.

"I understand," Nathan said simply. Sam looked down to avoid the inquisitive stare and noticed Nathan wore bright red flip-flops. His toes were long. As were his legs. Nicely muscled too and richly tan. Sam had often wondered if Nathan had Italian ancestry in spite of his English last name.

"—imagined myself."

Sam looked up when he realized Nathan had been speaking to him and he'd been daydreaming about his legs.

"Yeah, yeah." He nodded and tried to stifle a laugh. "I hear you."

Nathan arched an eyebrow and smirked like he detected Sam's bullshit, which made Sam irritable. The heat wasn't helping. Nor was the fact that Nathan's cheeks dimpled when he smiled. *Straight guy. Married guy. And I like his wife.*

"Ah, well. I better get back to work." Sam thanked Nathan again for the drink. He had two more properties to tend after this and had to hustle if he wanted to get lunch in.

Just as he'd expected, Nathan was in the pool when Sam finished mowing. Arranged with native plants and sustainability in mind, the natural grounds in the backyard didn't require as much time for upkeep. Off to the side of the pool, Emma had a raised-bed kitchen garden that was already bursting with ripe tomatoes and herbs. Sam could see through the french pane windows directly into the tastefully furnished living room. He concentrated on his work and not on how the same glass reflected back Nathan's graceful strokes while he swam.

Sam wasn't exactly hard up. Years of working outdoors had toned and strengthened his once thin frame, and even though his face tended a shade too far in the direction of boyish for his own liking, men found his dirty-blond hair and large hazel eyes compelling. He'd gotten laid the night before, after all. His thoughts drifted to Yuri. They had a lot of history. Yuri was good looking, if a bit on the short side, with dimples and olive skin. He was smart and funny and had always been there when Sam needed him. Sam sighed and brushed away the sweat dripping into his eyes. Maybe the problem wasn't with Yuri at all.

A splash from behind made Sam look to see Nathan emerge from under water, sputtering, as if after a dive.

"Hey, Sam?"

Nathan stood up in the shallow end. His nipples pebbled into tight beads, and water ran in lucky rivulets down his chest.

"Yeah?"

"If you finish up and want to take a swim, feel free."

"I don't have a suit."

"You can use one of mine."

Sam licked his lips. If any other man had proposed the same, he would have read it as a come-on. Nathan, though, seemed genuinely concerned about Sam's comfort. There was nothing leering in his friendly expression.

"That's nice of you. Thanks. I've gotta get going, though, before it gets too late."

Nathan nodded. "Of course. But consider it an open offer."

By the time Sam finished up in the yard, Nathan was out of the water and lounging on a nearby deck chair. Sam said his good-byes before he could do any more ogling. Checking out Emma's husband didn't feel appropriate, no matter how attractive he was.

Still, as he drove away, he almost wished he'd said yes.

NOT MANY people outside of Sam's inner circle knew about Tim. It wasn't a secret, exactly, but in Sam's experience, people only treated him differently after they found out. And not for the better.

Sometimes he felt guilty for not visiting more often, but the doctors weren't sure Timmy could hear anything, anyway. Still, Sam knew better than to investigate his excuses too thoroughly. The long-term care facility greeted him with its familiar whoosh of automatic doors. Inside, the cool air-conditioning instantly dried his sweat.

A front desk nurse named Lisa, who'd worked with his brother for years, greeted him. She'd been the one who had first encouraged him to read to Tim, back when he couldn't breathe on his own. Sam had done it for hours a day, reading everything he could get his hands on. He'd read himself hoarse. Lisa had called him a wonderful brother, but Sam knew the main reason he did it, and he kept it his guilty secret. Anything was better than letting the words out.

"How's he doing today?" Sam asked, as he always did, even though he already knew the answer. Sometimes he felt like he was in a play, repeating the same lines over and over for an audience of one.

"Oh, sweetie, he's fine," she said. She gave him a warm smile. "I'm sure he'll be glad to see you."

Sam nodded and headed down the hall, averting his eyes from open doorways where death and illness hung thickly in the air, covered by the smell of antiseptic. Everything was the same pristine white. The floor shone under his dirty boots.

Tim's room was bright and sunny, white and clean. The insurance plan didn't allow for a single room, so Tim shared with another comatose patient. Her name, Sam had learned from her son a couple of months before, was Helen. She'd fallen down the stairs, and now she might never wake up to meet her grandkids.

"Hey Timmy." Sam stood next to the bed. Covered in a white sheet, his brother's thin, wasted limbs looked fragile. Only his open eyes and the slight rise and fall of his chest gave any indication he was still alive, kept that way by a feeding tube Sam'd fought tooth and nail for, though the doctors had advised against it. Bastards.

"How you doing, bud?" The words hung in the air, static. "Blink if you can hear me."

Tim didn't blink.

Chapter 2

SAM HAD never been a high-maintenance kind of guy, but living in a fourth-floor apartment during a July heat wave, he longed for a working elevator and central air. The little unit in his bedroom window wasn't cutting it anymore.

He peeled his sweaty skin from the faux leather of his desk chair, sighed, and rubbed his temples to relieve the beginnings of a tension headache. The *Gazette* had called him, after all, for the obit piece on Feldman, and it was due the following morning. It still looked like crap, even though he'd taken the day off to work on it.

Most of the time, if they didn't want to write their own, families provided him with information and he'd piece together a narrative of life that painted their beloved—or, in some cases, not-so-beloved—in a positive light, highlighting major life events and celebrating those they'd left behind. With someone like Feldman, it was hard to know where to start. His widow had refused to speak with Sam when he called. He got the daughter instead—a twentysomething product of Feldman's failed first marriage. She told him the family's stance politely but firmly. Her father hadn't committed suicide. It was an accident, and there was nothing more to say. His accomplishments would stand for themselves. Her stepmother was too distraught and too busy to talk to him. Then she hung up and left Sam sitting with his mouth open.

Since he was getting nowhere fast, Sam decided to take a trip to the station to see Emma. Maybe she'd at least have the preliminary autopsy report.

The building where Sam lived had once been a warehouse. It still felt like it too, with high ceilings, utilitarian fixtures, and blessedly cheap rent. The neighborhood was mainly working class, and Sam liked the cracked sidewalks lined with caged trees and the old lampposts that fritzed out in the middle of the night. He liked them because they reminded him this city was more than the drug deals and gang violence outsiders saw. The people who lived here knew the truth. Their community wasn't perfect, but it was real, and Sam had seen generosity the likes of which he'd never known growing up in the suburbs of West Stonebridge, where everyone inhabited their own insulated bubble.

It was a quick ten-minute walk to the station, and soon Sam was climbing the gray stone steps that led to the interior of Stonebridge's central police headquarters.

Unfortunately Rich Petersen was manning the station's front desk with one of the rookies, McCormick. This meant Petersen was in charge, which was a shame. Sam would much rather have talked to the cute, all-American jock sitting next to his old high school nemesis.

Petersen folded his arms across a chest that could have been muscular but had long since taken an unfortunate turn toward saggy. His curly, dark hair had started thinning at the temples, and a doppelganger threatened his already round chin. It was a case of the ugliness inside being reflected on the outside, so Sam didn't feel particularly bad about being superficial.

"Look what the cat dragged in." Petersen gave Sam his characteristic sneer. "What are you doing here, Flynn? We didn't order any blowjobs."

"You sure about that?" Sam arched an eyebrow at McCormick, who flushed scarlet, puffed out his chest even farther, and crossed his arms to mirror Petersen.

"Cut the crap, Flynn. What do you want?"

"I need to see Officer Walker. Is she here?"

"I dunno anyone by that name." Petersen was all feigned innocence, while McCormick stared uncomfortably at the ceiling.

"She's in with the chief," said McCormick finally, earning a dirty look from Petersen.

"All right. Well, when she's done, let her know I'm looking for her."

"We'll think about it," said Petersen.

An instant later Emma appeared from the staff offices beyond. She smiled when she noticed Sam and gave the others a wary glance. "Are you two behaving yourselves?"

"Of course," said Petersen innocently. McCormick examined his fingernails.

"Are they bothering you, Sam? I can ask the chief to give them extra paperwork."

"No more than usual." Back in high school, Petersen had led the asshole brigade—the group of kids who got their rocks off teasing the gay kids, the slow kids, the nerds. Some things never changed.

Emma patted McCormick on the arm. "Behave yourself, or you'll end up like Rich." He smiled up at her, flushing slightly at the attention, which Emma then turned back to Sam.

"What can I do for you?"

Sam held out the iced coffee he'd brought for her. "You have a minute?"

"For you? Of course."

Sam followed Emma to the break room, which was empty late in the afternoon. He pulled up one of the ugly orange plastic chairs and parked it.

"I take it this isn't a social visit." Emma said. "You're after the autopsy results?"

"Guilty as charged. Any word yet?"

She nodded. "Yeah. Report came in this morning. There was no sign of natural disease, only the water in his lungs. His stomach contents revealed pills, but we don't know what type yet. Once we get the toxicology back we'll be able to tell if the pills were enough to knock him out and cause the drowning."

"So it's a suicide?"

"It's probable, but with no note, it's hard to gauge intent. I'm on my way to talk to his pharmacist right now. Then I'm going to stop in and talk to his wife later today."

"Good luck," Sam said, snorting. "I got nothing from her, not even for the obit."

"She's probably in shock, Sam. I can't imagine what I'd do if anything happened to Nathan. At least we don't have kids yet."

Sam shook his head. "I know." He lowered his gaze. "It's awful."

"Speaking of...." Emma opened the file she'd been carrying and slid a photo over to Sam. The Feldman family beamed up at him— Mark, his wife Patricia, and their two young boys. Twins. Sam was the first to admit photos could be deceiving, but this one felt real. It was possible things had been going down behind the scenes, but there was nothing to indicate any trouble in the photo. They all seemed perfectly happy. Feldman had one arm around his wife and the other slung around the shoulder of one of his sons. The other boy sat next to his brother. Both of the kids reminded Sam of Tim at that age, smiling mischievously at the camera.

"Can I take this?"

"Sure. I've got another copy. But I've got to get going. Good luck on your piece, Sam."

"Thanks, Emma."

Later, back at his apartment, Sam stared at the photo, looking for clues about what might have gone wrong. Maybe Feldman had been a pill popper. He presented one face to the world—successful entrepreneur and benefactor—but maybe in private he couldn't deal. There was a story there, a real story. Sam's fingers itched to trash the fluff piece on his laptop and start fresh. When he first told Emma he intended to write a blog exposé about Feldman, he'd only been half-serious. Now it felt like something he could do.

The rise and fall of Mark Feldman. But what had happened that night?

Sam yawned and slapped his face to wake up. When that didn't work, he retreated to the kitchen to brew some coffee and grab a bite. His stomach rumbled a complaint as he debated the questionably old takeout containers stacked in the fridge. Diving into one of those would be living dangerously.

He slipped on his sneakers and headed for the Star.

A blast of air-conditioning scented with stale beer welcomed him graciously. Rachel was behind the counter helping a customer. She looked over when he approached the bar, smiled, and gave him a gesture some would call rude. He gestured right back.

"Damn, you look like crap," she said once she'd finished up with the other guy.

"Gee, thanks."

"You're working too much. You need a break."

"Yeah, well, you know how it is."

Before she could say anything else, he gave his order—a car bomb and a double cheeseburger, hold the onions. The Lucky Star doubled as a gay bar on Tuesdays, and you never knew how the night would progress.

Rachel nodded and turned her slim frame toward the tap. Her cropped shirt showed off her belly ring, which she'd gotten on a dare. Rachel was one of his oldest friends—they'd met freshman year of high school and stayed in touch through college. She was also the only woman he'd ever kissed—just once, as an experiment at a party. It had pretty much proven he was gay. If he couldn't fall for Rachel, he'd never fall for another woman.

When she turned back with the pint in one hand and the shot of whiskey and Irish Cream in the other, her sarcastic smirk was firmly back in place.

"Not writing tonight?" she asked.

"I am, but it's too hot. I can't even think in my place. This should help." With a practiced motion, Sam dropped the shot glass into the pint and brought the whole foaming concoction to his lips. He drank half the contents in one huge gulp as Rachel watched.

"Flynn, you're a freak."

"Thanks." He finished the rest of the drink and gently slammed the glass back on the bar, feeling better already.

"So what're you working on?"

"Feldman obit. It's due tomorrow. Same old, same old."

Rachel sighed. "Poor dude. Poor Patricia."

"You know her?" Sam's eyebrows shot up.

"We go to the same synagogue. Well, when I go to synagogue."

In high school, Rachel had become a devout Zionist, a phase which lasted about six months. She used to brag about being the only African-American lesbian Jew in Stonebridge. Since then her zeal had faded and she only attended services on the High Holidays.

"Oh?" Sam asked casually. "What's she like?"

"Quiet, keeps to herself. Sweet, though. Alex used to babysit the kids when they were really little."

Alex was Rachel's girlfriend. They'd met during college but had only recently become serious. They seemed happy, but Sam was keeping his eye out. He hadn't allowed himself to get attached to Alex.

"They're still little."

"Yeah, they are, huh." She gave him a thoughtful look. "So, I take it you're having a hard time with it?"

"Did you know he was into pills?"

"It's not a surprise. So are half the people in this town. Everyone's got their poison." Sam looked down at his empty glass. Yeah. He'd probably been drunk three times in the past week, and tonight wasn't shaping up to be much different. A sting of something like shame wormed into his gut, but he tamped it down. It wasn't like he was an alcoholic or anything. He pushed the glass forward.

"I'll take another."

"I thought you were supposed to be working."

"Don't give me any shit, Rach. I've had a helluva day." Her eyes grew concerned again, but Sam didn't feel like talking about the letter he'd received from his insurance company. Maybe if he ignored it, it would go away. Yeah.

"So where's Yuri tonight?" Rachel asked. She poured him another pint of Guinness, but this time left out the shot. Sam didn't argue.

"How should I know?"

"You two seem to be spending a lot of time together lately—off the clock. I thought—"

"We're just friends."

"Yeah, and I'm your monkey's uncle."

"Nice to meet you." Sam raised his glass. "I didn't know my monkey had an uncle."

"Don't be a jackass." More customers entering the bar cut their conversation short. The Star was a popular after-work hangout for people in the neighborhood, but shit always got more interesting on gay night. As one of the only options in town, it drew men from a thirty-mile radius. One of the new arrivals was Sam's type—dark hair, long legs, cowboy boots, and lips that looked like they knew their way around a cock. His dark eyes flashed when they met Sam's, and Sam smiled over his pint.

Another server brought Sam's burger. He ate it carefully, every so often letting his eyes drift to Cowboy Boots to maintain the connection. He didn't want to think about Feldman and his kids anymore. And he certainly didn't want to think about the possibility Rachel was right about Yuri.

They'd seen each other at work since the last time they'd fucked, and it had been fine. They hadn't talked about it, of course, but they never did. It wasn't that Yuri didn't mean anything to Sam. They'd been friends for years and then business partners when Sam had bought into the company. He thought Yuri knew where they stood, but you could never be sure. After all, he didn't want to fuck up their friendship or working relationship if things got weird. That might be one of the reasons he felt a little guilty making eyes at Cowboy Boots. The guy returned his look with a subtle nod that asked "your place or mine?"

Shit. He needed to get back and finish up before his deadline, but he couldn't face the photograph again. Not yet. He grabbed his wallet to pay the tab. A familiar voice said his name.

Sam swiveled in his bar stool as Yuri slid into the seat next to him. He gave Sam a sunny grin, but the circles under his eyes told another story.

"I thought I might find you here," Yuri said. His Greek accent had faded over the years, but it was still damn sexy, and the smell of his fresh aftershave provided added enticement.

Sam cleared his throat and looked away. "What's up, man?"

"I've been meaning to talk to you, but you ran off today and you never answer your phone."

"Sorry. I have a thing due tomorrow."

"Finish it?"

"Nope." Sam emptied his pint. "Working on it."

"Seems that way." There was a pause in the conversation as Rachel noticed Yuri and came over.

"Hey, stranger. What can I get you?"

"Whiskey, neat."

"All right, baby."

"You might as well bring me another too," Sam said.

Rachel took Sam's empty plate away as she went, but not before mouthing something along the lines of "play nice."

The bar, which wasn't large to begin with, had begun to fill up with a sizeable crowd. He liked the lively atmosphere, but not when the mass of bodies interfered with his eye fucking. He couldn't see Cowboy Boots or his friends at their table anymore, and with Yuri sitting here….

Yuri nudged his arm as their drinks arrived. "What's with the Guinness? You going full Irish?"

"I think it's Rachel's attempt to throw me on the wagon."

"Good luck to her."

"So," Sam said casually. "How're we shaping up for the flatwork tomorrow?"

"I didn't come here to talk about that." Yuri sipped his drink, Adam's apple bobbing as he swallowed.

"All right. Well, if you can handle it on your own with Pete and Juan—"

"How long have we been friends, Flynn?"

It didn't take Sam long to think about. They'd met during a time when Yuri's own life was at a low point, watching over his father dying from lymphoma at the same hospital where Tim was a patient. They'd bonded over shitty hospital cafeteria food one day, and the rest was history. And then, once Yuri's dad died and he took over the family business, he offered Sam a job.

Sam had taken it gladly. After the accident that had killed his parents and stolen his brother, his childish dream of becoming a journalist didn't seem to matter anymore.

Now, with Yuri looking at him like a stranger, Sam wanted to lean forward and rest his head on his friend's shoulder.

"A while. Dammit, Yuri, listen—" He slid a hand onto Yuri's thigh and squeezed.

Yuri pushed Sam's hand away. "Hey, it's all right. We've been over this before. But after last week, I think it'll be better for both of us if we stick to the plan this time."

Sam stared. "What?"

"I'm saying it's better if we don't sleep together again."

"Okay," Sam said slowly. "That's fine with me."

Yuri's smile looked more like a grimace. "You think I don't know you? A few drinks and you're looking to score. And when I'm around, it's convenient. I don't really feel like being a convenience anymore, especially when you pass out as soon as it's over."

"It's not like that." His protest sounded feeble to his own ears. He'd barely been able to remember the last time. Not a good sign.

"What's it like, then?"

The question wasn't asked with malice, but with genuine curiosity. Sam flailed for an answer that didn't make him look like a major dick and came up with nada.

"Are you saying you didn't want—Come on, there're two of us." Yeah. He was totally full of shit.

"I'm not saying that at all." Yuri sighed and sipped his whiskey. "Don't pretend like you don't know how I feel about you."

The words, so long unspoken, sucked the air out of the room. Rachel caught Sam's eye mid-drink-mix and gestured conspicuously in a way Sam couldn't interpret. It might have been a reprimand or an indication of constipation. He ignored her.

Yuri went on. "I know you don't feel the same way, so please spare me. Let's go back to how it used to be, all right? You keep your hands to yourself, and I will too. We'll both be happier."

"But we'll still be friends?" It sounded so stupid, but Sam didn't have many people in his life he could designate with the term. Rachel and Yuri were about it. His family. Fuck. He took a long sip of beer and waited for what seemed like forever. Yuri took his time with his drink too, to draw out his suffering—the sadistic bastard.

"What do you think?" Yuri slapped him on the back and finished his drink, then threw a few dollars on the bar. "I've gotta head out."

"Hot date?"

Yuri winked. "Wouldn't you like to know? See you tomorrow."

Once he was alone again, Sam stared at the wet rings his beer made on the coaster and traced one with his finger. It could have gone a lot worse, he supposed. So why did he suddenly feel so goddamn lonely? He didn't get a chance to think too long on it. Rachel approached and leaned forward on the bar, not even trying to disguise her nosiness.

"What was that all about?" she asked.

Sam shrugged. "I think I just got dumped."

"I thought you said—Oh, never mind. Men are so fucking weird."

"But dicks are awesome."

"Are they? That hasn't been my experience." She stuck her tongue out at him and retreated before he could rally a comeback.

Sam nursed his pint for a few more minutes, trying to decide what to do. He had to get back to work, but the thought of his apartment wasn't very appealing. It was only ten, after all—plenty of time to finish the article later on. His eyes drifted back to Cowboy Boots.

The crowd parted as he advanced in the general direction of his mark. There was a good chance the guy had already found another hookup and left while Sam was distracted, but no—there he was, sitting in the same place with his friends. He looked up and raised an eyebrow when Sam approached the table.

Sam mustered his most seductive smile. "Hey. I'm Sam."

"Xavier," Cowboy Boots said. "And these are my friends so-and-so and so-and-so."

Sam nodded at the other guys but kept his eyes focused on Cowboy Boots. Actually, now they'd been introduced, the name seemed too formal. Boots, then.

"You want to join us?" Boots asked.

"Actually, I'm thinking of heading out." Sam scratched the back of his head.

Boots drew his lips into a knowing smile. He had the kind of handsome, nondescript face that belonged in a menswear ad, Sam mused as they made their way out of the bar. He had an incredible ass, though.

Boots's apartment was on the other side of town in an area that had been recently gentrified, but Sam didn't care about the gigantic flat screen or the saltwater fish tank. Luckily, Boots cut the tour short.

"Bedroom's back here."

Sam found himself in a room with a bed, which was good enough for him. His cock was already pushing against the seam of his jeans. They didn't waste time on preliminaries. Boots backed Sam up against the bed until his knees buckled, then crawled on top of him and kissed him. His stubble scraped Sam's chin. He was a good kisser, and Sam was only hazily aware of the guy kicking off his boots. Sam had forgotten his name—something unusual. Didn't matter.

When the guy pushed Sam's hands overhead and held him down as they kissed, Sam groaned his approval.

"So, what do you want to do?" the guy asked. "I don't fuck on the first date."

Sam nodded, oddly relieved. "I wanna suck your cock." He grabbed the guy's ass and urged him forward to straddle his chest.

The guy smirked and reached for his zipper. His erection sprang out and grazed Sam's bottom lip. Sam licked the slit with the tip of his tongue, testing the waters before finally opening his mouth to take it in. The guy fed his meat deeper until it hit the back of Sam's throat, and still Sam wanted more. He moaned as the guy withdrew and started to slide in and out, his salty precome coating Sam's tongue. Sam wanted to suck out every last drop.

It was a good thing they had all night.

Chapter 3

THE FOLLOWING week when Sam visited the Walkers' place, only Emma's car was in the driveway. Sam mowed the lawn and did an upkeep of the gardens, once in a while glancing over his shoulder at the inviting, empty pool. It was probably for the best Nathan wasn't around to distract him. It meant he could get on with his work and stop in sooner to see Tim. The increased summer workload of his day job meant he hadn't been able to stop by Shady Brook the previous Saturday. Sam didn't like to think about leaving Tim for so long, with no visitors save the nurses who attended him. At one point, Tim's high school friends had dropped in on holidays and special occasions, but they didn't come anymore. Of course Sam couldn't blame them. They'd grown up, gone to college, met new friends—and in their minds, Timmy was already dead, forever fifteen.

Not forever. Fuck. There was always a chance Tim would emerge from his wasted body, one day. Six years was a long time, though. He couldn't believe it had been almost six years.

Sam worked quickly. Once he'd stowed his tools, he jogged to the front door, planning to remind Emma about her outstanding bill. Usually he and Yuri didn't mind so much about immediate payment with regular customers, but it had been a couple of months since they'd gotten a check from the Walkers. Sam rang the bell. It broadcast his presence with a three-part chime that brought up bad childhood memories of church.

When Emma opened the door, the words of greeting poised at the tip of Sam's tongue died there. She looked like she'd been crying. Her red-rimmed eyes starkly contrasted with her pale, freckled cheeks. Sam hadn't seen her since he'd gone to the station the previous week to ask about the autopsy. She gave him a tight smile.

"Can I help you, Sam?"

"Actually, I was just heading out, but I thought I'd stop by and see about the check for June and July."

"Oh, right. Of course." She shook her head and held the door open. "Come in."

While Emma rummaged through a hallway drawer for her checkbook, Sam looked around. He'd only been in the house a couple of times, but the clean tidiness impressed him. They must have a service. With a car like Nathan's and a house like this, they had to be loaded or mortgaged to the hilt.

Tasteful, substantial pieces furnished the house. An overstuffed leather sectional dominated the living room to his left and complimented its companion, an oak coffee table with a neat spread of magazines. Evidence of Emma's green thumb was everywhere in potted plants that gave the place a lived-in feel. At least fifteen types of orchids with blooms of various colors and sizes were arranged near the eastern-facing windows at the front of the house. Emma had shown him how to care for them once, before she and Nathan had gone on vacation.

"Five hundred, right?" Emma asked.

"Yep. Make it out to Manella's."

Sam peered toward the kitchen beyond the foyer, surprised to see an overturned carton of eggs on the floor. Most had smashed and now formed a pool of viscous liquid on the stone tile.

Emma cleared her throat, and Sam flushed at being caught looking.

"The doorbell startled me," she explained.

"Sorry."

She passed him the check and he took it, folded it carefully, and slipped it into his back pocket. "I don't mean to bother you, but did you ever find out about those stomach contents?"

"I talked to the chief yesterday, but I'm sorry, no. I don't have any information for you." Emma considered Sam for a moment. "You want a drink?"

Sam shrugged. "Sure." He thought she meant water or, like last time, iced tea, but she pulled two beers from the fridge, and then stepped around the broken eggs like they weren't even there.

Sam cracked both bottles with the opener on his keychain and took a swig, then handed Emma's over. He couldn't help being disappointed the Feldman story seemed DOA, which meant the blog post he'd never actually started was too. After a morning of hot, uncomfortable work, the cold brew went down smoothly, but the strange look on Emma's face concerned him. She seemed lost in her own thoughts.

"You ever think about quitting, Sam?"

"What, you mean give all this up?" He didn't mind the work, though the load had increased since he'd become a partner.

"Yeah." She smiled. "I'm curious if this is what you always wanted to do?"

"I wanted to go to New York when I was younger. I had an internship lined up after college."

"And you didn't do it?"

"I had to stay and take care of family." He said the words without bitterness or malice. He had never once regretted the decision.

"If you didn't have any obligations, if you could go anywhere, do anything, what would you do?"

Sam thought as he drank his beer. It had been a long time since he indulged in any sort of fantasies regarding life goals.

"I guess I'd like to write. Travel. I've always wanted to go abroad." All of those things cost money, though, and the insurance letter sat heavy in his pocket. "What's with all the questions?"

"I don't know. I guess I've just been thinking a lot about my life lately, the choices I've made. Do we ever really know someone? A friend, a lover? Do we ever get close enough to anyone to *really* know them, or is there some part that's always hidden away?"

Her eyes grew bright again, and she wiped at her face. He wondered if she was talking about Nathan.

"I don't know." His mind drifted back to Yuri's confession and to Tim lying in his ergonomic bed. "I guess there're some things you're better off not knowing, you know? I think people have a right to privacy." He took another sip of his beer and put it down, irritated with himself at how hard it was to leave the bottle unfinished. It wouldn't do to drink more, because then he'd want another—and he had to visit Tim.

"But what if you trusted someone." She stared at the floor, where the cracked eggs slowly drained from their shells. "If you ever found out you weren't right about someone. That you didn't know that person, after all. What if they did something terrible? Could you ever forgive them?"

"I don't know. I guess it depends on what they did." He didn't know why he said it or even if it was a lie. This wasn't exactly the time to debate the relative severity of particular crimes, though. And fuck, he wasn't good at this, but he reached out and touched her shoulder anyway. She seemed so delicate, so unlike the confident woman he knew. For some reason, he liked seeing this more vulnerable side. Maybe he could talk to her about Tim.

"Thank you," she finally said, sniffing. "I'm sorry. You must be busy. I'll see you out."

They walked to the front door without speaking. The tick of the clock in the living room seemed almost loud as he reached for the door handle.

"Are you okay, Emma?" he asked before he left, thinking of the eggs she hadn't even mentioned or bothered to clean up.

"Yes, of course." She smiled, and this time it seemed genuine. "Thank you for all of your hard work, keeping the yard beautiful. I know it isn't easy."

"It's my pleasure."

THE CONVERSATION with Emma faded from his mind on the drive to Shady Brook, and a new kind of worry replaced it, making his stomach sick.

The letter he'd received a couple of weeks before wasn't exactly news. Tim's long-term care had surpassed the cap the previous year. Since then, Sam had paid the excess with the residual life insurance from his parents' deaths, but that money was running low too. Both of his still-living grandparents had retired on a fixed income to Florida, and the business didn't bring in enough money to support both Sam and the ever-increasing medical tab. He could only imagine what would happen once the funds dried up. And imagination would become reality in six short months unless something changed, and soon.

"I'm going to think of something. I promise," Sam told his brother. Tim stared at the ceiling and breathed in and out, in and out.

Shady Brook couldn't exactly put Tim out on the street, but Sam had nightmares about state-run care facilities for the poor. He couldn't let Tim wind up as just another lump in a bed, ignored by people who didn't get paid enough to care about who lived or died. He wouldn't. There had to be a way. Not for the first time, he contemplated bank robbery. Maybe he could sell drugs on the street. Lord knew there was enough money floating around in Stonebridge for that kind of thing. Just a week before, another bust at a warehouse down by the docks had taken in millions of dollars of product. Of course those were all fantasies and not very good ones. Sam needed a miracle.

"I won't let anything happen to you, bud." He patted his brother's arm and stood, wondering how long he could keep lying.

Later that evening Sam stretched out on his bed and flipped on the television. He rubbed his hand over his stomach and thought about the book he'd been reading to Tim, *The Road* by Cormac McCarthy. Depressing as hell, but something about it resonated with Sam. People did a lot of crazy shit when times got desperate enough.

Heading down to the Star for a nightcap was tempting, but his eyelids grew heavy as a commercial break announced cash for unwanted gold jewelry at the highest prices in years. He was on the verge of sleep when the local newscast returned. Two reporters, both of whom looked as though they'd been dressed and styled sometime in the late nineties, stared steadily at the camera. The older one spoke.

"An alleged break-in this evening has left one person dead. The victim was thirty-year-old Emma Walker, an officer with the Stonebridge Police Department. Police arrived on the scene when the victim failed to report for duty. Suspects are at large and all area residents are urged to stay in their homes and report suspicious activity."

"Ah, yes. It's a sad night indeed for—" The younger reporter droned on, but Sam had stopped listening. His body went numb as the picture they'd shown of Emma faded from the screen.

It couldn't be. This had to be someone's sick idea of a joke.

Sam grabbed his laptop and performed a quick search, only to find a brief mention of the robbery on several local pages with no more information than what had been offered on the news. Suspected break-in. Victim dead at the scene. Bile rose in his throat, and he hurried to the bathroom before his last meal made an appearance, barely in time to heave into the toilet. He retched his guts out even as he thought it couldn't be true. He'd seen wrong. He was dreaming.

He rinsed his mouth and waited for the nausea to subside, but it didn't. Hot tears pricked his eyes, and his stomach clenched again, an aching hollow. The floor was solid and comforting, and he allowed himself a moment to rest on it to stop his head from spinning. But every time he blinked, he saw Emma.

Some time later, another thought wormed its way into his head and made him shiver. He might have been the last person to see her alive. The check she wrote…. Was it the last thing she'd ever done? Sweat broke out on his brow.

Maybe he'd go have a drink after all.

BEFORE SAM could even grab his wallet and keys, a harsh knock sounded on the door. The cops who waited outside didn't cuff him but requested he come down to the station for questioning, all the same.

The Stonebridge Police Department hadn't been renovated since the late eighties, and whenever he visited, Sam always got the impression he'd stumbled onto the set of *Lethal Weapon*. Unfortunately, however, the detective interviewing him wasn't Mel Gibson. Of course, it was Petersen. Of course.

Sam leaned back and sipped the tepid coffee they'd brought as a token assurance he wasn't a suspect. It tasted like burned cat hair. He grimaced, his empty stomach churning, and set the cup back down. The corner of Petersen's fishlike mouth turned up in a smirk from across the table. Even though he had nothing to hide, Sam's blood chilled when he considered the possibility they'd analyze the cup for his prints. They sat in a little dingy brown room with uncomfortable folding chairs. It was an interrogation room, but they'd propped the dull metal door open to give Sam the illusion he could walk away from this interview.

"You don't like the coffee?" Petersen asked. "I made it myself."

"Explains why it tastes like piss."

Petersen clucked disapproval, and his double chin wobbled. "Sam Flynn. You never change, do you? Have you given up on being a fake reporter? I haven't seen you around here much lately."

"I thank God every day for small favors."

"I take it you two know each other?" Chief Sheldon raised his bushy eyebrows as he breezed through the open door and closed it firmly behind him. He had the bluest eyes Sam had ever seen and was handsome in a grandfatherly, old Paul Newman way. But those eyebrows. Sam had never encountered such impressive specimens. He'd often marveled at them as a child when he'd seen the chief at holidays or the occasional dinner parties his parents held.

"I'd like to say no," said Sam. "I really would. But I can't."

"So you've picked up murder as a hobby. I thought you only *wrote* about dead people."

"That's enough, Petersen," said Chief Sheldon. "Sam came in on a voluntary basis, and he's not a suspect."

"Not yet."

"Aw, still sore I wouldn't suck your dick after gym class?" said Sam. True story, but the chief didn't catch on.

Petersen blanched. "I always knew there was something off about you, Flynn. Besides the obvious. Watch what you say around him, Chief, or you'll wind up on his stupid blog. Not that anyone reads it."

Sam rolled his eyes. "Do I have to put up with this?"

"No, you don't." Sheldon gave a half nod toward the door. "I'll take it from here, Petersen."

Petersen scowled. "Just so you know, he's probably hiding something."

"Talking about yourself again, Little Pete?" Sam smiled sweetly and watched the departing backside with vicious pleasure. He'd had a rough enough night without having to deal with that sonofabitch. Even though Sam had a hard time believing in God, he believed in karma, and someday Rich Petersen would get his.

Sheldon sat down across from him. "Thanks for taking the time to come and talk to us. How are you, son?"

Sam answered automatically. "I'm fine, thanks."

As the chief of police, Sheldon had been close with Sam's father, who'd served as state's attorney before his death. Even though Sam hadn't seen the chief much in recent years, Sheldon looked out for him. He'd gotten Sam out of a DUI on the first anniversary of his parents' death, a stupid mistake made in a moment of grief, and Sam had never done it again. He didn't expect the same leniency a second time, family friend or no.

"And how's your brother?"

"Same. That's where I was today, by the way. I didn't kill Emma."

"You shouldn't let Petersen get under your skin." Sheldon straightened up and pushed the record button on the tape player sitting on the table. "Now for the formalities. I assume you know the drill? Let's start by stating your name and occupation." Sam did. "And when did you last see Emma Walker?"

It hurt to hear her name. She'd been alive merely hours before, and now she was gone. "I saw her earlier this afternoon."

"You work for the Walkers?"

"Yes, I co-own a landscaping business, and the Walkers are a client."

"And how many times would you say you've been to the Walkers' house for yard maintenance?"

"I'm there once a week on Thursdays, sometimes alone, sometimes with a crew." He shrugged.

Sheldon jotted down a few notes, those huge caterpillars knotting together. Then he glanced over his notebook at Sam. "Earlier today, when you saw Emma Walker, what happened?"

"I mowed the lawn, and then I stopped in to ask for payment. Emma let me inside while she wrote out the check. We had a drink, and then I left."

"You had a drink?" Sheldon sounded curious. He tapped his pen against his pad of paper.

"Yeah. I was thirsty, and she invited me to join her. I consider Emma a friend."

"What did you drink?"

Sam breathed deeply to calm his nerves. He had no reason to feel guilty. "A beer. Just one."

"While you were in the house, did you notice anything out of the ordinary?"

He hesitated a moment, and Sheldon picked up on the beat. "Was Emma acting strangely?"

"I thought you said this was a home invasion?"

"We're just trying to make sure we've covered all the bases. So you had a drink, cooled down a little. What did you talk about?"

The conversation he'd had with Emma, what had it been about— lying to someone you love, or rather, finding something out about someone you loved, something bad? Sam hadn't given it much thought after he'd left, distracted as he'd been by his own situation with Tim.

"A little about careers, what I might want to do with my life aside from landscaping. She seemed like she'd been having a bad day."

"Oh? How would you describe her state of mind?"

"Like she'd been upset earlier but had calmed down. She was... tired, I guess. She'd been crying. I did notice she'd dropped some eggs on the floor and hadn't cleaned them up."

"Did she tell you what she was upset about?" Sheldon's pen paused on the paper.

"No. Like I said, I didn't stay very long. And we weren't exactly confidants. She could have had a fight with someone, maybe a girlfriend."

"Or her husband?"

"Maybe. She didn't mention anything specific."

Sheldon started writing again, squinting down at the words. "If you remember anything else, don't hesitate to call anytime, okay?"

"Okay."

"And you're free to go, but before you do, one last question. What do you know about Nathan Walker?"

The way Sheldon said the name evaporated the pretense from the room, and all of the oxygen seemed to go with it. Walker was a suspect, and if Sam was reading the chief's face correctly, a serious one.

"I don't know much about him. I only mow his lawn." After all, he could hardly tell Chief Sheldon that Nathan had featured prominently in more than one of Sam's late night jerk-off sessions. He tried to think back to interactions he'd witnessed between Emma and Nathan, some indication their relationship could have devolved into such a sinister end. In the few conversations Sam had had with Emma about her home life, he knew she and Nathan had been married for nearly ten years and that Nathan was several years older. They seemed happy enough, from what he saw. Comfortable. Even a little boring. Of course, his own observations didn't mean anything. Every day stories came out about marriages falling apart and ending in murder, though to outsiders, the couple might seem perfectly normal.

Sam's gut swam with unease as his mind churned. Suddenly the full weight of the situation crashed down upon him. Whatever he said might be used to either condemn or vindicate a man who may or may not have killed his wife.

"I think you know why I'm asking," said Sheldon, breaking Sam's reverie. "Have you ever seen the two of them arguing?"

"No, Chief, I haven't."

"You're a hard-working kid, Sam. You know I respect what you do. A guy like Walker, though. Now he's the type born with a silver spoon. He's not like you and me. Sometimes men like that think they can do anything and get away with it."

"Yeah." Sam nodded. "I'm sorry, but I can't say. I've never seen them argue. They always seemed to get along."

"All right." Sheldon gestured toward the door, which opened. Petersen poked his head in, and Sheldon raised those bushy eyebrows in some sort of Morse code signal for the conclusion of their interview.

"I'll be in touch if we need you to come back down," Sheldon said as he pushed back from the table and stood. "Thanks for your cooperation. You can let yourself out. And Sam?"

"Yeah?"

"I hope you know your dad would be real proud of you."

Sam blushed and stood, relieved to have his freedom once again. He brushed by Petersen in the doorway before retreating down the hall to the exit. A few people gave him curious glances, but he kept his eyes focused straight ahead. McCormick, the rookie, was manning the front desk with another woman Sam vaguely recognized. She was white as a sheet, and he didn't look much better. Another few officers stood around the front door in close conversation, their grim tableau a reminder the department had lost one of its own. Their talk became more animated when a new arrival entered the station.

Even partially shielded by the cop leading him in, Sam knew the handcuffed man. Sam froze as Nathan Walker was urged forward in his direction.

Their eyes met. At first Sam didn't think Nathan recognized him. Sam knew that particular look well—the look of a person in deep shock. He'd seen it on his own face when he looked in the mirror.

"Nathan," he said automatically. A flicker of awareness appeared on Nathan's handsome face. His eyes searched Sam's.

"She can't be dead. She's not dead, is she?" He choked the words.

33

Sam nodded. "I'm sorry."

Nathan crumpled. His head sagged and his shoulders slumped as if under an unbearable weight. "That's what they told me." He sounded like a lost child.

"Move along," said the officer leading Nathan. "There's no time for chitchat."

"Can't you see he's not well?" Sam wanted to reach out and help when Nathan stumbled forward, but the cop gave him a narrow-eyed glare. They passed and left Sam staring after them.

"Sympathy for the suspect, huh? Suspicious," Petersen said from behind Sam.

Sam didn't bother replying. They still lived in America after all, and innocent until proven guilty meant something. Perhaps it was wishful thinking on Sam's part, because he didn't want to imagine the alternative.

He left the station, but he didn't go directly home. It was past closing time, so he wandered the neighborhood for a while, though he'd have to be up for work in only a few hours.

The streets of Stonebridge were empty except for the night creatures, those above or beyond the law who skulked corners and alleyways looking for a fix—something to take them out of their tedious existence, whether it be sex, drugs, or violence. A couple guys passed each other quickly, slapping palms as they went, and Sam wished for a wild moment he was the one pocketing the bag of whatever and slipping it into his veins or breathing it into his lungs. But his drug of choice had always been legal. He probably shouldn't be wandering in this particular neighborhood unarmed, but he didn't have any money to lose, and he felt reckless, untethered.

Life was so fucking strange. It chugged along blandly until one day, an ordinary day like any other, everything changed. Sam still didn't know how to get back to the person he'd been before the accident. That person was a stranger. He could empathize with Nathan because, whatever had happened, this was that moment for him. There was no going back.

Chapter 4

THE PROJECT Sam and Yuri started the next day required them to tear up an entire front lawn for replanting. The heat combined with 100 percent humidity to create a cocktail of misery. Juan, one of the contract workers, drove the excavator while Sam and Yuri took a quick break. A couple other guys smoked at a distance. The whole crew was in force and probably would be for the next week, at least.

"So do you think he was charged?" Yuri asked. He leaned against the side of his pickup and took a deep drink from his water bottle. Sam tried not to stare at his muscular arms.

"I don't know. He looked like shit when he was brought in for questioning."

"I'll bet." Yuri snorted.

"You think he did it?"

"I don't know, but if they brought him in, there must be a reason."

Sam shrugged. "They brought me in, and I sure as hell didn't do it. I don't know. Something about it doesn't sit right with me."

Yuri gave him a hard look. "I think it's probably best left to the professionals, Sam. Don't meddle."

"Who, me?" Sam widened his eyes, all innocence. "I never meddle."

"Ha, bullshit."

The sound of the machinery grating against rock was getting on Sam's nerves. He could practically see the heat rising in waves from the crackling asphalt. If the pavement couldn't stand the heat, it seemed unfair to think a human body could.

"We better get back to work," said Yuri to everyone. "Long day ahead of us, boys." The other two guys butted out their cigs on the ground and nodded. One of them was new to the crew, and Sam could tell he was uneasy with the whole gay thing. As long as he kept his mouth shut about it, there wouldn't be a problem. Sam and Yuri didn't tolerate bigotry on their team.

Juan idled the engine of the excavator, hopped down, and patted the seat for Sam.

"It's all yours, boss," he said.

"Gee, thanks, but I didn't get you anything."

Juan must have been at least fifty, but he still had the body of a much younger man. Only his leathery skin showed his age. It wrinkled around his eyes, evidence of too much time spent in the sun. "You're a funny one, *cabrón.*"

Yeah, he was a damn comedian.

SAM HAD never been able to shake curiosity. As the days passed, the mainstream press continued to treat Emma's death like an average break-in/homicide. Nathan had been released from custody with no charges, and it looked like maybe he was off the hook after all. Sam couldn't help wondering whether Nathan had friends or family nearby to help him through.

On the morning of the funeral, Sam dressed in the one shitty suit he owned and stationed himself in the back pew at the church. He'd never been a religious person, but he couldn't deny the comfort of ceremony. The whole police department was there, even Petersen. People filed in dressed in black—mourners and onlookers full of morbid curiosity. Sam wondered which category he fell into.

When the service began, he saw Nathan sitting toward the front, next to an older woman who bore a striking resemblance to him. She couldn't be anyone but his mother. Something eased inside Sam's chest. Yet after the funeral ended, he went home feeling strangely vacant. He thought maybe he should write a blog entry, but he had nothing to say.

RACHEL LET herself into his apartment in the middle of a Sox/Yankees game. She flopped down on the couch and propped her feet up on the square inch of the coffee table that remained uncluttered. "It smells like a shithole in here, Sam."

"I like to think of it as my own personal potpourri—beer and old Chinese food. It's got a certain je ne sais quoi."

"Don't forget the dirty socks. Jesus, how do you even bring guys back here?" She nudged a can out of the way with one of her pointy-toed shoes.

"I don't." In fact, he hadn't hooked up since Cowboy Boots—over a century earlier.

"Right. Never show them where you live. I forgot."

"How could you forget my golden rule?" Sam flipped the channel. He hated commercials. And he'd finished all the beer in his fridge.

Rachel cleared her throat. "Are you all right, Sam?"

"Why wouldn't I be?"

"Yuri told me about what happened."

Shit. Yuri and his damned big mouth. "I'm fine."

"He says you knew her, the policewoman who was killed."

"Yeah, I knew her."

"It's terrible. Jesus, to die so young." She winced.

Sam sagged back against the couch. Even so many years later, he hated being reminded of his parents when he didn't expect it. He felt like a deep-sea creature suddenly yanked from the bottom of the ocean and exposed to air and light. Sam took a deep breath, but oxygen felt like poison.

"Sorry, Sam. I didn't—"

He waved his hand. "It's all right. Listen, what are you up to tonight? You feel like going out?"

"Can't. Alex and I have a date."

"Oh, wouldn't want to interfere with the beaver brigade."

She punched him. "Don't be an asshole. I better go, though, or I'll be late. I wanted to stop by and see if you needed anything."

"I told you, I'm good. I don't need anything except more beer, if you wouldn't mind?"

"That's the last thing you need, Sam. Hey—" She punched him again, hard, and he grunted.

"What the fuck, Rach?"

"I'm worried about you. Yuri's worried about you."

"I'm fine."

"You're not fine. I thought you were going to write something about Feldman? What happened with that?"

"There's no story. And I don't feel like it."

"How many have you had tonight?"

"Sorry. I can't hear you over the sound of this annoying whining in my ear."

The door slammed behind her. Sam flung the remote onto the coffee table, upsetting the precarious balance of trash he'd worked so hard to cultivate. He was fine.

Chapter 5

EVEN IN relation to all the dumb things Sam had done in his life, standing outside the Walkers' home late on a Friday night ranked as one of the stupidest. When he'd gotten in his truck and started driving, he hadn't planned a destination. It just sort of happened.

Darkened windows gazed back at him, blank and vacant, but the Mercedes was parked in the drive. Sam rang the doorbell again. Once the chime faded, only the sound of crickets in the fields beyond the house remained.

It occurred to him the killer had stood right here, had maybe even rung the doorbell as he did for the second time. And Emma had come to the door to greet the stranger, unsuspecting, vulnerable, and at ease in her own home. His gut twisted, chased by the doubt in the back of his mind that perhaps it hadn't been a stranger, after all. So why had he come?

Try as he might, he couldn't forget Nathan's devastated expression at the police station. Maybe Sam was a sucker for lost causes.

He paused, finger hovering over the doorbell a third time. Maybe Nathan had cut out of town after all and left his car behind. Or maybe....

The pool glowed a luminescent blue-green. Empty deck chairs lined the perimeter, giving the surroundings a lonely, expectant feel, waiting for a party that would never happen. Empty except for one. In the far corner by the herb garden, Nathan sat with a bottle in one hand and a cigarette in the other. He didn't say anything, and when Sam

39

came closer, he realized how unfocused Nathan's gaze was. Made sense given the half-drunk fifth of Jack clutched against his chest. He looked up at Sam and lifted the bottle in salute.

"Want some?"

Sam eased the bottle away and took a small sip, just enough to feel the burn, before he set it down on an adjacent table. Nathan didn't seem to notice. He fumbled in his front shirt pocket for a pack of smokes and lit a new one off the back of the other. "I quit, you know. A few years back. Emma didn't like it. It's like riding a horse, though." He inhaled deeply and shuddered, suppressing a cough. "Well, maybe not exactly. You smoke?"

"Nah, I never smoked, not even in college. Did pretty much everything else."

Nathan let out a laugh that sounded more like a sob and leaned his head back against the chair. He took a drag of the cigarette. "I don't know what the fuck to do."

"I'm sorry for your loss." God, how many times had Sam heard the same lame comment himself? It was the kind of phrase people used when they didn't know what else to say, exactly his position now. Nathan's dark eyes flicked to his.

"You know, outside of my family, you're the first person who's said that to me? This whole town thinks I did it." He shook his head and stretched his arm to reach for the bottle. Sam had half a mind to take it from him and pour it out, but he'd dealt with the kind of grief that rattled your bones so hard nothing could put you back together. Still, he winced a little when Nathan drank so deeply he choked on the liquor. He was a man intent on drinking himself into oblivion. It was strange seeing it from the outside, for a change.

"Gimme some more of that." Sam dragged over a chair and tucked the bottle behind him when he sat—an old trick Rachel had pulled on him more than once.

Nathan didn't complain. He looked Sam over, his gaze watchful despite his near stupor, as though observation were an ingrained reflex. The attention made Sam mildly warm.

After another beat, Nathan butted out the cigarette and struggled to stand.

"I'm tired."

"Whoa, whoa, whoa." Sam stood as quickly as he'd sat down, and in good time too. Nathan almost dropped like a sack of rocks before Sam got his arm around his waist. For a moment, Nathan sagged against Sam, resting his weight against Sam's shoulder, and Sam realized the full extent of Nathan's height. This close, he seemed to tower over Sam's five-foot-nine frame. His warm muscles flexed underneath his thin cotton shirt, and his hot, alcoholic breath tickled Sam's ear almost like an invitation. Sam couldn't help responding despite the inappropriateness of the situation. Drinking and tragedy always made him think about sex.

"Maybe we should get you inside."

"I can walk." Nathan didn't try to push himself away, however. If anything, he seemed to press even closer to Sam.

"All right. Well, show me your stuff, then."

Somehow they managed to negotiate the chairs and Nathan's discarded shoes without any major incident as they skirted the edge of the pool on their way toward the house. The crickets, singing their chorus into the night, were louder in the tall grass beyond the yard. Sam remembered a lesson from grade school about what made the sound. There'd been controversy in his class over whether crickets rubbed their legs or their wings together. The teacher had held up a jar of crickets and instructed the children that male crickets made chirping sounds with their wings, which served as both a mating call to females and a warning to other males. Later, one of the boys who'd been embarrassed to be wrong ripped off all of the crickets' wings. This, of course, only proved the teacher right. They couldn't sing anymore.

As they entered the house, Sam disentangled himself from Nathan's grip to search for a light switch. The living room flooded into view. From the looks of it, Nathan had been sleeping on the couch. A messily bunched blanket and a pillow decorated one side of it, and the cushions were slightly askew.

"Is this where you're crashing?"

Nathan blinked slowly. "All of her stuff is upstairs."

"I got you."

For lack of anything else to do, Sam shook out the blanket and fluffed the pillow, feeling self-conscious all the while. Aside from the observation out by the pool, Nathan had yet to ask him what the hell he was doing there.

"Here," Sam said, gesturing to the pseudobed he'd created. "Why don't you come and lie down?"

"I would, if I'd be able to sleep. Unfortunately…." Nathan swayed on his feet. "I can't."

"The amount you drank, I'll bet you pass out in five seconds flat."

"Whoever killed Emma is still out there. I can't sleep until I find who did it." His eyes gleamed and sharpened. Sam noticed a black handgun on the coffee table, in reaching distance of the couch. Nathan picked it up and a chill ran up Sam's spine.

"Well, you're not going to find anyone drunk as a skunk. Better sleep it off, Nathan, and save it for the cops."

"Who the hell are you to tell me what to do?"

Sam threw up his hands. "Whoa. I'm only saying you're no use to anyone like this, certainly not to Emma. If you want to help the investigation, this isn't the way to do it." He gestured toward the gun.

The fight seemed to go out of Nathan again. "I don't think I can stay in this house tonight. I need to get out of here."

"Do you want to sleep at my place?" The words escaped Sam's mouth before he could stop them. Nathan stared at him dumbly. "I mean, it's not much, certainly not anything comparable to what you're used to. I've only got the one bed and it sags in the middle. But you're more than welcome to take it, and I'll sleep on the couch. That is, if you want." Sam ran a hand through his hair and stared at his feet. "Never mind. It was a stupid idea."

"No, no, I… yeah."

Sam stood awkwardly in the hall and waited while Nathan gathered a few things, like they were going to a slumber party. He should have kept his mouth shut. He never thought Nathan would actually say yes, and now he had to play host to a grieving man in an apartment full of takeout containers and dirty laundry. His sheets were probably ripe enough to get up and walk away on their own.

"My truck's out here." Sam led the way after Nathan locked the door. He carried a small bag and had managed to get a pair of shoes on his feet and tie them. He left the gun on the entryway table. Maybe the random invitation had sobered him up.

Nathan climbed into the passenger's seat and nearly fell back out trying to close the door. Maybe not.

"It's about a twenty-minute drive. You need me to pull over, let me know."

"I'll be fine." The haughtiness in his tone made Sam smile to himself as he started the engine. His truck rumbled loudly to life. The muffler and exhaust needed replacing, but Sam hadn't gotten around to it. He'd probably need a new car altogether before the winter set in. Fat chance given the state of his finances.

By the time they reached Sam's neighborhood, Nathan had nodded off. He startled awake when Sam shook his arm.

"Here we are," Sam said. "Home, sweet home."

Sam got out of the truck and helped Nathan up the four flights of stairs. If Nathan leaned a little too hard on Sam or got a little too close, Sam didn't say anything about it. He had left the TV on, so some sitcom laugh track greeted them as they entered. It was hot and loud inside the apartment. The asshole upstairs was having a party.

Sam's hand-me-down couch, a floral eyesore courtesy of his grandparents' retirement to Florida, seemed to catch Nathan by surprise. He blinked and looked around, and Sam's stomach squirmed with shame. How could he expect a guy like Nathan to be comfortable here?

"It's nice."

"It's terrible, but it's home." Sam gestured for Nathan to follow. "I'll show you where you can sleep."

He made use of Nathan's delayed reaction time to tidy up the floor and kick some dirty clothes under the bed. Fuck. No wonder he never brought guys back here. The place really was a shithole. He vowed to be more diligent in his cleaning enterprises and turned on the light. Nathan watched him from the doorway.

"Sorry it's kind of a mess. I don't usually have guys over. Or girls. Er, anyone, really."

"It's okay. I appreciate your hospitality, and to be honest, I'd rather sleep in a pit of vipers than at home."

"Indiana Jones fan, huh? I guess this is one step up from vipers."

"At least two, I'd say."

They smiled at one another for a moment, but then Nathan's face shuttered. "Thanks again, Sam."

Taking it as his cue, Sam headed for the door. "It's no problem. I know what it's like not to be able to sleep."

He didn't stay for further explanations. The last thing Nathan needed to hear was Sam's own sob story. One of the worst memories Sam had of the time right after the accident was people sharing the tragedies in their own lives to make him feel better. As if hearing how much the world sucked could ever do that.

Sam punched one of the overly fluffy couch pillows and settled down with the TV still on. It always helped him fall asleep.

The next morning he awoke with a crick in his neck to the sounds of someone trying to be quiet in the kitchen and mostly failing. He found Nathan, still wearing his clothes from the previous night, knocking back a couple of painkillers with a pint glass chaser of water.

"How're you feeling?" Sam asked.

"Like hell." He grimaced. "It's a good thing you came over when you did, or I'd probably be face down in the pool by now."

"I'm glad you weren't. It would have been a pain in the ass to drag you out."

Nathan gave him a half smile and refilled his glass from the tap. He drained it in a few long pulls, looking lean and graceful with his head tilted back. After he'd finished and wiped his mouth with his hand, he set the glass on the counter. "Why did you come over last night?"

Sam grasped for a rationale that wouldn't sound creepy or stalkerish, but he had nothing. "I thought you might need a friend."

"Emma always liked you, you know."

"I liked her too."

"She thought you might have a crush on me."

"What?"

Nathan's face paled. Sam's first instinct, to reach out and steady him, took him by surprise. He had no idea if such a touch would be wanted. "Maybe you should sit down."

44

"I realize I said *liked*. It will never be *like* again. The present tense is gone. She's gone."

"Shit, Nathan."

Sam had a small table and chair set in the kitchen, which he normally used to store mail and newspapers, but he figured it could also serve its real purpose. He cleaned it off, piled the papers in a stack on the floor, and set about brewing coffee, aware of Nathan's eyes on his back. The guy seemed tied together with string, and Sam figured he better tread with caution.

"How do you like your coffee? Cream and sugar?" He peered into the fridge.

"Black is fine."

"Perfect, because I don't have either." His cupboards were bare, and he didn't have much to offer by way of breakfast save bread and butter barely hanging on to its expiration date. He made toast for both of them and set plates down on the table along with the coffee. Nathan eyed the meager spread with a strange expression. He picked up a piece and stared as if toast were a new thing.

Sam cleared his throat. "Sorry it's not much. Haven't had much time to shop or cook lately." Not that he'd cook even if he had the time, but Nathan didn't need to know. The comment seemed to be enough to break Nathan out of his quiet, though. He nodded.

"You work a lot."

"Yep, twenty-four seven, feels like."

"Emma was similar. Always at work. Working at home when she was off. She wanted to make detective."

Silence descended as Nathan sipped his coffee, and Sam took the opportunity to study him. The pronounced dark circles suggested he hadn't slept well again, and his skin had the unnatural pallor of a hard night of drinking. But the expression in his eyes—dull and resigned—bothered Sam the most.

"What do you do for work?" Sam asked.

"I guess you could say I'm a consultant." He punctuated the words with an efficient bite of toast. "I don't think I'll be going back to work any time soon."

"Sometimes I find it's a good distraction."

"With all due respect, I don't think I want to be distracted. I have to find who did this."

"You don't trust the police to find out?"

Nathan pursed his lips. It seemed like he wanted to say something but was weighing his options. "I don't trust anyone."

"I can't say I blame you."

"You're awfully young to be so cynical."

"Yeah, well I've had my fair share of shit thrown at me, and living in this neighborhood gives you reason not to trust the police. You know Rich Petersen?"

Nathan nodded. "There're always a few bad eggs. But I like to think most people go into it for the right reasons."

"Of course." Sam glanced down, abashed. "The chief is a good guy. And Emma, of course. Was." God, he'd really put his foot in it.

"I should go." As Nathan pushed the plate of half-eaten toast away and stood, a tightness lodged in Sam's throat. He'd made a misstep and he didn't know how to fix it. He didn't want Nathan to leave in this state.

Still, he said, "If I can help in any way, I will."

Nathan's eyes softened. "You've already done far more than anyone else, and hell if I know why. But thank you."

"Do you need a ride home?"

"I'll catch a cab."

"All right. Nathan—" Sam restrained himself once again from reaching out and grabbing the man's arm. "What will you do now?"

"I don't know."

Chapter 6

SAM PULLED up in front of Nathan's house the next evening after work. He hadn't been invited, but he couldn't rest easy without finding out if the guy was okay.

This time Nathan was in the backyard doing laps. He covered the length of the pool in seconds, then performed some sort of fancy underwater flip, and headed back toward Sam with the butterfly stroke. He finished the lap and then held onto the edge, breathing heavily.

"What are you doing here?" Water droplets caught in Nathan's long lashes as he looked up at Sam.

"I came to make sure you didn't drown yourself. How long have you been out here?"

"I don't know. A couple hours."

Sam whistled and hooked his thumbs in his pockets. Though the water looked inviting, illuminated in the pool lights, he couldn't imagine swimming for hours. "What are you, training for the Olympics?"

"I figure it's a healthier way of tiring myself out than what I did last night."

Sam didn't mention he'd almost expected to find more of the same. "You're probably right."

"Do you want to come in?" Nathan's muscles flexed as he pushed himself away from the edge.

The evening had begun to cool the air, but it was still sticky and hot. Sam hadn't even thought to bring trunks. He remembered Nathan's invitation weeks before, when he'd told Sam he could borrow a pair, but Sam would look ridiculous in anything of Nathan's, what with the height difference. And nudity was out of the question. He shook his head. "I'm good."

"Suit yourself."

Nathan started another lap, this time at a slow crawl. For lack of anything else to do, Sam stationed himself on one of the deck chairs and watched as the sky darkened.

When he finally heaved himself out of the pool, Nathan's usual grace was gone. He grabbed a towel and stood there staring across the pool at Sam, dripping wet.

"You're still here?" There was actual surprise in his voice.

"You're kind of freaking me out, to be honest. I've never seen someone swim so long, except maybe a seal."

"I'm fine. I am… tired, though." He approached with wobbly steps. "I'll be okay."

Right. He seemed hardly able to move, let alone towel himself off and go to bed. Sam imagined a different life, one where he could do the honors of drying Nathan's muscular torso, his lean, strong legs—and then quickly pushed the thought from his mind.

"Good. Okay."

"Good night, Sam." Nathan started to walk away but then paused and turned his head. "I take it I'll see you tomorrow?"

"You betcha."

SAM MADE good on his promise. He showed up the next night, and the next. Most of the time, Nathan swam and they didn't talk. It became a strange routine, the peaceful evening turning into night with only the sounds of gently lapping water and crickets to break the stillness. Out here in the country, millions of stars appeared once the sun set, and Sam wondered why he'd never given much thought to their beauty before. There was probably something to be said for looking up once in a while, instead of straight ahead, but Sam didn't feel inclined to delve more deeply into the thought.

After the first night at Nathan's, Sam made sure to bring his trunks. He never swam as long as Nathan did, but he did laps and then lounged by the pool's edge, feet dangling. They spoke very little, except for passing comments about the weather or sports. But on the fourth night, Nathan seemed different. He smiled when Sam arrived and continued his lazy backstroke. "I was wondering if you were coming."

"Of course."

Sam nodded and went into the house to change. When he came back, Nathan was still idly circling the pool. Sam took a running leap, cannonballed into the cool water, and popped up only a couple of feet from Nathan.

"Quite an entrance."

"Yeah, well, what can I say? I'm a drama queen." And then, for no reason whatsoever, he splashed Nathan right in the face.

Nathan wiped the water from his eyes, which he then narrowed dangerously. "You splashed me."

"Hell yeah, I did. And I'll do it again." So he did.

"Do you seriously want to play this game?"

Sam shivered, and not because of the coolness of the water, which had warmed considerably. Nathan's predatory smile grew.

"You better swim fast."

Sam dove to get a head start, but Nathan had the advantage. Before he knew it, Sam was trapped in Nathan's strong arms and dragged toward the deep end of the pool. They wrestled, laughing, until Nathan finally got the better of Sam and dunked his head. Sam grabbed Nathan around the waist to pull him under as well, but the water made everything slippery. Their bodies slid together, and Sam suddenly realized he'd wrapped his leg around Nathan to get a firmer hold and had wound up in a very compromising position. His cock was hardening against Nathan's thigh. Nathan exhaled against his cheek.

The struggle continued for a moment before Sam froze and, with a laugh to cover up his increasing embarrassment, pushed himself away. Nathan let him go without protest. Sam swam to the other end of the pool and then hoisted himself out, deciding to pretend nothing had happened.

"There's water in my ear," he explained, tilting his head to the right.

"I'm sorry." Nathan sounded contrite.

"It's not a big deal." Maybe Nathan hadn't even noticed Sam's response to the roughhousing. A guy could hope.

"It's getting late."

"Yeah," Sam agreed. Better leave before things got even more awkward. "I… I've got plans tomorrow night, so I probably won't come by."

Nathan glowered at him. "I appreciate what you're trying to do, but I don't need a babysitter, Sam. I'll be fine."

"Are you sure?"

"Of course I'm sure. I'm always fine."

Nathan got out of the pool too and dried himself off. Sam pulled his shirt over his head and wrapped a towel around his wet shorts. "Do you mind if I borrow this?" It would help keep his truck seat from getting soaked, not to mention hide his misbehaving erection.

"Not at all. Hey—"

"What's up?"

"Thank you for the company. I do appreciate the distraction, but it almost doesn't feel right. Like I shouldn't be distracted. I don't deserve to be."

Sam nodded. He had a feeling there wouldn't be any more late-night swims. "I understand what that's like. But call me if you ever need to talk, okay?"

"I will."

NATHAN DIDN'T call the next day, or the next. Sam got an assignment from the *Gazette*. In honor of Mark Feldman's work, the mayor had made a two-year pledge to get drugs off the streets of Stonebridge. Sam's editor insinuated his article should take a positive spin on the plan, and Sam wondered, not for the first time, just how deep in the pockets of local government she was. He suspected the whole thing was nothing more than a publicity stunt.

Still, the article would pay more than his usual fare, so he swallowed his distaste and went down to the station on his day off to find someone to talk to. Since Emma was gone, he would need a new connection, and he didn't like exploiting his relationship with the chief.

Petersen was loafing at the front desk with his hands resting on his paunch. His upper lip curled when he noticed Sam. "I knew I'd see you back here. Missing the interrogation room already?"

"Spare me your prison-rape fantasies, Petersen. I'm here to talk to someone about the mayor's plan."

Petersen crossed his arms. "And why should I help you?" Someone behind Sam cleared his throat. Sam turned around and got a face full of beefy and blond McCormick.

Sam smiled. "McCormick isn't it? I was wondering if I could ask you some questions."

McCormick looked from Petersen to Sam, as though unsure. "Uh."

"I'll take that as a yes." Sam grabbed out his notebook and pen. All he really needed were a couple of stock quotes. "How many officers has the mayor designated for the cleanup downtown?"

"Uh. Twenty."

"And are you one of those officers?"

"Yeah, I am."

"Can you tell me anything about your strategy going forward?"

The interview proceeded in fits and starts. McCormick got a little more enthusiastic and talkative once they were out of Petersen's earshot. He seemed very concerned with saying the wrong thing or critiquing the mayor's policy. By the time Sam left the station, he had collected enough bland praise and positivity to write his softball article and earn his check.

He went back to Nathan's the next week for maintenance, but no one was home. The same was true the next week, and the next. Either Nathan had gone away on a trip, or he'd decided to avoid Sam altogether. The following week, Sam sent another team.

Chapter 7

SAM STARED at the stupid, shiny balloons he'd tied to Tim's bed frame. They danced in the cool fall breeze from the open window. Most other visitors had already left for the evening. Helen's son had come and gone about an hour before, along with his wife and their baby. Sam should have given them the balloons. They were something you bought for a child, not for a brother turning twenty-one. Maybe that was the problem. He considered popping them, one by one, and imagined the sounds they would make. Loud enough to wake the dead.

At his own twenty-first birthday, Sam had relied on the kindness of his friends to get him shitfaced, but Tim didn't exactly have that option.

"Wake up, Timbo," Sam said. "Wake the fuck up, will you?"

His brother's white face remained impassive. "I'll take you to a strip club, and we'll do tequila shots. Don't you want to get laid?"

Nothing. Every day that passed meant Tim was slipping further away. Miraculously he'd held on this long, but even with the physical therapy designed to keep his muscles toned, he didn't look much older than he had the day of the accident.

"You're a real asshole, you know?"

He imagined Tim sitting up and shouting back at him, *"You're the asshole, asshole."*

When Timmy was twelve and Sam was seventeen, their family took a trip to Florida and all of those hot, crowded amusement parks.

The whole time Sam had remained resolutely unimpressed. He refused to hang out with his family and ended up spending most of his time in an arcade near the hotel, playing *Street Fighter* and checking out cute boys. He'd been embarrassed and filled with wanting, without having any idea how to channel those emotions. That is until one of those boys noticed him looking and didn't mind.

Paul, pretty and quiet, had freckles across the bridge of his nose and the most luscious lips Sam had ever seen. It started out innocently enough. The two of them met up each morning to play games or swim in the hotel pool. Paul wore low-slung board shorts that showed off his slim waist and hips, and at night Sam dreamt about grabbing hold of Paul's smooth body and pressing close.

And one day, away from the sharp eyes of his family, Sam had his first kiss. The shock of it hit him like a revelation. He didn't know where to touch, how to get close enough, how to understand the brilliance of another boy's mouth on his. The intensity blotted everything else out. So when Timmy begged and pleaded to join them on that final afternoon, Sam had said no and hurried off to meet his friend. They spent hours alone in Paul's room, and that night when Sam boarded the airplane to return to New England, he left his virginity behind in Florida too.

Tim pouted for a few days once they got home, mad at Sam for the exclusion, but then things went back to normal. Sam finished up his final year of high school and went to college. When he came home for breaks and holidays, he filled his time with old friends and crappy jobs. Sometimes he ate dinner with his family. But then a friend would call or he'd hear about a party, and he'd be off again, thoughtless and full of the promise of life outside the confines of home.

Sam thought about that summer a lot, but never figured out how to forgive himself for the missed opportunities. His brother grew up without him, and Sam never found out Tim's favorite movies or if he liked girls. And then there were the things Sam never told Tim or his parents. That he was gay. That he loved them.

Of course they knew about the love already. But still.

Part of him understood he'd been acting like any normal teenager finding his way. Another part of him, no matter how irrational, felt like he should have known. He should have known about time.

Tim's hand lay lifeless and warm in his, and Sam squeezed it. "I'm sorry. You're not an asshole. Happy birthday, buddy." Visiting hours were over.

Sam pulled out of the parking lot at breakneck speed and headed south down the freeway. He needed to put some space between himself and his life, and a night in New York was just the thing. Calling Yuri was an afterthought, but he did it anyway, keeping one eye out for cops as he hit the speed dial.

"Hey, Sam." Yuri sounded wary. He knew what day it was.

"Hey. So I'm thinking about heading down to the city for the night. Hit up a club or two. You in?"

"I've got to work tomorrow, and so do you."

"That never stopped us before. We can be in for seven, take an early train."

"It's a big job tomorrow." But Sam could hear the hesitation in Yuri's voice, and he wasn't above exploiting it for the company. He hummed. "Come on. For old time's sake. Don't make me dance alone."

Yuri snorted. "You never dance alone, Sam."

Shit. He'd lost the thread with that one. Perhaps guerilla tactics would be more effective. "Get ready. I'll be at your place in ten minutes, and I won't take no for an answer."

"Yes, you will." This time it sounded final. "I can't come. You have a good time, but be safe. Okay?"

"You're no fun anymore, old man."

"Yeah, maybe not. I'll see you tomorrow."

The line went dead, and Sam tossed his phone onto the empty passenger's seat. It didn't matter if Yuri didn't want to come. Rachel was the other obvious choice, but she'd be working until closing time. He really needed to make some new friends.

By the time he parked at the commuter rail and paid for his ticket, the sun had already dipped low in the sky. The train hurtled into the station like a steel cage filled with oblivious captives, lost in their cell phones and laptops. Sam grabbed a seat facing forward and stared out the window as they began to move again, first slowly, then gaining more speed. The sway of the train and the loud clatter of the rails lulled him into the first calm he'd felt in days.

The clubs would be dead for a while once he arrived, but he could spend some time in the Village, maybe, or grab a bite to eat. It would be far better than another night in Stonebridge, another night at the same bar or at his apartment, in his neighborhood. An old woman sat across from him, sleeping with her head pressed against the window. Her gray hair was mottled through with sickly yellow, and even with several feet between them, Sam could smell the stink of old clothes and unwashed flesh.

He wondered what contentment felt like. Did anyone live a charmed life, or was it a myth designed to make everyone feel like shit?

This woman's face and worn, dirty clothes spoke of hardship and suffering, but maybe all of that was misleading. This woman, with all of her seeming vulnerabilities on display, had courage. So did Tim. They didn't deserve Sam's pity. Better pity a man like Feldman who had every advantage, yet lacked the strength to show his true face to the world, or someone like Nathan or Sam, who hid pain away behind closed doors and socially condoned anesthetics.

Maybe Sam was getting too maudlin for his own good.

He turned his gaze again to the window and watched the evening zoom by.

Once the train left them off at Grand Central, Sam decided to walk downtown and stretch his legs. The heavy traffic of the city filled the air with exhaust, which combined with the sweet smell of roasting peanuts as the skyscrapers of midtown gave way to shorter, picturesque brownstones. After about an hour, he entered a familiar neighborhood, lively with late shoppers and groups of friends heading out for the night, meeting and mingling at cafes and trendy bars. Even for early fall, the city was noticeably warmer than it had been in Stonebridge. Most of the guys wore jeans and tees to show off their sculpted muscles and tattoos, their hair artfully mussed. A few of them gave Sam appreciative once-overs, which he returned in a noncommittal way.

When he and Yuri first met, they'd come to the city often—usually to pick up guys, but sometimes to hang out, just the two of them. It had been a while, though, and Sam wondered how things had gotten so fucking weird. Maybe it was his fault. He'd sensed Yuri's feelings for him had grown more serious, but he'd been too caught up in his own desires and the convenience of their relationship to think too hard about it.

Hours passed. At around midnight, Sam found himself in a club he'd never been to. The patrons tended toward the leather end of the spectrum, muscular and barrel-chested. After a few shots, he made his way onto the dance floor, pushing through the sweaty male bodies. Everyone was smiling and laughing as they gyrated to the strong bass rhythm, and Sam found himself swept up in the crowd. Before long he was sandwiched between two guys, clearly a couple looking for a third. Both of them were big—taller than Sam and broader—and their arms snaked around him to find each other. Sam felt a hot, wet mouth on the back of his neck, kissing down to the nape. The other guy moved closer so Sam could straddle his thigh. A hard erection pushed against Sam's pelvis and another against his ass, and Sam's body responded.

"Haven't seen you around here," the guy in back said, loud enough to hear over the music.

"Yeah. I don't come down to the city much."

His partner grinned and nosed forward, kissing Sam's jaw. His head fell back against a powerful shoulder.

"That's a shame. Well, now that we've got you, whatever will we do with you?"

Another drink and a couple of songs later, and the answer to that question was "anything you want," which was exactly how Sam wound up back at an apartment on all fours, with one of the guys eating his ass and the other thrusting powerfully into his mouth. The cock was thick, and Sam did his best to swallow it down, sucking hard despite the unpleasant taste of mint latex.

He gripped his own erection and pulled as the guy behind him spread his ass and pushed in one lubed finger. Sam willed himself to relax as his body adjusted to the girth of the cock pressing into him from behind. A hand on his jaw guided him gently, distracting him from the pain of the stretch. For such big guys, both of them were surprisingly careful and affectionate. They kissed across Sam's back, and he was only vaguely aware of the sounds they made. Every thrust shattered something inside, making him want to come and cry at the same time.

When he came, neither of them had finished, so he lay back on the bed while they jerked their cocks and painted his chest and face. The guy with the anchor tattoo on his left pec rubbed his softening prick against Sam's cheek, smearing his jizz and shuddering with the last aftershocks. The bad porno move made Sam sigh and wonder what the fuck he was doing. He wiped his face off with the back of his hand.

"Damn," said the other. "That was so fucking hot."

"Best anniversary ever," said Anchor Tatt, giving his lover a long, open-mouthed kiss.

Sam watched them in a daze, suddenly wanting to be anywhere else. He was a fucking anniversary present—literally.

"How long have you two been together?" he asked as he groped for his underwear, more out of the need to break the awkward silence than any real curiosity.

"Five years," said Anchor Tatt. "We met in the navy."

So that explained the tattoo. "How nice," Sam said lamely. He found his clothes and quickly dressed, his back to the bed. When he turned around, both men were watching him with their arms wrapped loosely around each other.

"Are you sure we can't convince you to stay for another round?" Anchor Tatt asked. He had a pretty smile, and he bestowed it on Sam with interest.

Sam shook his head. He was going to be feeling that thick cock in his ass for days. "I've gotta head out. But thanks, I had a great time."

"Well, you've got our number. Call us the next time you're in town."

"Sure thing."

Outside in the wee hours of the night, Sam walked quickly toward Houston to catch a cab back to the station. His mouth tasted like yesterday's garbage. He could already imagine the look Yuri would give him if he showed up to work like this, hung-over and stinking like sex. A quick trip home first was definitely in order. He pulled out his cell to check the time and noted a couple of missed calls, both from a number he didn't recognize with a Stonebridge area code.

There was one voice mail, and Sam listened to it on the ride to Grand Central. His heart started pounding as soon as he recognized the voice.

"Hi, Sam, this is Nathan Walker calling. I was wondering if you had any free time. If you'd like to talk. Or rather, I'd like to talk to you, if you have some time. Call me back."

He had to replay the message twice more just to make sense of it. At first, his tired, semidrunk neurons couldn't process what Nathan meant, but then he remembered telling Nathan to call if he wanted to talk. Nathan had said he would, but after two months of radio silence, Sam had almost forgotten the initial offer. Now, out of nowhere, Nathan wanted his help.

The idea appealed for reasons Sam tamped down. He'd call Walker back at a reasonable hour and see what he wanted. If he could offer help, he would. Nothing more to it.

Chapter 8

SAM THOUGHT about calling Nathan for days before he finally did. The remembered awkwardness of their last encounter made dialing the number a daunting prospect. But the guy had sounded ragged around the edges on his message—not much different than he had right after the murder. No new information had come to light about Emma's death. In the few times Sam had gone to the station to ask around, he'd been given the typical "this case is still open" brush-off. Either they had no leads, or the police were still gathering evidence and biding their time.

Even though weeks had passed since he'd seen Nathan, nervous adrenaline kicked in once Sam hit send and the phone started ringing. There was no formal greeting or hello. Instead Nathan launched right in over the din of background noise.

"You called back. I wasn't sure you would."

"Sorry it took me so long." He flushed as he thought about what he'd been doing when Nathan originally left the message.

"It's all right. I'm glad you did."

A car honked in the background. It sounded like Nathan was out of town. Stonebridge didn't bustle anymore.

"It's nothing. So what's up? How are you?"

"Oh, not great. But better since the last time I saw you. I apologize for how I acted, by the way."

Sam wasn't exactly sure what Nathan was apologizing for—not calling? Avoiding Sam? By now Sam had concluded his hard-on in the pool had made Nathan uncomfortable. Still, he said, "There's no reason for you to apologize."

Loud construction noise jackhammered through the phone.

"Sorry about the commotion," said Nathan. "I had to leave town for a couple of days on business, but I'll be back tomorrow. Can you meet?"

"Yeah, sure. Where and when?"

"Eight o'clock at La Fronde. I'll make the reservation."

"Are you sure you wouldn't prefer someplace a little more casual?" La Fronde had an excellent reputation, but Sam had never been. A five-star French dinner would put him out at least a hundred bucks.

Nathan cleared his throat. "What did you have in mind?"

"My local—the Lucky Star. It's a little more in my price range, if you know what I mean. They have excellent burgers and fries. French fries."

Nathan didn't laugh at the joke. "If you'd rather, sure, though I was planning on paying, just so you know."

Fuck. Had he misread this entire situation? Had Nathan asked him on a date?

Ridiculous.

"That's generous of you," Sam said. "But I'll feel more comfortable at the Star. I don't think I even have anything to wear to such a fancy place."

"All right, Sam. Eight o'clock tomorrow at the Star. I've got to go. I'll see you then."

Without another word, the line went dead. Sam stood with his cell phone in his hand, staring at it as though it could explain what had just happened.

He spent the rest of the night scouring the Internet to see if he'd missed any developments in Emma's case over the past couple of weeks. The incident—the murder—had been fading from his mind under the avalanche of his regular worries. It had faded from the news too, it seemed. Nothing turned up. After a few newspaper mentions and an obit that Sam—thankfully—hadn't had to write, the case disappeared from the headlines, replaced by the news du jour.

He leaned back in his desk chair, sighed, and rubbed his temples to ward off an impending headache. Sam's parents' deaths had been accidental, and he still hadn't figured out how to make it stop hurting. He couldn't imagine living with the knowledge that a killer was on the loose, possibly never to be found.

It would be like hell on earth.

AT A little before eight, Sam left his apartment to head down to the Star, hoping to get there early and station himself before Nathan arrived. Rachel was behind the bar, wearing a black leather vest. She'd streaked her Afro with purple, and it suited her. Sam sauntered up and took a seat.

"Hey, Rach." He leaned forward and fished his wallet from his back pocket. "I'll take a triple Jack on the rocks."

"It's Monday. Are you serious?"

"I consider Monday part of the weekend. And anyway, I'm meeting a friend."

"Oh, Yuri's coming?"

"I'll have you know I have more friends than you and Yuri, thanks very much."

"Oooh." Her eyes went devilish. "A date, then."

"It's not a date." In spite of himself, his cheeks warmed.

Rachel arched an eyebrow and grabbed a pint glass. "You get Guinness."

The place was pretty quiet, but he recognized a couple of guys sitting at one of the high tops beyond the bar as friends of Cowboy Boots. One of them gave him the eye and smiled. Maybe old CB had given him a good report.

By the time Nathan showed up, Sam had been nursing his beer so long it had grown warm. He knocked back the last sip with a grimace and stood up to face him.

Nathan looked like he'd come straight from work. He wore one of his trim-fitting suits and a dark tie. The whole ensemble made him stick out like a sore thumb at the Star.

"Hi." Nathan extended his hand. "Sorry I'm a little late. It's good to see you, Sam."

"You too."

They shook, and Sam relished the warm touch. He wondered if he imagined Nathan brushing his palm gently as their hands released. Surely the gesture hadn't been intentional, yet the mere fantasy of Nathan's interest made Sam's heart speed up.

"You want to grab a table?" he asked to settle himself.

"Sure. Can I get you another?" Nathan gestured toward the empty glass and beckoned to Rachel. She did a slight double take, a flash of recognition passing over her face before she schooled her expression and cleared her throat.

"Nathan, this is a friend of mine, Rachel Mayer. Rachel, Nathan Walker."

Unlike most of the men in the place, Nathan kept his gaze on Rachel's face as they shook hands and he placed his order.

"My condolences to you and your family," Rachel said. "I hope they find the asshole who did it, and he gets what he deserves."

"Thank you."

"This round's on me." She looked again from Sam to Nathan. Sam could see the wheels turning, but he didn't have time to explain. He followed Nathan away from the bar to a quieter corner of the room. The lights dimmed as they sat, and Sam contemplated murdering his best friend.

"Sorry about that back there," Sam said. "Rachel's a little on the outspoken side."

Nathan shrugged as he stretched his long legs under the table. "No apologies needed. I appreciate her directness, to be honest. Everyone else is afraid to talk about it."

Sam nodded, rubbing his finger over a bead of condensation on his glass.

"That's one of the reasons I asked you to meet with me," Nathan said. "I confess I have an ulterior motive."

"I figured. I know there aren't any leads so far."

"And you're a reporter. So tell me what that means—months without an arrest."

"It's not good."

"I want this case solved. For Emma," Nathan added quietly. The flash of fresh, real pain across his face cut like a blade deep into Sam's gut.

"So, how can I help?"

"You can tell me, for starters, what happened that day. I remember—well, I don't remember much, aside from seeing you down at the station. But you'd been to the house, before...."

Sam took another sip of beer, relieved Nathan wasn't going to bring up the swimming and ensuing awkwardness. Good. "It's hard to remember all the details."

"Try."

While the conversation he'd had with Emma had grown foggy with time, he still remembered the gist of it. Nathan might not like what he had to say, but if it would help, he had a right to know.

"We had a bit of a strange conversation, to tell you the truth. Pretty personal. She seemed to be having a rough day."

"How personal?" Nathan leaned forward.

"Well, it was a little vague. She asked what I would do if I ever found out someone I cared about did something terrible. Whether I would forgive them."

Sam kept his eyes down given the awkward nature of the conversation, but the silence from the other side of the table compelled him to glance up. Nathan had gone rigid and pale. His dark eyes focused on a place beyond Sam's head, as though he were seeing something horrible played out in detail, like a man caught in the midst of a revelation—or a memory. The dull noise of other bar conversations faded, and an uncomfortable pressure squeezed at Sam's chest.

Once-clear facts started to blur and twist. Sam had been so convinced of Nathan's innocence the night at the police station, and then later during their nightly swims, that he hadn't even bothered to consider the alternative. Nathan's shock and grief didn't rule out the possibility he'd killed Emma. Out of pity, empathy, or something else entirely, Sam had let that possible reality slip away, and now it stared back at him through the hollows of Nathan's eyes. Guilt.

Sam's thoughts must have been plain as day, because Nathan's face changed, the emotion traded for a wary expression.

Instead of speaking, Nathan knocked back the rest of his drink, squinting his eyes shut as he did so. When he finished, he stood and asked "another?" before going to the bar.

It didn't add up. Nathan had been devastated when Sam took him back to his apartment, and since the last time they'd seen each other, he'd obviously been having a rough time. And what about his obsession with bringing the killer to justice? If he were guilty, he wouldn't be pressing for further investigation now that the police had lost the thread. Or would he?

That thought kept Sam in his seat once Nathan came back with two more drinks—whiskey, this time.

He got straight to the point. "You think I did it?"

"I admit the thought crossed my mind."

"I don't blame you." Nathan sighed and ran a hand through his dark hair. "I'd probably think the same thing, in your position. But I want you to know, I didn't. I would never—Listen," he said, his voice a harsh whisper. "Whatever was wrong between Emma and me, I would never have hurt her. What you told me threw me for a loop."

"So she *was* talking about you? I'm sorry, and I don't mean to pry into your personal life, but I'm totally lost here."

Nathan seemed to be considering Sam's words as they stared at one another. The intensity of the moment stretched for several beats, until Nathan folded his hands on the table and leaned even closer. "I'm sorry I'm being cryptic. Let's say I have a solid alibi for the night Emma was killed, and it's not what you think. Not exactly, anyway."

"You weren't having an affair?" The liquor burned a path down Sam's esophagus, warming his stomach. He resisted the urge to knock back the entire drink in one go.

"Honestly, I can't say any more."

Sam couldn't stop himself. "James Bond fan?"

At that moment one of the guys from earlier, the friend of Cowboy Boots, decided to make his presence known. "Hey," he said to

Sam, standing a little too close to the table for friendly conversation. "Don't I know you?"

"Yeah. We met a few weeks back. Briefly. I'm Sam." Sam hesitated, torn between wanting to flirt back and feeling awkward with Nathan sitting at the table. He didn't hide his orientation. He simply knew from experience most straight guys preferred to be kept in the dark about gay mating rituals.

The guy—cute, a little shorter and more twinkish than Sam usually liked—smiled. "I thought so. Richard." He extended his hand, and Sam took it. Richard's youth showed in his eagerness and lack of finesse. He bit one pretty lip between his teeth, eyes flicking between Sam and Nathan, whose expression remained impassive throughout the exchange. "Anyway, sorry to interrupt your date."

"Oh," Sam gave the kid's hand a squeeze before releasing it, and a small piece of paper slipped into his palm. "We're not on a date. Just friends having a drink."

"Oh—*cool*." Richard's smile widened. "I'll see you around, then."

"Sounds good."

The kid sauntered away, swinging his little ass, and Sam had to stifle a laugh. He tossed the number onto the table.

Nathan watched him with an inscrutable expression, but his jaw was ticking—a barely visible movement.

"That doesn't bother you, does it?" Sam gestured to the piece of crumpled paper. Thinking better of it, he picked it up and tucked it into his pocket, where it couldn't cause further offense.

"It seems pretty easy for you."

"What, getting hit on?" Sam snorted. "Yeah. It's not exactly rocket science. Sorry if you're weirded out." He didn't bother to mention the hookup apps on his phone that made finding guys even easier.

Maybe Sam imagined it, but Nathan seemed to stare at his mouth for a moment before glancing away. He chalked it up to wishful thinking.

"Wait a second," Sam said to get them back on track. "Let me see if I've got it right. You admit you and Emma were having some problems, but say those issues have nothing to do with her murder—for which you have an alibi that you can't tell me about, but must have been good enough to keep you out of jail."

Nathan ran his thumb over his full bottom lip. "I'm not answering that question. You can think what you like. None of it matters now. What does is the fact I'm not giving up on this case. And I think you can help, if you want."

"How do you expect me to help when you won't tell me what's going on?"

"Think about it, Sam. Why don't you tell me what you think happened to Emma?"

The basic details arranged themselves into order. It did seem cut and dry. "I think whoever planned to rob your house freaked out and shot her when she drew her gun."

Nathan frowned. "Interesting theory, and I'd be inclined to agree with you, but you don't have any of the facts. For one, there was no sign of forced entry."

"Maybe she left the door unlocked."

"Emma never left the door unlocked."

Sam nodded. He couldn't remember ever going to the house and finding an unlocked door.

"And Emma hadn't drawn her gun. It was missing."

"Her gun was stolen?"

Nathan took a sip of his drink. "And so was her cell phone. By the time I got home, the whole place had been swept clean by the cops. There were no broken windows. Oh, and aside from a few cracked eggs on the floor, which seem to suggest she was surprised, nothing was out of place. Nothing else was stolen save some petty cash in the front-hall drawer. No real valuables were missing, aside from the phone."

"Wait a minute. Those eggs were already there."

"What?"

Sam scrunched his forehead and closed his eyes. He remembered the eggs on the floor and how Emma had walked right by them as if she didn't even see—evidence of her troubled thoughts, but now so much more. "When I saw Emma that day, when we talked, I was in your kitchen. The eggs were there on the floor, already broken. She said she dropped them when I rang the doorbell. It startled her. Almost like she was expecting someone."

Nathan narrowed his eyes. "And then there's the way she was killed."

"I thought—"

"Emma wasn't shot. She was strangled. Her hands were tied. There was an impact wound to her skull...."

"Jesus." It didn't sound like the type of crime committed by a random burglar.

Nathan's mouth went tight, his lips whitening. "I have a friend at the coroner's office. Whoever did this was careful not to leave any traces behind. Even though she was small, Emma was a fighter. She would have gouged the hell out of the person's eyes, at the very least. Fuck." His eyes glazed over.

"Do you think she knew her killer?"

"I don't know. Nothing else makes any sense. Emma would have protected herself with her weapon if a stranger broke into the house. Someone surprised her and then killed her. A strong man with large hands. And it wasn't me."

Sam hesitated before he spoke his next thought out loud. He had no idea how Nathan might react. "Do you think it was possible she was having an affair?" he said, as gently as possible. "I mean, I know you think she was talking about you, but what if she was talking about herself?"

Nathan stared at him with obvious shock. "I don't know. I hadn't even...."

"I'm sorry, and I know it hurts to consider the possibility, but if you two were having problems, it isn't so unusual to go looking for comfort somewhere else."

If they did something terrible, could you forgive them? Yeah. It sure as hell could have been Emma's way of working out her own guilt, maybe even getting the courage to break it off with whoever she was seeing on the side. And then tell Nathan.

And if the guy knew what Emma had been planning to do....

At the other side of the table, it appeared the same gears were turning in Nathan's mind. He looked like he might be sick. "I need some air."

"Let's take a walk."

After Sam settled up with Rachel, he met Nathan outside. The cool fall night cut through the hazy warmth of the alcohol and invigorated Sam almost instantly. He motioned toward the right, away from some of the seedier neighborhoods and down along the waterfront. It wasn't exactly a picturesque scene, what with the cargo ships and industrial docks. But in the darkness, the glowing lights shimmered on the water of the bay, lending it a sort of lurid beauty. The Baptist Street Bridge rose in the foreground, a gateway between the inner bay and the cold waters of Long Island Sound. They headed toward it, lost in their own thoughts.

Once they'd made it halfway across the bridge's narrow pedestrian walkway, Nathan stopped and looked down into the black, oily water.

"Can you think of anyone, Nathan, anyone who it could have been? Maybe someone from the force? Someone she spent a lot of time with, or talked a lot about?"

Nathan's frown deepened. "She was helping to train a new guy. McCormick."

Sam nodded. McCormick was beefy and tall, definitely strong enough to strangle someone. The day Sam went to the station to ask about the mayor's plan, he'd seemed hesitant to speak too freely. At the time, Sam had attributed it to his newness to the force. Looking back on it, maybe he'd just been cagey talking to a reporter who knew Emma. He didn't give off a violent vibe, but a couple of brief interactions didn't prove anything. Sam tried, and failed, to remember if Emma and McCormick had flirted at all, or seemed closer than normal for colleagues when he'd seen them together.

"You ever meet him?" Nathan asked.

"A couple of times. We talked about the mayor's two-year plan."

"Streets Clean for 2015?"

Sam snorted. "That's the one. I'm insulted you didn't read my article."

"I didn't know you'd written one."

"Yeah, for the *Gazette*. It was pretty crappy, so don't worry about it." It hadn't even been published until after they'd lost touch. Sam shivered and wished he'd worn something more substantial than a button-down. The wind had picked up, making it feel at least twenty degrees cooler than it had been near the bar. "So, she mentioned him to you?"

"I've been traveling a lot over the past year, but she did talk about him on a pretty regular basis. I always thought it was sisterly affection."

"Listen, I know Emma loved you very much. Whatever happened, that much is true." He patted Nathan's arm and let his hand linger there.

Nathan smiled sadly. "It's not about jealousy. If she'd told me she was unhappy, yeah, I would have been upset. But if this is true, and she put her trust in someone, maybe even loved them, and they—" He turned away and squeezed his eyes shut. "God, I'm a mess."

"Maybe we should let this go for the night, all right?"

"Too bad it's so cold." Nathan returned his gaze to the water under the bridge. "I could use a swim."

"Not tonight."

"No. Not tonight." Sam thought he detected a hint of wistfulness.

"Do you want to crash at my place? You probably shouldn't be driving. My bed's all yours." Nathan had downed several double whiskeys at the bar. He was a tall guy, but Sam got the feeling he didn't drink much under normal circumstances.

Nathan seemed to consider the proposition seriously, and Sam's stomach did a little flip. The look he'd given Sam at the bar returned for an instant. This time he didn't imagine it. But maybe he did. By the time Sam got his bearings to insist he hadn't meant what Nathan thought he meant, Nathan had turned away and started walking back toward the bar.

Chapter 9

SAM GROANED as he regained consciousness. His phone was ringing close to his ear.

He cleared his throat. "Hello?"

"Sam, where the hell are you?"

"Hey, Yuri," Sam said, his voice gravelly. "What time is it?"

"It's after ten. You were supposed to be here an hour ago."

Sam realized several things at once. He was naked. There was another person in his bed. And his bed was actually… not his bed. Or his room. There was a Madonna poster on the wall. Shit. The curly-haired kid from the bar. He smiled sleepily at Sam and stretched, yawning. Sam turned away and started searching for his clothes.

"I'll be right there," he said into the phone. "I'm sorry."

"Yeah, well sorry isn't good enough. Sam, I know you're my friend, but if this happens again, you're fired."

"You can't fire me, I'm your partner."

"Not for long if you don't get your act together."

"Goddammit." Sam found his socks under the bed and sniffed them before pulling them on. His head pounded, and the foul taste in his mouth reminded him of all the whiskey he'd drunk after Nathan had left him at the bridge the night before.

At least the adrenaline shocked him out of his hangover. The kid reached out and touched his shoulder.

"Shit. Was that your boss? Are you going to get in trouble?"

"Nah, it'll be fine. My partner's a little testy before he's had his morning coffee."

"I had a great time last night," said the kid.

"Me too," said Sam absently, shoving a foot into a shoe. "Hey, I'll see you around."

"Sure. You've got my number."

Sam hit the gas and caught up with the rest of his crew in record time. He hopped out of the truck, avoiding Yuri's gaze as he did.

Juan gave him a pat on the back, but his expression said he wouldn't want to be in Sam's shoes for anything.

Sam hated letting Yuri down. He felt small, like the time he'd gotten suspended for fighting with another boy at school—one of Petersen's minions. The asshole had deserved it. He'd been tormenting Sam all year, calling him a fag, leaving hate-filled notes in his locker, tripping him in the hall. Sam had taken it and taken it, letting it roll off his back until the day he couldn't bear it anymore. He'd punched the guy so hard, he'd bruised his own hand.

God, his father had been so disappointed in him. He'd come to pick Sam up that day and hadn't spoken to him for almost a week. His mother, always the peacekeeper, had tried to intervene, but Sam's father could be a stubborn asshole when he wanted to be. He was angry because Sam wouldn't tell anyone why he'd done it. And Sam had feared outing himself over everything else, even his father's silent treatment. With Yuri casting dirty looks his way, he felt suspiciously like his teenaged self again.

After they finished the last job, Sam tried to slip into his truck unnoticed, but Yuri caught him.

"I need to talk to you, Sam."

"Look, I'm sorry about being late." He shuffled on his feet.

"I'm not going to ask you where you were or why you were late, because I don't care."

Ouch.

"Okay. Well, then I guess there's nothing else to say."

"There's a lot more to say. You can't keep living like there's no future."

"I don't know what you're talking about."

"Yes, you do. Hey." Yuri grabbed his arm before he could turn. "I know what it's like to lose someone too. You're afraid to move on with your life, and it's killing you."

"I'm not afraid. And this isn't about Emma."

"You think I'm talking about Emma? I'm talking about your brother and your parents. It's the worst thing in the world. It hurts. It's horrible. I know. But that doesn't give you an excuse, not anymore. It's been years, Sam. You're so goddamn smart. You could be doing anything you want. You wanna tell me this life is really what you want? No wonder you drink yourself stupid every night."

Sam's face burned. "I'm not wasting my life. I do things."

Yuri scoffed. "Yeah. Getting laid and talking about your blog, which you write in, never."

"I've been busy."

"It makes me mad, because it could be something great. You could have a job you actually liked, and you could make enough money to take care of Tim too."

"It's not that easy. I've tried—"

Yuri cut him off. "You haven't tried. You really haven't tried."

"You have no idea what you're talking about," Sam gritted through his teeth.

Yuri didn't seem to care about arguing in the middle of a suburban street with half the neighbors watching, including their customers. His eyes flashed with anger.

"Oh, cut the crap, Sam. You pretend you don't care, but inside you're scared as hell. You're scared as hell." He started backing away, and the dismissal stung as keenly as his words had. But Sam wasn't going to let go so easily, not with Yuri so clearly spoiling for a fight.

"Don't stop now. Tell me how you really feel." Sam could barely control the quaver in his voice.

"See? You always have to turn it around. Rachel told me about you and that Walker guy at the Star last night."

"So now you two are talking behind my back. Wonderful."

"Do you think it's a good idea to get involved with him?" Yuri asked, quieter now.

"I think you're jealous. I think that's what this is about."

Yuri frowned. "Believe whatever you want. I don't care. But if I were you, I'd seriously consider straightening out my own life first, before I started worrying about anyone else's."

WHEN NATHAN called again, Sam almost didn't pick up. Yuri's words still echoed in his mind, circling around and around, little bits of truth breaking off and lodging like daggers in his brain. He hadn't touched a drop of booze in days, and it was starting to make him irritable.

"Sam," Nathan said when he answered. "I'm sorry about the other night. I shouldn't have left like that."

"It's all right."

"No, it's not, and I think I owe you an explanation. Can you come over?"

It was like Nathan's voice had a direct link to Sam's sympathetic nervous system. He started looking around the living room for his shoes. "What's going on?"

"I'll talk to you when you get here."

Nathan looked better than he had the last time Sam saw him. He'd shaven, and the absence of dark circles indicated he'd gotten some sleep. When he unlatched the door and let him in, Sam immediately noticed other changes too. A stack of large cardboard boxes almost blocked the way to the kitchen. In the living room, the sofa had disappeared, along with the bookshelves that had lined the far wall. Emma's piano had been removed too. Sam spun around, disconcerted.

"Going somewhere?" he asked.

Nathan tilted his head and stuck his hands in his pockets while he surveyed the room. "I'm taking an apartment downtown. This house is too big—too many memories."

"I get it." Sam swallowed. Unloading his own family home on the nearest paying customer had been one of the most painful, and necessary, things he'd ever done in his life. He'd needed the money, but more importantly, he couldn't imagine ever living in the place again.

"This is all going to Goodwill," Nathan said. He gestured toward a large flat screen television wedged between two boxes. It was much nicer than Sam's.

"Are you moving or joining the priesthood?"

Nathan scoffed. "Hardly. I never watch TV, though, so it's not really a sacrifice."

"Still, you might want it someday. And the rest—maybe you should put it all in storage or something instead. Wait awhile before you make a decision. There could be some things in here you end up wanting to keep." He still had several boxes of family belongings in a small storage unit, including a bunch of Tim's stuff. Just in case.

"I don't think so."

Most of the plants were still in place near the windows. A few orchids that looked like they had seen better days sat sadly among the boxes. Sam picked one up, recognizing it as Emma's favorite.

"It's dying, like all the others." Nathan's voice came as a surprise from over Sam's shoulder.

"The soil's too wet." Sam prodded the plant at the base of the stem. "You've got to let them dry out in between watering."

"You'd think with all the time she spent with those plants, I would have learned how to take care of them."

"It was her interest, not yours. And I think they seem more complicated than they are. All they need is light, humidity, and a little bit of temperature modulation." Sam hesitated, aware of Nathan's proximity behind him. "If you want I can show you—"

"Take it when you go."

Sam shook his head. "I couldn't—"

Nathan smiled grimly and touched the bloomless plant. "It's just going to die if you leave it with me."

Sam nodded and set the orchid aside. It seemed right he should take it.

"So, where are you moving to in the city?"

"My agent's still looking for a place. Of course, my mother wants me to move closer to her and my father." He snorted. "I think she still thinks of me as a child, especially now." His expression softened in spite of his tone. "I think I'm overdue for a visit home."

"Where's home?" Sam couldn't help being curious—he'd imagined so many things about Nathan but knew very little about his background.

"I grew up in California, mostly."

"Ah. You don't want to move back west?" Sam hedged, hoping Nathan would say more.

"No."

The finality of the word told Sam not to push further. Nathan didn't seem inclined to give details. Maybe he didn't get along with his folks.

"What about you?" Nathan asked. "Do you have any family nearby?"

"My parents died in a pretty bad car accident a few years back."

Nathan's head shot up like he'd been slapped. "Oh Sam, I'm so sorry."

"Yeah, well, it happened a long time ago." He hated the inevitable awkwardness of this part. It was best to cut it off at the pass, but before he could, Nathan spoke again.

"How old were you?"

Sam toed the Persian carpet he'd often admired and wondered if Nathan would get rid of it too. "Twenty-one."

"That's not so long ago. I don't suppose you ever get over losing someone close." Sam's attention drifted from the soft curl of Nathan's hair to the full line of his mouth, which appeared alternately severe and sensuous, depending on his mood. Nathan's eyes caught and held Sam's. They were dark and focused. Sympathetic, but not pitying.

"I guess not," Sam said.

"Do you have any siblings?"

Sam nodded slowly. "Yeah. I have a younger brother."

"And he…?" Nathan trailed off, leaving the question hanging gently in the air.

"He's been in a coma ever since. Or I guess a vegetative state, technically. But yeah."

Nathan reached out and squeezed his arm. The warm solidity of Nathan's hand was comforting in a way Sam couldn't name. He swallowed and leaned into the touch for a moment before it fell away.

Nathan cleared his throat. "I shouldn't have pried. I'm sorry."

"It's okay. Sometimes it feels good to talk about it."

"And there's nothing they can do for him?"

"Only wait. But it's been so long, they don't think he'll wake up." He swiped the pad of his thumb under his eye and pretended to examine one of the paintings on the wall. Then he shrugged and forced a smile. "I don't think you called me to listen to my sob story."

"I didn't know you had one. But I don't mind."

"Listen. Before you tell me why you did call me over, I've been thinking. I'm not sure I can help you with this case."

"What? Why?" The surprise in his voice caught Sam off guard.

"To be honest, I think I'd be more of a liability to you than anything else. I'm not… dependable."

"You're the one who came up with the lead in the first place."

"I'm sorry." Sam ran his fingers through his hair, feeling awkward. He probably should have told Nathan over the phone and skipped the visit. But somewhere along the line, he'd started thinking of Nathan as a friend.

"Come with me."

With slight reluctance, Sam followed Nathan to the kitchen, the only room in the downstairs area still relatively untouched by the imminent move. Nathan snagged two bottles out of the fridge—water, Sam realized with a twinge of disappointment. They sat down at the kitchen island, and Sam remembered another day, an almost-identical situation. His throat tightened.

Nathan perched on his stool and leaned his elbows on the counter. "I'm about to tell you something that's considered classified information. I need your word it will stay between us."

"Of course."

"I told you before I was a consultant, but that's not entirely true." He looked slightly contrite. "I work for the government."

"I knew it. Fucking CIA."

"Close, but no."

Sam rolled his eyes. "FBI, then. Jesus, I'm sitting in the kitchen with a James Bond wannabe."

Nathan smirked. "It didn't start out like that. After I graduated Yale, I worked as a member of a think tank—mostly domestic criminal policy, strategy and execution, that sort of thing. It was fine for a while, but I wasn't happy. After I met Emma, she encouraged me to change careers."

Sam nodded, afraid if he said anything, Nathan wouldn't continue. He had a feeling whatever he was about to hear wouldn't be pretty.

"I have to omit certain details, you understand. The case I've been involved in is still in progress. But the long and short of it is, I'm part of a human trafficking task force that deals mainly with sweatshops, sexual slavery, and prostitution. About a year ago, I was called in to investigate a sex ring in the Midwest. There's an underground club that caters to all sorts of tastes. Very discreet, very elite." He paused, as if to gauge Sam's response. "There were rumors of children."

"Shit."

"As you can imagine, there's a lot of money involved. Lots of high-profile people. Everyone in the place is required to wear a mask to maintain anonymity. But even so, even with all of the privacy, it's not until you get in really deep that the worst... illegalities are an option."

Nathan took a long drink of water, which made his Adam's apple bob. Meanwhile, Sam's brain raced to catch up with what he'd heard so far and what he suspected was coming.

"Did Emma know what the case was about?"

The question went right to the heart of the matter. Nathan sighed. "She knew the general area in which I worked. This case was different than what I'd done before, though. She wasn't particularly thrilled about it, but she trusted me. They gave me a partner for the job, an insider. He had connections with some of the club's clients. We went in under deep cover as a bored couple looking to branch out and experiment with other people. Share, if you will."

Sam wondered if his brain might explode. "You posed as a couple."

"Yes. My boss felt going in alone would be too dangerous, especially since I was a novice. I'd had some training with my partner, of course."

Training. As a gay couple.

"Huh." Sam eyed the glass cabinets, looking for bottles. He had the feeling he was going to need something stronger than water. "Did you... um...."

"You're asking if I fucked him?"

"Yeah." Sam's pants felt uncomfortably tight. He shifted in his seat.

"In order to be convincing, we were affectionate with each other. But no, we didn't have sex at the club."

Sam noticed the evasion but didn't comment. "Okay. So what happened?"

"I always thought I'd be able to get away with being an observer. Some people just like to watch. But after a while, management started to get suspicious. My partner fucked other people, but I never did, and we were no closer to finding the kids. I realized that if I didn't start participating, I might ruin the case and get us both killed while I was at it."

"So you started participating." Participating. Fucking. That's what participation meant in this situation. Sam wiped his sweaty palms on his jeans.

"I justified it to myself because I knew there were children being abused, somewhere, and I could never help them if I blew my cover." Guilt and regret mingled with arousal in Nathan's voice as he recounted his story.

"You had to, for the case." Sam's own speech sounded breathy, and it shamed him.

"Yes, but I liked it. I liked it with the women... but I liked it with the men too. I've always known I found men as attractive as women, but I'd never—I loved Emma."

If Nathan wanted reassurance, Sam had no idea how to give it to him. The words he'd spoken only seconds before still hadn't quite sunk in. In fact, Sam wasn't entirely sure he'd heard right. He didn't know whether he should be outraged for Emma's sake, sympathetic to Nathan, or turned on. While his mind was deciding on the first two options, his body had settled on the third.

"So what happened?"

"I traveled back and forth for almost a year, and eventually we gained the confidence of the people in charge. Money can buy anything." Nathan sighed.

"You found the kids?"

Nathan's eyes turned cold. "One of the owners asked if I wanted to try someone a little younger. He brought me a boy who couldn't have been more than thirteen. He didn't speak a word of English."

"Fucking hell." The statement quashed Sam's arousal, replacing it with sinking horror.

"I could have killed the sick bastard right then with my bare hands. I might have, but the most important thing was to get the kid out of there. So we made the bust and shut the whole place down."

Sam nodded slowly. "And you never told Emma."

"I was ashamed of what I'd done. I like to think I would have come clean if I'd had the chance. But I never did."

Sam had begun to put the puzzle together, and it was even worse than what he'd first imagined. His stomach churned at the cruel irony. "Wait, that's not where you were when—"

The devastated expression on Nathan's face said it all.

"I helped save those kids, but the cost was Emma."

Chapter 10

SAM WONDERED if anything he could say would change Nathan's mind. Even though they didn't know each other well, he had the feeling the answer was a big, fat no. Still, Sam considered himself pretty much an expert on the whole self-blame thing. He'd been going around that hamster wheel for years. And even though he knew it was useless, he shook his head. "You can't think about it like that."

"I can, and I do."

"It wasn't your fault."

"If I had been here, she'd still be safe." Nathan crumpled his empty water bottle. He looked like he wanted to throw it. Sam figured that might not be such a bad idea.

"Nathan, I know you don't want to hear it, but facts are facts. If a killer has a motivation, he's going to find a way. You had no idea something like this would ever happen. How could you predict it?" The man had risked his life for the sake of children who would otherwise still be living a nightmare. That had to count for something.

"I understand what you're trying to do, and I appreciate it. But it doesn't change the fact she's dead." He braced his hands against the granite counter and let his head fall forward. For the first time, Sam noticed a few white hairs among the nearly black strands.

"No. I know it doesn't."

Another drift of silence stretched between them, and Sam's stomach rumbled audibly. He hadn't eaten all afternoon. Nathan probably hadn't either. He seemed to have lost weight over the past couple months. Despite her busy schedule, Emma had loved to cook, which was the reason for the robust kitchen garden outside. He supposed the garden would die with the oncoming winter. Whether new tenants would revive it in the spring remained to be seen.

"You hungry?" Sam pulled out his cell phone.

"Not especially."

"You should eat anyway. What's there for delivery around here? Anyone come out this far?"

"Sam, you don't have to stay."

"Do you want me to go?"

Nathan blinked twice, as though surprised by the question. "No." And then, more softly, "Nero's delivers."

"Well that settles it. I'm staying and I'm hungry. So what do you like on your pie?"

"Anything is fine."

"Pineapple and anchovies it is," Sam said. And then, when Nathan gave him a look halfway between skeptical and scared, he amended, "Kidding, kidding. I'm a pepperoni kind of guy, myself."

"Like I said, anything is fine—anything except anchovies and pineapple."

After Sam made the order, they returned to the packed-up living room. Sam found a clear spot on the floor to sit, and he watched as Nathan picked through a pile of stuff he hadn't boxed yet. Tchotchkes, most of it. Nathan weighed each item in his hands before placing it into either the box on the left or the right. A small mantelpiece clock went to the right. A vase to the left. He carefully wrapped framed photos in newspaper and stacked them in a pile without looking at the pictures. Sam, however, managed glimpses before they disappeared into the black-and-white print. A picture of Emma standing in the garden. Nathan and Emma somewhere tropical, then at a winter cabin bundled in fashionable ski gear. All of them typical photos you would expect to see in any middle-class, married couple's home. They spoke of easy times, financial security, and happiness.

Instead of feeling sad for Nathan, however, Sam's chest twinged for a different reason. He'd never wanted that type of relationship with anyone. But maybe, even though it hurt like a sonofabitch, having someone to lose would be worth it.

On the heels of that thought came another. Those pictures, this house, all of the trappings of a happy life meant nothing if the people in them were lying to each other. Nathan and Emma had seemed content, but everything Sam had learned since her death suggested otherwise. And if that was true, maybe love didn't fucking exist. Or if it did, it didn't last.

Satisfied with the return of his cynicism, Sam closed his eyes and leaned his head against the wall, lulled by the quiet *thunk-thunk* of discarded or kept items being tossed into boxes.

"It got to me, you know."

"What?" Sam asked, his skin prickling.

"Doing what I did with strangers. Oh, sure, I got to know their bodies, but never faces. Never real names."

The darkened space of the imagined club and other, more secret chambers opened up before Sam. People twining together, half-dressed. Sam shuddered. He could see Nathan there, surrounded by willing men—the easy, controlled strength of his every movement and his dark, dark eyes. He'd fit right in. No wonder he'd been chosen in the first place.

"You said you liked it."

"I did and I didn't. I—It was more like an addiction. At first I hated it. I didn't want people I didn't know to touch me, and I didn't want to touch them. So I made rules. I was very strict. And then, yes, it became like an addiction. I was good at it. Jesus, I can't believe I'm telling you this."

Sam didn't trust himself to speak, afraid he'd give himself away. He was thankful Nathan had his back turned.

The whole thing seemed strange. If Emma had suspected Nathan's infidelity, she'd apparently never confronted him about it. And yet some of the things she'd said to Sam suggested she not only suspected, but knew. Perhaps she had spoken to the man who'd been working with Nathan on the case, this enigmatic new partner Nathan had mentioned.

Nathan's shoulders tensed. When he turned around, Sam almost didn't recognize him. His expression had grown shrewd, calculating. The eye contact made Sam uncomfortable, but he didn't look away.

"I need you to remember what she said, exactly." Nathan's voice took on a hard edge.

"I told you. It was about trust, and what I would do if I ever found out someone I cared about did something terrible."

"That's not good enough. I need her exact words."

Nathan crossed the room and suddenly the air suffused with a sharp tension that fired Sam's blood. He stared up at Nathan, defiant.

"I'm sorry, but that's all I remember."

"You said she seemed to be having a bad day. How could you tell?"

Sam swallowed and tried not to stare at the bulge of Nathan's crotch, eye-level and only a few tantalizing feet away. "I hadn't seen her since I talked to her at the station about the whole Feldman fiasco, before she went to break the autopsy news to Patricia Feldman. When she answered the door, she looked like she'd been crying. Her face was pale."

"And she let you inside."

"Yes. She wrote a check for the landscaping. Your bill was past due. And then I noticed the eggs in the kitchen."

"She said she'd dropped them?"

"That's what she told me. The doorbell startled her when I rang it."

Nathan crouched on the floor. He rested one of his hands on Sam's knee, and his expression changed. His mouth curved into a seductive smile. "But she didn't clean them up while you were talking?"

"No. She sort of acted like they weren't even there." If Nathan handled his suspects like this—all fierce interrogation one minute and sex the next—Sam actually pitied them. How could anyone resist? The pressure of Nathan's hand on his knee didn't abate.

"She was distracted."

"Yes. And to be honest, I'm not entirely convinced she wasn't talking about herself, Nathan. Remember the McCormick theory?

Maybe she was waiting for a visit and she wasn't expecting the doorbell to ring so soon."

Nathan seemed to be considering what he'd said, so Sam pushed further. "How would she even have found out what you'd done for the case? Did she know your new partner? Could she have asked him?"

"No. It was important for him to remain anonymous."

"Anyone else you work with? Your boss?"

"Unlikely." Nathan's eyes darted to Sam's lips. Sam definitely hadn't imagined it this time.

"What? Is there like a bro code or something?"

"There are female agents too, Sam. It's more of an honor code. Or a dishonor code, depending on the situation. But yes. We take care of our own, ugly secrets and all."

"So why are you so convinced she was talking about you?"

"Because it started to affect the way I was with Emma. Certain things weren't enough for me, anymore. I wanted things she couldn't give. I wanted—"

"Hey." Sam squeezed Nathan's shoulder and was amazed at the tightness there. "It's okay."

Nathan continued, his words tumbling out in a flood "It hadn't been right between us for a while, even before the case. We hardly slept together. It was more like living with a friend than a lover, but I guess I thought it was the inevitability of marriage. We were both busy. I tried not to think about it."

"Until you started experimenting," Sam said.

"When I think back on it now and I realize how selfish I was, it makes me sick. It wouldn't have taken much for her to put two and two together. And she died thinking—" He removed his hand from Sam's knee. "She died knowing I was a goddamn liar."

The guilt eating at Nathan couldn't have felt much better than being feasted on by a school of piranhas. Cheating on your wife was one thing, but cheating on your dead wife and living with the knowledge she probably knew about it was another.

"You must think I'm a terrible person," Nathan said. He sounded more resigned than regretful.

"I think you made mistakes. Did Emma know you liked men too?"

Nathan seemed to consider this while Sam braced himself. He'd known a guy in college who'd had girlfriends on and off but, when he was drunk, liked to slip into Sam's room and blow him. One day Sam got tired of the secrecy and called him on it. It resulted in a bruised jaw and a helluva shiner. But Nathan didn't seem angry, only contemplative.

"I don't know. I never told her. But maybe she did. All I know is, I used the investigation as an excuse, told myself I was doing what I had to, when all along I knew it was more. I did it because I wanted to."

Sam sighed. "Okay. So let's leave the whole saving-abused-children part of it out for a sec. You cheated on your wife. What would have happened if she'd lived?"

"We couldn't have gone on the way we were."

"Maybe you would have gotten a divorce?"

"I don't know. Maybe. But now there's nothing I wouldn't do to have her back." His voice cracked. "I'm no good, Sam."

"Sometimes shit doesn't work out, despite good intentions. My hunch is Emma was as unhappy as you, or near as. She had to feel it wasn't working." Nathan stayed quiet, so Sam continued. "I can't tell you not to feel guilty about cheating, but Emma's death wasn't your fault, and thinking about it like that is only going to make you crazy. It's not gonna solve the murder. And the same is true for wondering what she knew or didn't know. How will that help anything?"

"I don't know, but I can't stop myself. I worry I'm too close to this case, and there's something I'm not seeing."

"That's understandable." Nathan had come to lean against the wall next to Sam. Their arms pressed lightly together. Sam wished he knew Nathan better, if for nothing else than to offer the hug he most certainly needed. The revelation about Nathan's sexuality had thrown him for a loop, though, and he couldn't help thinking back to that time in the pool, when his own arousal had been so obvious. Maybe Nathan had felt something too.

Lights in the front of the house and a rattling car engine announced the arrival of the pizza. Sam left Nathan in the living room and fished his wallet out of his pocket, figuring he should pay, since he was the one with the rumbling stomach.

"There's cash in the hall drawer," Nathan called after him. His warm, deep voice betrayed a slight tremor. Sam wondered if he'd pushed too far.

"I hope you're hungry," Sam yelled back, kicking the door shut with his foot. "I got extra cheese."

"Sounds good."

They grabbed plates and drinks from the kitchen and settled at the counter to eat. Nathan ate with a gusto unexpected in a man who'd been unenthusiastic about ordering in the first place. He'd nearly polished off his second slice by the time Sam finished his first, and Sam considered commandeering his half of the pizza before it disappeared completely.

Nathan swallowed his last bite and smiled sheepishly. "I guess I was hungrier than I thought." He licked a crumb from the side of his mouth, and Sam tried not to stare at the pink sweep of his tongue.

"Have you been eating?" Sam asked and then immediately regretted the question. It was none of his business.

"When I remember. I've never been one for cooking. I'm fine, Sam, seriously. I shouldn't have dumped all my baggage on you back there. For some reason, I find you easy to talk to."

"I've been called easy before, but not in that context." Sam smiled at his own joke, but Nathan seemed unsettled. His eyes flicked away from Sam's face to his empty plate. A strange, twisting tension anchored itself in Sam's gut, and he pushed the remainder of his dinner away. He wondered again about the pool, and all those looks and smiles they'd exchanged over the past few years, and he hated himself for wondering. It wouldn't be right. But once his mind started churning, he couldn't stop it. Worst of all, he wasn't sure he wanted to. The electricity from their earlier conversation—or interrogation—still lingered.

"So what now?" Sam asked. Nathan returned his stare with equanimity this time, but there was something challenging about his gaze.

"About?"

"About the case, of course." Sam wondered if Nathan noticed his quickening breath.

"Are you back on board?"

Sam thought about asking why a trained FBI agent like Nathan wanted someone like him around, anyway. He didn't. "I shouldn't have gone back on my word."

Nathan nodded. "Good." Then he stood. "There's something I want to show you."

"Lead the way."

The way turned out to be up the stairs and down a long, carpeted corridor toward the rear of the house. Nathan flicked a switch and illuminated a modest office filled with bookcases. A small desk faced a curtained window that looked out over the backyard. Nathan obviously hadn't made it this far with his packing. Though it was dark outside, from this vantage, Sam imagined the pool and garden would be visible, and he wondered whether Emma or Nathan had ever sat here while he worked below.

"My confession wasn't the only reason I called you over here." Nathan pressed the switch to the desktop computer, one of those fancy-schmancy, huge-screen Macs. It flashed to life, and he ran his hand over the keyboard absentmindedly before taking a seat. "We shared this office, but it was mainly Emma who used it."

He clicked a few more keys and brought up a browser and then a search history. "Take a look at this."

Sam peered over Nathan's shoulder. "It's blank."

"Exactly. She deleted her history."

"Hmm." He didn't want to add the obvious, but the insinuation was there, and it only confirmed the theory from the other night. Nathan frowned up at him.

"And it's not only the search history. The entire hard drive has been wiped. I did a sweep. No prints except for Emma's."

"So either she did it, or someone else did it with gloves on."

"Exactly." To prove his point, Nathan opened a file marked with the current year. It was empty. Everything on the computer had been erased, save the basic programs.

"Okay." Sam rubbed his hands together. "In scenario one, Emma decides to break off her affair with McCormick, or whoever it was, and knows that she's kept some incriminating evidence on the computer. So she deletes it, calls him over, and then...."

Nathan nodded as the words faded to silence. "Yes. And in scenario two, the killer gets rid of the evidence after he kills Emma. He would have had plenty of opportunity. The coroner estimated time of death at between three and five p.m. Emma was supposed to report for duty at six, and the cops didn't arrive here until after eight."

"Why not take the hard drive?" Sam scratched his head.

"Disposal would be a problem."

"True."

Nathan glared at the blank search history page, as though by concentrating hard enough he could conjure answers. He spun around in the desk chair and clasped his hands together. "Think about it. How can it have been anything but intended murder? Hardly anything stolen, and then this."

"I'd say it sounds pretty likely. Did you tell the police about the computer?"

"No. I have no proof it was wiped at the time of the murder. And if it's McCormick.... Well, let's say I want to keep my cards to myself until we have something more substantial to go on. If we don't have proper evidence, no charge is going to stick."

"Do you know who found Emma?" Sam asked.

"It was Petersen—and McCormick."

"Petersen's the type of asshole who likes to torture animals. It could have been him."

"Maybe. But what's the motive?"

"Besides being a sadistic fuck? Yeah." Sam wrinkled his nose at the thought. No way anyone would screw around on Nathan with that toad. "So we need to get the evidence. Do you know her e-mail password?"

"Yes. I guessed it. But nothing incriminating there."

"You said her phone was missing. Can you get her call history from her carrier?" Nathan nodded as Sam spoke, like he predicted the question.

"Unfortunately I don't have any jurisdiction on this case. A judge has to grant a court order for any phone record requests."

"What about girlfriends or other close friends she might have confided in?"

Nathan smiled up at him, and it took Sam aback. "What's so amusing?"

"You. These are all good thoughts, Sam. But believe me when I say I've done that and turned up nothing, so far. Whatever Emma was hiding, she was doing a damn good job of it. Or...." He straightened and turned back to the computer.

"Or what?"

"What someone else was hiding." The roster of officers at the Stonebridge Police Department loaded on the screen. There were about thirty pictures, most of them familiar to Sam. Emma's had already been removed. They sure didn't waste any time.

"Hmm." Nathan stared at the screen. After he'd scrolled all the way through, he blew out a breath. "She never had a serious problem with anyone, so far as I know, but that could have changed during the past few months of her life. We weren't exactly on a sharing basis by then."

"Someone down at the station has to know something. It's just a matter of who."

"And how to get the information."

"Why don't you get your FBI cronies to come in and use some muscle? Isn't that what they do in the movies? I guess I still don't understand why you think *I* can help you."

Nathan closed the laptop. "I've got some buddies looking into leads, but it's a delicate balance. If anyone gets suspicious, that could be it. Any remaining evidence might get destroyed. It's best for everyone to think I've accepted the break-in theory. And I haven't entirely ruled out the chance these two cases are connected. Until I do, I can't trust anyone."

"Wait. You think the child trafficking thing might have something to do with Emma's death? What about the honor code?"

"At this point, anything is possible."

Sam rubbed small circles on his temple. All this talk of conspiracy was giving him a headache—and making him thirsty.

"Okay. So if Petersen and McCormick were the first ones on the scene, they're the ones we should target."

"We? No. All you need to do is to keep your eyes and ears open. If you go asking questions down at the station, people are going to get suspicious, and you're going to get yourself killed."

"I thought you wanted my help."

"You are helping," Nathan insisted. "Just having someone to talk to about this has helped. I never would have gotten the McCormick lead if not for you."

Sam ignored the little thrill of pleasure and crossed his arms over his chest.

"Sam? Are you all right?"

"I'm fine. I was just thinking maybe I could talk to Chief Sheldon. He was a friend of my father's."

Nathan shook his head. "I think it's better if we keep this between us for now. Sheldon isn't going to take baseless accusations about his staff lying down, family friend or no. Leave the investigation up to me."

"Because you're doing such a stellar job of it yourself."

"Are you saying I'm a shitty detective?"

Sam grinned. "Uh, I plead the fifth?"

Nathan laughed, this time for real. His deep, rich chuckle made everything about him seem lighter. Happier.

As the sound faded and the seriousness returned, Sam remembered the time in his life when every laugh, every smile, felt like a betrayal. Some days it was still like that. It didn't take a genius to conclude why Nathan stood without another word, exited the room, and disappeared across the hall into a darkened doorway.

Sam went downstairs and waited. It was already nearing midnight, and he had to work in the morning, but his body didn't feel ready to sleep. Nervous energy and concern kept him pacing until Nathan rejoined him a few minutes later. He didn't mention his sudden disappearance.

"So are you going to tell me what you're thinking?" Sam asked.

Nathan stood so close Sam could feel his breath and the warmth of his body in the otherwise cold space. The proximity jumbled his mind and made him stupid. He mumbled something inarticulate and waited for Nathan to laugh at him, but he didn't. He didn't smile, either.

"The other night on the bridge, you asked me if I wanted to come home with you."

Sam swallowed. "Oh, that. I only meant—"

"I know what you meant. But I thought something else."

"Oh?" His heart thumped against his ribcage.

"I wanted to. I've wanted to for quite a while." Nathan's gaze tracked down Sam's body, and the sudden rush of heat to his groin made Sam dizzy. Still, he anticipated the next words. "But I can't."

"I know, of course. It wouldn't be right." He tried to hide his disappointment with a shrug. He'd known nothing would come of his attraction to Nathan. Finding Emma's killer so justice could be served was their one and only purpose and the extent of their relationship. As it should be.

"You're a good friend, Sam. Did you call that guy who left his number the other night at the bar?"

"Yeah." Sam flushed, unsure why he'd confessed. Nathan remained expressionless.

"Good. Now go home and get some sleep. I'll be in touch."

As Sam turned to go, Nathan held up his hand. "Wait a second." He jogged to the living room and returned with the bloomless orchid from earlier. "Don't forget this."

Sam took the plant and wondered if something so fragile would survive the winter ahead.

Chapter 11

THE NEXT week dragged by at such an excruciatingly slow pace, Sam could barely stand to be in his own skin. He hadn't spoken to Nathan since the night of unexpected confessions, but he had been doing a pretty good impression of a thirteen-year-old, checking and rechecking his phone for missed calls and texts so often he'd started to drive himself insane.

True, he didn't expect anything to happen between them. But to have the attraction confirmed as mutual, only to be told two seconds later it could never happen, was like telling a little kid he deserved dessert but was never going to get it. The circumstances couldn't have been worse. Then again Sam had never been very good at portion control.

Still, he did as he'd promised and kept his eyes and ears open around town. The neighborhood where McCormick lived wasn't far from Sam's, and it didn't take much digging to turn up people who knew him. He found McCormick's local hangout and spent some time there, striking up conversation with the bartender as he sipped a light beer and tried not to want another. From those casual conversations, he concluded people generally liked the guy. He seemed to be an honest cop, if a bit wet behind the ears. While a few people mentioned they'd seen Emma with him at various times, every incident seemed connected with work. Still, that didn't mean anything. A lot of people carried on secret affairs and never saw each other in public. Even so, though it was entirely possible Emma had been seeing someone on the side,

Sam's instincts said otherwise. He was beginning to think his theory was bunk.

At the end of the day, he'd turned up nothing. He wondered if Nathan was having better luck.

It turned out, he was.

"I've got a lead." Nathan's voice on the end of the line was so whisper quiet, Sam had to strain to hear.

"What? On who? What is it?"

"I'm sorry, but I can't tell you yet."

"What the hell, Nathan? I've been dying here all week waiting for some news, and you just randomly call and tell me you have a lead, but it's a secret?"

A sigh from the other end of the line. "I'm sorry. You have a right to be angry. I'm going to have to ask you to trust me, though, and sit tight on this one. I know you've been talking to people about McCormick, and I need you to stop."

"How do you—"

"It doesn't matter. Listen. This is important, okay? Please, for your own safety, stay out of this. There are a few things I need to do, and I won't be able to concentrate if I'm worried about you."

"You don't need to worry about me."

Nathan said something softly, something that sounded like "apparently I do."

Sam clutched the phone to his ear. "Will I see you?"

"Soon."

The next night was a Friday. Sam wanted to see Nathan, but not for the right reasons. He needed to do something to diffuse the tension building inside him, making it impossible to sit still. He'd been good for weeks, and a night on the town would be just the distraction he needed.

Without thinking about it too much, he dialed Yuri's number.

"Hey," Yuri said when he answered. They hadn't seen each other much since the fight, but the time had come to patch things up. Sam knew the perfect thing.

"Hey, man. What are you up to tonight? You wanna go out?"

"I can't. Sorry."

Old stick-in-the-mud Yuri. "I thought we could hit the town, maybe check out the new bar Rachel was telling us about, the one with all the craft beers."

"Maybe another time."

"What? You have a date or something?" Sam snorted.

"Actually, yes. I've been seeing someone, and we're hanging out tonight."

Sam frowned. "Who? Anyone I know?"

"No, you don't know him. Sam, I know why you're calling me, but I don't feel like being used tonight. You can't screw around forever before you burn your bridges."

"I wasn't trying—"

The line went dead and Sam almost threw his phone across the room. He hadn't been trying to use Yuri. He only wanted to see his friend, grab a few beers, and shoot the shit.

"Fuck."

Guilt wormed its way under his skin like a flesh-eating virus. What kind of friend was he if it had gotten to the point where they couldn't hang out without Yuri interpreting a latent, selfish motivation? He had to get out of his apartment. He wanted to go far away, somewhere he could be a stranger in a crowd. He'd go to the trendy new bar across town—by himself. He didn't need Yuri's company.

Just as Rachel had said, the bar was one of those places with a hundred different brews and homemade ketchup for fries crisped in duck fat. He took a seat on one of the dark wood stools, ordered an eight-dollar beer with a high percentage, and stared at it when it was brought over in a snifter. The bartender's rolled-up shirtsleeves displayed intricate forearm tattoos, the kind Sam usually thought particularly hot. Even though he gave Sam a pearly white, appreciative smile, Sam remained uninterested. He was too depressed—and too sober—to think about sex.

The clientele consisted of young yuppies and hipsters, mainly between twenty and forty—the type of people who shopped at organic markets with their reusable grocery bags. They all seemed friendly enough, and no one paid him any attention.

After a few minutes, Sam ordered another beer, and his thoughts drifted back to Nathan. He'd sounded so distant on the phone, and Sam wanted to see him so badly. He wanted to be a part of whatever plans Nathan was hatching, not sitting alone at a hipster bar wondering whether he should go home or find some guy to fuck. Some meaningless stranger. Sam remembered what Nathan told him about how addictive the anonymous sex had been. Sex could be like a drug, a moment of pleasure in the midst of dull existence, and it had served that purpose for him on more than one occasion. Sure, he had fun, but loneliness always returned after the rush. Yet the second a guy expressed interest in starting something more serious, he panicked. He couldn't even remember the last time he'd been sober in bed. Or the last time he'd gone a day without having at least one drink.

Yuri had said some pretty hurtful things, but they only hurt because they were true. Maybe Sam couldn't have a meaningful relationship. Maybe he wasn't cut out for it. Maybe that was the reason he insisted on believing such relationships didn't exist.

The long day of work and stress had tightened Sam's shoulders. He rubbed at the knot of muscle at the back of his neck and sighed, then drained the rest of his beer.

"You want to order some food with that, friend?" asked the bartender. "It packs a punch."

"Nah, I'm good."

After that, the place started to fill up, and another bartender joined the first. Sam kept to his seat and watched the ebb and flow of the crowd, anonymous on his barstool island. The beer had made his head fuzzy, but he wasn't yet drunk. He wondered if Nathan had finally found an apartment and whether it was close.

No. Sam had said he understood, and he did. Some secret part of Sam hoped Nathan would change his mind, but what did he expect? For the guy to show up and forget about his dead wife—Sam's *friend*. She hadn't even been dead for five months. What kind of asshole was he?

Another beer, and his thoughts became a little unclear, a little less focused. He stopped caring so much.

"Gimme that one," Sam said, pointing at the bar menu on the wall behind the taps.

"Sorry, but I'm going to have to cut you off."

"I feel fine," he insisted, "and I want another beer."

Hot bartender frowned, looking a little like Nathan with his dark eyes.

"It's against our policy to serve to visibly intoxicated people. I'm afraid I'm going to have to ask you to pay your tab and leave."

Sam shook his head and leaned forward. A half-baked plan had begun to take shape. "I'm not paying anything, and I'm not leaving. Now give me the goddamn beer."

The guy crossed his arms over his chest. It made him look even more like Nathan. "Sir, pay up and go. I don't want any trouble." Sam noticed he wasn't "friend" anymore.

"Well if you don't want any trouble, you should do what I tell you. I'm a paying customer."

Playing the part of belligerent drunk didn't come naturally. Sam had always been affectionate—Yuri would say horny—while intoxicated. Still, if he could piss off the bartender enough, maybe then he'd have a chance of getting some intel for Nathan. He could help with the case after all, and show Yuri he cared about people. Yes, this was a great idea.

"I don't want to have to call the police," said the bartender.

"You don't have the balls."

It didn't take long. After a little more back and forth, the minor altercation turned into a scene. Patrons who'd been pretending not to stare now gawked openly. The people nearby shifted nervously in their seats. Sam could feel their disapproval reflect off his back and turn to outrage as he pulled a move he'd once seen on TV and downed another customer's drink. The guy shoved him in response, and Sam hurled back an insult about his mom.

By the time the cop showed up a couple minutes later, Sam was almost relieved. Any more time in the bar, and drunk and disorderly wouldn't be the only charge slapped on him. Luckily he'd avoided getting physical with the guy who shoved him, and he sat with his head lolling on his chest while the cop, who he only vaguely recognized, approached to question the bartender. Other patrons were whispering and sending him dirty looks. Sam pretended not to notice.

As the cop—his badge said Officer Jain—led him out of the bar into the empty squad car, he realized with crushing disappointment he'd gotten himself arrested for nothing. He'd hoped to find McCormick, or even Petersen, but they were alone. Sam slumped against the back seat as the door of the cruiser slammed behind him.

Once the car was in motion, Sam tried to kick-start his brain. Maybe all wasn't lost. It was possible he could still learn something, but he had to do it without arousing suspicion. He trailed his finger over the ripped seam of the faux leather seat and poked at the yellow stuffing inside.

"How long you been on the force?" he asked.

The cop gave him a look in the rearview. "What do you think, I'm straight off the boat?"

Sam raised his hands. "No, no! I was just wondering. I know some people at the station, s'all. I knew Emma Walker. She was a friend of mine."

The other man's eyes flashed with sympathy. He seemed to shake off the perceived insult. "I didn't know her well. But I'm sorry for your loss."

"Thanks."

After a couple more failed attempts at getting Officer Jain to engage in conversation—clearly he wasn't a talkative sort—Sam gave up. Outside, the night was cold and clear. It made the window cold too. Sam closed his eyes and leaned his head against it, feeling a little woozy.

When they entered the station for processing, Sam stumbled. He was a little drunker than he'd originally thought.

"Sam." A familiar voice startled him. When he looked up, he came face-to-face with a frowning Chief Sheldon. His blue eyes narrowed, making his big eyebrows seem even bushier. "I didn't expect to see you here tonight."

"Sorry, Chief." Remorse crept up the back of his neck. He looked like a complete idiot in front of a man who'd respected his father—and no doubt wondered what sorry excuse for a legacy he'd left behind. He remained quiet while Sheldon spoke with his arresting officer and then led him toward the staff offices, forgoing the normal booking procedures.

"What were you thinking getting yourself arrested, son?" Sheldon asked once he'd closed the door to his office.

"Dunno."

"You're lucky the owner of the bar decided not to press charges." Sheldon's chair creaked as he sat down on the opposite side of the desk. "Most places would have."

"Does that mean I get to go home?"

"I'm afraid not, Sam. You're headed to the tank to sleep it off."

Sam stiffened in his chair. Now that his harebrained scheme had turned out badly, he wanted nothing more than to go home, bury his head under a mound of pillows, and forget it had ever happened. When Nathan found out what he'd done, he'd be upset—especially after the previous day's conversation. "Are you trying to scare me straight?"

The chief chuckled, but Sam hadn't even intended the pun.

"I'll never understand why you do this to yourself. Is it worth it? You're going to have a helluva hangover in the morning."

He didn't feel like talking or telling Sheldon he wasn't as drunk as he could be.

Sheldon leaned forward and cracked his knuckles, one by one. "Drinking ruins lives, Sam. Sure. You're young now, and it's all fun and games. But wait until you're forty, fifty years old. It won't be so pretty then." He tutted and shook his head. "I always say it's the people you associate with who influence your choices. You hang out with a bad crowd, you turn bad, yourself. I've seen it time and time again. Bad choices."

Sam didn't bother responding. When he was a kid, Sam used to wonder if dead people could still see the living. After his grandmother passed, one of the kids at school teased him after the funeral, warning she might be in the room watching, at any time. He'd been afraid to get undressed for almost a month.

He wondered if his parents could see him.

"I hope you don't mind my saying, Sam, but this association you have with Nathan Walker is a bad choice. The man is dangerous. I say this as a friend of your father, since he's not here to say it himself. I'm concerned about your welfare."

"Nathan's not dangerous. He's a good guy."

"Sometimes it's the ones who seem good who are the worst kind. Most people who seem too good to be true have secrets. Eventually those secrets drag you down." Sam met Sheldon's eyes. He was about to defend Nathan when the radio on Sheldon's desk crackled to life.

Available units in the Clarksboro area report to Baptist Bridge. 10-56A in progress, repeat, 10-56A in progress.

"Jesus, lord above," Sheldon cursed.

"What's that mean?" Sam asked as Sheldon stood and grabbed his jacket before heading toward the door and barking orders down the hall. Twisting around in his chair to watch, Sam asked again what was happening. Instead of clarifying, however, Sheldon urged him up and into the custody of another cop, a short, stocky woman with plain features.

"Get him in the tank," he told her. "I've gotta head over to the bridge."

The officer nodded and took Sam's arm. Her grip dug unpleasantly into his bicep, but he didn't mention his discomfort.

"What's happening on the bridge?" Sam asked.

"It's none of your business."

The officer unceremoniously deposited Sam in the old-fashioned holding cell still used to house drunks. It was adjacent to the squad room, and from his vantage point, Sam could see a flurry of activity. He'd already begun to put two-and-two together. The Baptist Street Bridge was a favorite for suicides. Not only was it impossibly high, once a body hit the surface, waterlogged clothes would pull a person under quick. Sam had heard some jumpers loaded their pockets so they'd sink even faster.

"A suicide?" All of the blood rushed out of Sam's face. His lips felt numb. "Hey. Is it a suicide?" he asked the officer who'd brought him in.

"Sleep it off, buddy," she replied, shutting the barred door behind her with a clang.

There were two other men in the relatively spacious cell. One of them had pissed his pants and lay with his soggy ass pointed in Sam's direction, completely passed out. The other, a younger man with a scraggly beard, mumbled incoherently and shuddered as a tremor shivered through his body. He seemed to stare right through Sam with his wide, bloodshot eyes.

Sam chose the least offensive corner and sat on one of the peeling benches. If he'd expected to find someone to talk to, he'd been sadly mistaken. The younger man suffering the DTs turned to Sam and murmured.

"What?" Sam asked, unconvinced the man even knew he'd spoken.

The man muttered again, and Sam realized he'd asked for booze. His eyes grew wider still as anticipation filled them, and then they shuttered, the hope going out like a light. He let out a quiet, broken moan that chilled Sam's blood, and Sam looked away.

He didn't want to see this. His head started to pound as the rancid smell of vomit and urine filled his nostrils. He tried not to breathe too deeply. He wished he were home and not sitting numb assed on an unpadded metal bench. This wasn't why he'd come.

He must have waited for an hour, maybe more. After the initial commotion, the station quieted down, and only an occasional officer was visible in the adjacent room. Sam started to get used to the sound of his companion's incomprehensible mutterings.

And then a few cops, Petersen and McCormick among them, reentered the squad room. They seemed to be arguing. One cop looked incredibly distraught, and Sam recognized her as a friend of Emma's. Sam's buzz had long worn off, leaving him tired, but not terribly so. He moved closer and strained to hear what the cops were saying.

"I'm so tired of this," said someone to McCormick. "This city is like hell on earth sometimes." McCormick shrugged and stayed quiet.

"Petersen tossed his cookies like a rookie," said another guy.

"Yeah. Even McCormick held it together."

"Shut up." Petersen's voice.

When he finally got a look at Petersen's face, though, Sam almost thought he had the wrong guy. Under the fluorescent overheads, Petersen was white as a sheet, tending toward green, and gripping the back of a chair with both fists. His whole face had broken out in a cold sweat, like he'd had the shock of his life. Grief.

He'd never known Petersen to regret anything.

The chief entered a few seconds later, cutting the chatter short.

"We've all seen something terrible tonight," he said. "But that's no reason to fall apart." He directed a pointed look at Petersen, who responded by straightening up. "In fact, it's the reason you have to keep it together. Remember you represent this station, this precinct. No matter what you do, always remember. Now excuse me. I have to call the jumper's family."

Jumper. So it had been a suicide, after all. A chill ran down Sam's spine. Over the past five years he'd written many obituaries, and it was never fun, but a suicide brought a whole new level of pain to the survivors. All of that wondering about what they could have done differently, if they could have stopped it. He wondered who the jumper was and what family would have the misfortune of receiving Sheldon's call. Sam wouldn't wish it on his worst enemy, and he could sympathize with Petersen's reaction. *That* was something new.

"I get what the chief's saying," said Emma's friend. "I do. But I can't see how we're supposed to not feel anything, or act like we don't feel anything. I mean, this woman's husband just died, and now she's dead too. And they both did so much for this community."

"It's terrible," someone else agreed.

Sam wondered if they even knew he was still there or if they'd gotten so used to people in the drunk tank being wasted that they didn't worry about being overheard.

"People die in this town almost every day," said the guy who'd teased Petersen. "I don't know why we should feel worse because the person had a lot of money. I mean, the Feldmans were loaded, but who cares? What makes them better than anyone else?"

Sam's breath caught at the name. Feldman. Had Patricia Feldman jumped?

Emma's friend spoke again. "It doesn't make them better. But at least they've tried to do something to help. Listen, they're calling in the Coast Guard to search for the body, and I'm going home to bed. You guys can do whatever you want."

AT SOME point during the night, Sam must have dozed off. He woke to the sound of unoiled hinges screeching. He blinked and remembered where he was. Oh yeah. Jail.

His companions were still asleep. The guy with the DTs seemed to be having fitful dreams, and Sam hoped he'd sleep for a long time, at least until it didn't hurt to be awake.

"You're free to go now." A grim-faced Chief Sheldon stepped into the cell. "I'm sorry I had to do this, but it was for your own good."

Sam was too tired to muster indignation or anger. He turned back to the guys on the floor. "What's going to happen to them?"

"What happens to all addicts, son. They get clean, or they die."

AFTER SAM retrieved his truck from the bar, he went back to his apartment to shower and change. His voice mail had two messages, including one from an unfamiliar number. It was Nathan, asking him to meet at a diner downtown. His stomach squirmed at the prospect of telling Nathan what had happened the night before, like a naughty child who wasn't sure how his parents would react.

He spied through the thick, dirty glass of the diner's front window before going in. Nathan sat at the counter sipping a cup of coffee. The relief of seeing him there, safe—although Sam had no idea why he wouldn't be—almost bowled him over. He'd missed him.

"Did something happen to your phone?" Sam asked, sliding onto the vacant stool next to Nathan at the counter. He'd texted Nathan back to say he'd received the message and gotten no response.

"Yeah, in a manner of speaking." Nathan gave him a tired smile. He looked like he'd been up all night. Sam hadn't gotten much rest in the tank either. He'd spent most of the night remembering the smiling middle-aged woman in the photo Emma had given him when he'd been writing Mark Feldman's obit. Thinking about the kids too. It pissed him off that they'd grow up without a mother or father. He hated thinking badly of the dead, but suicide seemed so cowardly and selfish with kids in the picture. When you had someone depending on you, how could you just throw in the towel?

"I take it you heard about Patricia Feldman?" Sam asked. Nathan nodded and gestured to the television hanging on the adjacent wall. Sam squinted at the words. "A bereaved lover's suicide?"

"That's what they're calling it."

"Have they found the body?"

Nathan took another sip of his coffee. "Not yet."

They watched the rest of the newscast in silence, but once the reporter gave his over and out and topics turned to other news, Nathan nudged Sam. "Are you hungry? Get whatever you want."

They ordered, and Sam gratefully downed some coffee while he tried to think of the best way to broach the subject of his arrest. He didn't want to keep secrets. "I was there last night."

"What?" Nathan's face paled. "What are you talking about?"

Sam quickly realized his error. "No, not at the bridge. Sorry." He winced. "I went out to a bar and I… sort of got arrested."

"What do you mean, you sort of got arrested?" Nathan whispered harshly.

"I thought maybe I'd be able to help get some intel for you about Emma. So I pretended to be shitfaced and I got in a fight with the bartender. On purpose. A little." Thinking about his stupid not-plan in the light of day made him flush. He started fidgeting with his napkin to distract himself from Nathan's piercing gaze.

"Are you crazy?"

"Maybe. Anyway, once they hauled me to the station I had a conversation with the chief. I think he was trying to give me some tough love."

Nathan's mouth formed a thin, angry line as their food arrived, sparing Sam for a moment. He took the opportunity to deflect.

"What's up between the two of you, anyway?" Sam asked. "He doesn't seem to like you very much."

"I told you to stay out of this. You promised me—"

"I didn't actually. Technically. But yeah. It was stupid, and I shouldn't have done it. It was pointless, anyway."

"Sam—"

"Please spare me the lecture, okay? I know it was stupid, but I'm fine. Fine except for the fact I spent last night in the drunk tank with two guys who'd pissed themselves. I did see the cops come back, though. They were pretty shaken up about it, especially Petersen."

Nathan paused. "Oh?"

"Yeah, one of the other guys teased him for puking on the bridge. He looked as upset as I've ever seen him, but that's not saying much. Apparently McCormick kept it together, which is interesting, given he's new to the job."

For a long time, Nathan didn't speak. He stabbed his eggs vigorously and ate, staring straight ahead. Sam got that naughty puppy feeling again, but he didn't know what he could do to make it better. He ate his breakfast, even though the toast tasted like cardboard.

The local news had turned to weather, showing a bleak ten-day forecast. November had never been Sam's favorite month, and ever since the accident, it had gotten worse. Christmas seemed to come earlier and earlier each year, and now the whole damn month seemed to be a lead-up to the worst day of his life. The weatherman smiled cheerily and spoke of rain, rain, and more rain. Sam wanted to punch him in the face. Sam gave Nathan a sideways glance. He looked like he might be on the verge of telling Sam off again. Or leaving.

"Nathan?"

Nathan put his fork down. "I understand why you did it. But Jesus, this isn't a game. I don't know if I can trust you anymore."

The statement hurt worse than a slap. "Of course you can."

"Can I?"

"If you would tell me what's going on, I wouldn't have done it in the first place."

They whispered, leaning close, and the waitress gave them a curious look as she refilled their coffees. Sam tried not to pay attention to how Nathan smelled, woodsy and warm, or the way Nathan's thigh occasionally grazed his under the counter. It was already difficult enough to muster righteous anger, since he knew he'd messed up.

"What did you say to Sheldon? You talked about me?" Nathan asked.

Sam brought his mug to his lips. He could only remember scraps of conversation. "No. I didn't. I didn't say anything. He was going on about me getting arrested, said I was hanging out with a bad crowd. He meant you." Something didn't sit right. "But come to think of it, how did he even know we've been—"

"I'm under surveillance." Nathan sighed.

"What?"

"My phone has been tapped. That's the reason I called you from a pay phone. And I'm being followed. Or I was, at least, the other day. I probably shouldn't be seeing you at all."

"You're still under suspicion."

"It would appear so."

Sam glanced around the room. An old couple sat in a booth behind them, and a few kids were crammed into another, probably skipping school. No one looked like a cop. Still, his scalp prickled at the thought of being watched. Maybe Nathan was right. Maybe Sam had been treating this too much like a game. It certainly didn't seem like one anymore. "What about your alibi?"

An almost imperceptible shake of his head let Sam know this wasn't the time or place. He let the subject drop—almost. He hated the idea of Nathan not being able to trust him.

"I am sorry, you know. I wanted to help you with the case. I never wanted to jeopardize it. So, if that's what I did, I apologize. I don't know what's wrong with me. I can't seem to be able to help people. Or when I do, it turns out wrong. My friends think I'm a fuck-up. I can't even help my little brother." Sam stared into his half-empty mug. "I won't try to get involved again." He waited for a laugh or scoff. Neither came.

"It's not about the case, you know. I don't want you to get hurt."

"Yeah."

"I mean it, Sam. And I don't think you're a fuck-up. I admire your courage."

"Courage?" Sam snorted. "It takes a real hero to get himself thrown in a drunk tank."

"I'm not talking about that. I'm talking about the fact you've been taking care of your brother all of these years by yourself. You lost your parents, but you built a life for yourself anyway."

Sam's eyes burned. "I did what I had to do." And according to Yuri, it wasn't much of a life.

"You don't know how to take a compliment, do you?"

"If he would wake up, I'd feel like I'd done something to be proud of, you know? Speaking of...." Sam glanced at the wall clock. "I've got visiting hours in a few."

"Let's get out of here." Nathan wiped his mouth with his napkin and set it neatly on the counter. He gestured for the check.

Sam grabbed for the bill when it arrived, but Nathan's hand covered his. "I've got this."

"It's okay. I can pay for breakfast." The rough warmth of Nathan's palm made it hard to concentrate on anything else.

"All right. Thank you."

Outside the diner, the gray sky had begun pissing rain, fulfilling the weatherman's prophecy. Nathan popped the collar of his jacket against the rain. "I've gotta catch a cab. I didn't want to risk driving."

"Do you want to come with me to see Tim?" Sam asked before he had a chance to think about it.

Nathan didn't hesitate. "I'd like that."

"Before we go, there's something I need to tell you. Emma's orchid... I was going to give it to the nurse who takes care of my brother. It's in my truck. I won't do it if it makes you uncomfortable. I don't want you to think it doesn't mean anything to me—"

"I think it's a nice idea."

They drove in comfortable silence, listening to the classic rock station Nathan had tuned in after Sam gave him permission to change the channel. He hummed a few bars of a particularly cheesy seventies power ballad and Sam held himself back from joining in, stealing a glance across the seat from the corner of his eye. Nathan was watching him too.

LISA GAVE Sam a smile and wave when he came in. She looked a little surprised to see another guest behind him.

"Good to see you, Sam," she said. "He's been waiting for you."

"I'm sorry I missed last week."

She nodded, something sad in her eyes, and glanced between the two of them. Nathan shuffled on his feet.

"This is Nathan. He's a friend of mine."

She extended her hand. "Nice to meet you." Her eyes drifted to the orchid. "That's pretty. A gift for Tim?"

"No." Sam set it on the desk. "You, actually."

"Oh, that's so sweet."

"I wanted to thank you for taking such good care of him." Sam flushed a little under her pleased smile. It was just a damn plant. "I guess we'll head down, then."

It had been a while since Sam had brought company with him to visit Tim. In fact, he couldn't remember the last time. There was something comforting about not having to be alone, but Sam knew it wasn't a feeling he could trust. This was a one-shot deal, born out of nothing more than Nathan's curiosity. It didn't mean anything.

Tim lay on the bed as he always did, staring blankly at the ceiling. A vase of flowers decorated the bedside table, and Sam thought Lisa must have put them there. He was glad he'd brought her the orchid.

"Heya, Tim," Sam said. "This is Nathan. He wanted to meet you."

"Hi," said Nathan. He stood close to the bed, looking down at Tim. When he glanced back at Sam, his eyes were soft. "You two look alike."

"Do we? You hear what he said, Timbo? You're as ugly as me."

"That's not what I meant."

Sam swallowed the hot feeling in his throat. "Yeah, well. You wanna sit?"

They grabbed two chairs and pulled them up to the side of the bed. Sam's leg brushed against Nathan's as they arranged themselves, sitting close together.

"So what do you usually do when you're here?" Nathan asked.

"I talk to him. Sometimes I read. You know, he never got to finish high school. When he wakes up, I want to make sure he's familiar with all the classics, so he doesn't fall behind." It sounded so stupid to say it out loud, Sam wanted to cringe. Nathan merely smiled.

"That's a good idea."

For some reason, the answer made indignant rage bubble out of his mouth. "No, it's not. It's a fucking dumb idea. He can't hear a goddamn thing I say."

"How do you know that?"

"Because if he could hear me, he'd wake up." Again, a child's answer. Sam suddenly wished he could kick Nathan out or reverse time so that he'd never invited him in the first place. He turned back to his brother on the bed. Tim's face was placid, as innocent as an angel's. The fact that Nathan thought they looked alike didn't make any sense.

"What do the doctors say?"

"That he can probably hear, or maybe…. They don't know. They don't know anything. They told me he'd never breathe on his own, but look, he's breathing. They say even if he wakes up, he'll be a vegetable, because of the brain trauma. He'll never regain anything but basic motor functions. They don't know my brother. He's smart, you know. An A-student. A helluva lot smarter than me." Burning threatened his eyes, and instead of blinking the tears away, Sam let them fall.

"They treat him well here?"

"Yeah, but the insurance won't cover the bill anymore, and after New Year's they're going to transfer him to some state-run place." He wouldn't get the care he needed there, and he wouldn't wake up. That was the reality, and he'd just confessed it to Nathan. He hadn't mustered the courage to tell Yuri or Rachel yet. He wasn't sure he could stand their pity.

"I wanted to keep him here to give him a chance, you know? To make up for the fact I was a selfish dickhead when I was young. And I've tried. I've tried."

"Of course you have. But we're all selfish when we're young. There's no way you could have known, back then, what would happen."

"That's true, but it doesn't change the facts."

"You sound like me." Nathan huffed a sigh.

"Yeah. I guess I do."

Nathan squeezed Sam's shoulder, and Sam thought about the times Nathan had touched him—at least three today. "What happened, with the accident?"

"They were driving to a Christmas party, and they hit a bad patch of road. My father lost control of the wheel. I was still on campus." He'd been so happy—with a real boyfriend for the first time—getting laid, being free. The thought of going home for the holidays had sounded like so much of a drag, he put it off until the last possible moment. And then he got the call. "My parents died. And Tim.... I can't help feeling I should have been there, but I wasn't."

Nathan's hand stilled where it had been rubbing, and Sam leaned into the touch, wanting it to continue even if he didn't deserve it.

"You once gave me some pretty good advice, and I want to return the favor. You shouldn't have been there. Thank God you weren't."

Sam didn't feel like arguing, not when Nathan started massaging him again. His warm hand cupped the back of Sam's head. His fingers scratched lightly, and Sam couldn't help the way his body responded. His cock twitched with interest, not confused like his brain. He closed his eyes and hoped Nathan didn't notice.

Thoughts jumbled in his head like wet laundry in a broken drier. Maybe Nathan was touchy-feely with all his friends. Maybe it was a little fucked up to be seeking comfort from a guy whose wife had been murdered not four months before. Maybe it was even more fucked up to be sporting a semi in the same room as his comatose brother.

"Feels good," he mumbled, letting his head fall to his chest.

With his talented fingers, Nathan sought all the places where the knots resided, and released them, one by one. Sam felt like he was floating. He couldn't remember ever being touched so tenderly.

"I have to go," Nathan finally said, a hint of regret in his voice.

"Oh? Where?"

"It's... work related."

The smell of mass-produced turkey and mashed potatoes wafted in from the hall, announcing the beginning of meal service for those patients who could still eat on their own. Along with Nathan's news, it was enough to break the spell. The sudden cold on the back of his neck hit Sam like a shock.

"I'll be gone for a few days or so." Nathan glanced away, as though embarrassed, and Sam's gut curdled with jealousy as he thought about the night Nathan had told him about his last case. Maybe this job would require Nathan to go undercover and fuck, or be fucked. Sam couldn't decide which alternative pissed him off more.

He nodded, keeping his eyes on Tim. "Right. Well, good luck."

"Thanks. And I'm sorry I have to leave like this, but I'm already late. I'll try to check in, see if you need anything."

"I don't need anything," Sam said, injecting hardness into his voice. When he turned around, Nathan was pulling on his coat.

"I'll catch a cab, all right?"

Sam stood and crossed his arms over his chest. "Fine."

Nathan looked like he might take a step forward, so Sam stepped back. He ignored the slightly hurt expression he received in return. "Thank you for introducing me to your brother."

"It's nothing." Sam shrugged.

"Sam—"

"You don't have to tell me to stay out of the way, okay? I get it. Go on… do whatever you have to do."

As soon as Nathan left, Sam regretted his behavior. He'd acted stupidly—out of some sense of entitlement, some false expectation that something was happening between them—in spite of what Nathan had told him. Maybe Nathan had seen his response after all and had wisely decided to put the brakes on. Or maybe he really did have to work. It didn't matter. Sam tamped down the hurt in his chest and let it bleed into numbness.

Chapter 12

IT KEPT raining. Sam and Yuri worked nine to five unclogging the last rotten fall leaves from drainpipes and readying their customers for the coming winter. According to the *Farmer's Almanac*, it was shaping up to be a real doozy. Even though Sam never put any stock in it, Yuri did, and it gave Sam something to tease him about. Or at least, it used to.

Things hadn't quite gotten back to normal since their fight. The ball was in Sam's proverbial court, but he didn't know how to broach the subject. He'd never been good at that. Besides, Yuri appeared perfectly content with his new boyfriend, smiling all the time in an aggressively cheerful way. To top it all off, over a week had passed since Nathan had left for work, and Sam had spent way, way too much time thinking about what he might be doing.

"Are you sure you don't want to come along tonight?" Yuri asked hesitantly as they packed up for the day. "Michael would really like to meet you."

Sam grimaced at his muddy boots and kicked one of them against the curb to release some of the dirt. "Doesn't this guy have a nickname? Michael?"

"What does it matter? So, do you want to hang out or not? Rachel and Alex will be there too."

"Oh fabulous, a double date. And I'm the fifth wheel."

"Fine. Don't come. Have fun getting drunk by yourself." Yuri turned away and opened the door to his truck, and something inside Sam gave way. He grabbed the handle.

"Wait a second. Yuri, I'm sorry. It's only—what you said to me—"

"Aren't you ever going to forgive me?"

"Of course. And I want to come along tonight and meet your new boy toy. I've had a lot on my mind."

"A lot of someone, at least."

Sam sighed, wondering when he'd gotten so transparent.

"You could always bring him along."

"It's not like that. Listen," Sam said, wanting to change the subject. "I've missed hanging out with you like we used to. I mean, I know it can't be like it used to. But you're still my buddy, right?"

"Of course, you idiot. So, will you behave yourself tonight?"

"I'm not making any promises." Yuri glared, and Sam threw up his hands. "I'm kidding. I'm kidding. I'll be an angel." He drew an invisible halo around his head.

"You'd better be." But Yuri was smiling.

It turned out the whole shebang wasn't half bad. For one thing, Michael was a lot less boring than Sam had expected. His freckles and fair skin contrasted with Yuri's dark looks, and even Sam couldn't deny they made an attractive pair. Michael had a sharp sense of humor too, laughing and telling horrible boss stories that rivaled Rachel's best. Alex, the quietest of the group, smiled indulgently at her girlfriend and her friends, twirling a strand of her white-blonde bob around one finger.

After dinner they decided to stop at the bar. Sam hung back with Rachel and Alex and let the new couple walk ahead. Once in a while, Michael slipped his arm around Yuri or moved in for a brief kiss. It seemed easy, comfortable, and Sam wondered if it would ever have been like that between him and Yuri if they'd made a go of it.

"He's nice, isn't he?" Rachel asked, giving Sam a meaningful look.

"Yeah, yeah. He's nice. I like him."

"Good. Now make sure you tell Yuri that." She nudged his shoulder.

"Okay, Mom, jeez. The two of you are ganging up on me like I'm some sort of a delinquent, lately."

"You are a delinquent."

"Oh yeah, I forgot." Sam made a face.

Alex giggled.

Once at the bar, Sam found himself on the end, sitting next to Alex, while a few seats away, Rachel and Yuri debated the political relevance of the under-thirty generation. Michael acted as mediator in the debate. It was a headier topic than Sam was into for a Saturday night.

He and Alex rarely spoke without Rachel around, though, and Sam found himself struggling for something to say.

"So what are you two doing for Chanukah?" he asked. "Your folks live in Colorado, right?"

She nodded and put her gin and tonic on the coaster. "Yep. And believe me, I have no desire to spend the holidays at home."

"They're still not okay with you being out?"

Alex rolled her eyes. "Dad's okay, but I think my mother's still in denial. She keeps telling me 'one day you'll meet a nice Jewish boy' and this whole 'phase' will be over."

"Ah, that's one good thing about not having parents," Sam said. "No one to dismiss your sexuality as a phase. No one who matters, anyway."

"Oh, Sam." Alex's mouth quivered. She drew her dark brown eyebrows together. "It must be hard for you. The holidays. I forget, sometimes."

Thanksgiving was only a couple of days away, and Sam had been doing his best to avoid remembering. "It's okay. I'm used to it by now." He finished the last of his beer and glanced around, looking for distraction. If everyone else was getting laid, he might as well scope out the scene.

Unfortunately however, pickings were slim. The place was filled with couples, mostly straight, as well as a huge gaggle of women out for a bachelorette party. There were two guys sitting at the other end of the bar, but one of them was eyeing up the prettiest girl in the group, and the other was… Rich Petersen.

"What the hell is that asshole doing in here?" Sam said aloud.

"Who?" Alex perked up.

"Rich Petersen. Went to high school with him. He's a cop now."

Petersen seemed to sense the attention. He looked up from his beer. In the split second before recognition kicked in and the familiar sneer plastered across his face, Sam saw something else in his expression. It could have been regret or maybe sadness. It didn't last long enough to decipher. Still, though, the guy looked awful enough for Sam to know something was up.

"Hang tight, will you?" he told Alex before grabbing his fresh beer and sauntering over to where Petersen sat brooding into his.

"You're in my local, Richie."

"I didn't see your name on the door." Up close he looked worse than he had across the bar. A patchy sort of five-o'clock shadow covered his flabby jowls, and underneath the black hairs, his skin had taken on a sallow, grayish tinge.

"I'm only curious as to why you're here, is all. Just making a little friendly conversation."

The guy who'd been sitting next to Petersen had moved on to the bachelorette party, so Sam commandeered his seat.

"I needed a drink, but if I'd have known it was a fag bar, I'd have stayed away."

Sam clucked. "Now, now. See, I think you're getting defensive, since I know you were looking for me." It was a long shot, but Petersen's movements—the way he wouldn't quite meet Sam's eyes, his uncomfortable shifting—pinged Sam's instincts.

"I was not looking for you."

Something inside Sam made him hesitate. He'd promised Nathan he'd stay out of the spotlight, but Nathan was away doing God knows what with God knows who. And this was an opportunity he might not get again.

"It's okay, Rich." Sam took a deep breath. He'd made his decision. "I was there, you know. I saw you after you got back from the bridge."

Petersen's jaw dropped open. "What do you mean, you saw me?" There was a panicked edge to his voice, but the next time he spoke, he managed to suppress it. "You couldn't have been there."

"I was. Got picked up for drunk and disorderly, and I was in the tank."

Petersen sniffed. "Figures."

"We all have our bad nights."

Petersen's large jowls trembled. "So you saw me all shook up and you came over here to rub it in. Real classy, Flynn."

"That's not why I came over." Sam let his voice drop an octave, so no one around could hear. "I know what it's like to see something terrible like that. How it feels when a person slips away right in front of your eyes." It was difficult not to let the emotion of the memory pull him under, and it felt even worse to exploit his recollection of his mother's last moments for the likes of Petersen. But it would be worth it on the off chance Petersen knew something.

Petersen seemed just as startled at the sincerity. He didn't rebuff Sam, but he didn't say anything else either. Then, finally, "I saw her jump. I tried to stop her." Like he still couldn't quite believe it.

"Did she say anything to you before she did it?"

Petersen's face turned a furious red. "I see what this is about. Well, you can look somewhere else for your damn story, because it ain't gonna be me."

Sam held his hands up and slid off the stool. He'd obviously touched a nerve—the question was why. "All right, Petersen, relax. There's no need to get angry."

"If you don't get out of my face this minute, Flynn, I swear."

Rachel arched her eyebrow curiously when he rejoined the group. Petersen stormed out almost immediately after the confrontation, not even acknowledging Sam and the rest as he passed.

"What was that all about?" Rachel asked. "You were all nicey-nice, which was weird, not gonna lie. And then, all of a sudden, he's about to tear your head off."

"He saw Patricia Feldman kill herself. I was asking him about it and I pissed him off."

"Patricia? He was the one who saw her?" Alex's voice trembled.

"Yeah. Hey," Sam turned to her. "You're the one who used to babysit the Feldman kids, right? Rachel said you knew Patricia pretty well."

"I did. Yeah."

"I'm only wondering, and there's no way you can know for sure, but did you see any signs, anything that said she might be suicidal?"

She shook her head. "No. Not even after Mark died. I mean, she was upset about it for sure, inconsolable even. But she loved her kids so much. That's why I've had such a hard time believing it. The Patricia I knew would never have left them behind."

SAM STARED at the frozen turkey dinner on the counter. The gravy resembled baby vomit, and the tiny ice crystals on the corn guaranteed the thing would taste of freezer. Still, it was better than nothing. He popped it in the microwave, then cracked his knuckles and sat down at the table where, for the past couple of days, he'd been considering every possible outlandish scenario. The funny feeling that had blossomed in his gut the night he'd confronted Petersen at the bar had taken over like a weed, consuming his sleep as well as his waking hours. He opened his word doc and reread the list. *Blackmail, murder, adultery.* Maybe it seemed like the synopsis of a *Law and Order* episode, but the stories weren't adding up. In less than six months, three prominent and respected citizens had either killed themselves or been murdered, and Sam would be damned if there wasn't a connection between all the cases. He just had to find out what it was.

Too bad he seemed to be on his own.

Two weeks had passed with no word from Nathan. For all Sam knew, he really had taken off for good. It shouldn't have bothered him, but it did, and it only got worse with each passing day. Especially when the delayed realization hit him—Nathan could actually be injured, or worse.

The microwave dinged, breaking the silence and Sam's morbid concentration. His stomach rumbled as he peeled back the thin plastic film that covered his crappy Thanksgiving feast, which only looked slightly more appetizing when hot.

He forked a bubbling bite into his mouth, burning his tongue in the process, and continued scrolling through the massive archive of newspaper clippings that described Feldman's myriad accomplishments—charity work, infrastructure repairs, prison reform. The Feldmans had a massive amount of wealth and their own foundation to distribute funds to those in need. Maybe if Mark Feldman had lived, he would have made a difference in this town. Which left questions. And several possible smoking guns.

Sam blew on his next bite to save his mouth some pain. His phone buzzed on the table and he grabbed it, still chewing. As powerful as it had been, his appetite vanished when he saw the unknown number. He swallowed the salty mush and answered.

"Hello?"

"Happy Thanksgiving, Sam. How are you?"

Oddly formal for a man who'd rubbed his neck for almost half an hour the last time they'd seen each other.

"I'm fine. Uh… how are you?"

"Back. For a while, anyway. Sorry I didn't call earlier, but I got in late last night."

"Did you have a nice trip?" He tried to keep the question neutral, but a note of sarcasm slipped in.

"I did what I had to do" was the cryptic and not-very-comforting answer. Sam decided he needed to stop acting like a jealous boyfriend. There were new developments to consider, and Nathan's input was far more important than his own misguided ego.

"Good. Some things have happened while you've been gone. I think I have a theory about Feldman's death, but I'd like to talk it over with you first—"

"Wait a second, Sam. Hang on. What's this about Feldman? You're not still working on the case?"

"Of course I am."

"But I said—"

"Yeah. I know what you said, but I've got this pesky habit of thinking for myself, and you know how I feel about this case. I'm part of this now, and there's nothing you can do about it."

A sigh. Sam could almost see Nathan rubbing the bridge of his nose in frustration. He didn't like to be contradicted, and suddenly Sam really, really wanted to see what Nathan would do in the right situation, with the right sort of contrary man.

"So, what do you think—" Sam started when a knock at the door surprised him. He frowned and turned toward the sound. "Hang on a sec. Someone's here."

Holding the phone to his chest, he walked to the front door and peered through the keyhole. Nathan. Sam's stomach swarmed with butterflies, the likes of which he hadn't felt since he was a teenager.

He opened the door. "How did you get inside without buzzing?"

"I'm an FBI agent, remember?"

"Oh. Right."

"Surprised?" Nathan's eyes crinkled at the corners. He wore a faded button-down under his leather jacket. His smooth face and damp hair were evidence he'd recently showered and shaved. The anxious knot in Sam's gut started to unwind. He opened the door wider.

"New phone?"

"A buddy of mine hooked me up. One of the perks of the job."

Nathan hesitated a beat before stepping into the apartment. He filled up the space with his tall, lean presence, and it hit Sam again how much he'd missed him. The coffee table between them made things awkward. It was a barrier Sam wasn't sure he should cross. Nathan's eyes traveled over him, cataloging his body in a concerned way, as if to see all the pieces still fit together. Sam did the same to Nathan.

"So," Sam said to break the tension. "Have you eaten?"

"Not yet. You? It smells like…."

"Frozen turkey dinner. Yeah. I had half of one, but I'd much rather go for a burger, if you're interested."

"Is anything open?"

"The Star is."

Sam ran to the bathroom to make sure he looked relatively presentable. His cheeks were flushed and his dirty-blond hair stood up at all angles, so he used some cool water to tame it and splashed some on his face for good measure. He needed to get himself under control and stop acting like a teenager.

Nathan stood waiting by the door when Sam rejoined him. "Is it cold out?" Sam asked, shrugging into his coat.

Nathan gave him a faint smile. "They say it looks like snow."

Sam wrinkled his nose. "I hate the winter."

"I know."

The two of them joined a surprisingly gregarious crowd at the Star. As one of the only places in the neighborhood open on Thanksgiving, the bar had attracted a motley crew of misfits and expats, as well as a group of hipsters protesting the holiday in support of Native American rights. Rachel had taken the day off to spend with Alex since Chanukah had already begun, so Nathan and Sam placed their orders with the relief bartender and got a pitcher of beer for the table—the same one they'd sat at during their first visit.

It didn't feel much like Thanksgiving, but that was fine by Sam. His leg grazed Nathan's under the table, and he barely resisted the urge to press closer. He had no idea why Nathan had come, but suddenly all of the details of the case seemed unimportant.

Nathan sipped his beer slowly, watching Sam over the rim of his pint glass, and Sam did the same. He didn't want to get drunk and risk ruining this.

"So, I suppose you can't tell me where you were."

Nathan shook his head. "Sorry."

"So damn mysterious."

"Am I?" Nathan chuckled.

"Why are you laughing? You are."

"You're probably the first person who's ever thought of me as mysterious."

"I doubt that's true. Most people would never say it." A heady, reckless feeling bubbled inside Sam. Something was changing between them.

"But you're not most people?" Nathan raised an eyebrow.

"Exactly."

"I'd like some examples."

"Examples of how you're mysterious?" Somehow they'd started flirting, Sam realized—that was the shift. It wasn't one-sided this time either. Naked amusement and interest shone in Nathan's eyes.

"Yeah. Out of curiosity."

Sam licked the foam off his upper lip and set down his beer. "Well, for starters, you are incredibly vague about everything."

"I have to be. It's my job. That doesn't mean I'm personally mysterious."

"You're evasive about yourself too." Sam paused as a server brought their food. His burger smelled delicious, but excitement had replaced hunger. He waited while Nathan squirted some ketchup—a lot—onto his burger and took a bite.

"Mmm."

"Good?" The word came out sounding husky. Sam held his breath as Nathan chewed with obvious enjoyment.

"Very."

Sam picked up a french fry and forced it down. He decided watching Nathan eat could be a new favorite hobby.

"So," Nathan said after he swallowed. "You think I'm evasive. I'm not trying to be. Ask me whatever you want, and as long as it doesn't relate to something confidential, I'll answer."

"The training you went through before your last case. Tell me about it."

Nathan's evident surprise quickly faded. He leaned forward, focusing his dark eyes on Sam. "What do you want to know?"

"Who trained you?"

"I spent three weeks at the home of a professional dominatrix in California. A crash course, if you will, so I would know what to expect at the club."

"So… you were like, tied up and stuff? Whips and chains?" Sam knew very little about actual BDSM, but the idea of Nathan being trussed up by a woman was strangely arousing.

"Sometimes. Most people in the community identify as a Dominant or submissive, and I had to learn both roles. There are some who switch."

"What else?"

Nathan wiped his hands on his napkin and tossed it on the table. He seemed to be choosing his words with care. "Kinks like breath control, edge play, spanking. What to do for aftercare. I hadn't heard of half the stuff Ryan taught me. It was eye-opening, to say the least."

Sam's dick was hard as a rock. He shifted in his seat.

"Did you have sex with her?"

"No. It wasn't like that. It was actually much more like being at school than you'd think. All very professional—and tiring. Ryan thinks of it as her mission to discover the true desires of her clients. She made me comfortable and taught me about how normal so-called deviant desires are, and how average people enjoy them. It was important for me to know, working on this particular case. Most people at the club were engaging in completely consensual and legal sex and had no idea about the horrible things going on."

"What about you?" Sam took another sip of beer to wet his throat. "Did she discover your true desires?"

Nathan's gaze grew hot. "I found I fit more comfortably into the dominant role."

Neither of them spoke, and the moment seemed to drag on forever. Sam bit his lip.

"So, is that what you wanted to know?" Nathan asked. His eyes had darkened to black, and he rubbed his leg against Sam's under the table.

"You said being at the club was like an addiction. That you hated it and loved it at the same time."

"I don't know how to describe it. There was the guilt, of course, and the anonymity of it. I don't think I'd ever been so free... or so trapped. If that makes any sense." The rubbing stopped, but Nathan didn't move his leg away.

Sam hesitated before asking the next question. His blood pounded in his ears. "Were you safe?"

"Of course. And I've been tested since."

Sam figured he could be making the stupidest mistake ever, but his hand moved anyway. He squeezed Nathan's thigh above the juncture of his knee.

"Thank you for telling me."

"Like I said, you're easy to talk to."

Nathan grabbed his hand. Sam could see the war waging behind his dark irises. Electricity buzzed between them, making Sam's cock throb in his jeans. "Do you want to go back to my apartment?" he asked, already fumbling for his wallet.

"Fuck, yes."

The frigid air that greeted them outside did little to alleviate the tension. Sam couldn't help thinking it was like balancing on a tightrope, and one false move would precipitate disaster. Nathan walked quickly, and Sam kept pace, their arms brushing together every so often.

Once inside and face-to-face, with the door shut behind them and their winter coats discarded, Nathan rubbed Sam's shoulders like he wasn't sure where to settle his hands, even as their bodies aligned in all the right ways. A hint of worry in his eyes contradicted the intimate position.

When the kiss finally happened, Sam wasn't sure who'd made the first move. Nathan's lips on his were tentative at first, searching. Sam wanted more and was afraid something would happen to end it before it even began. He needed to know Nathan wanted him just as much.

Sam hooked his fingers into the belt loops at Nathan's waist and pulled him closer to deepen the kiss. Nathan let out a soft grunt of approval and responded by wrapping his arms more tightly around Sam's back and sliding one hand through Sam's hair to guide his head. Their mouths slotted together and opened, and the first probing stroke of Nathan's tongue lit a fire at the base of Sam's spine. Nathan kissed with his whole body, insistent and possessive, and Sam's brain short-circuited. A fire in the building couldn't have torn him away. All reticence gone, Sam rubbed his cock against Nathan's, and the answering erection provided all the evidence he needed. The relief almost made him laugh.

Before Sam knew it, he was seated astride Nathan on the couch, grinding down on him as they kissed. Nathan rubbed his smoothly shaven face against Sam's stubbly chin and then sucked and licked his way down Sam's neck to his collarbone. Sam closed his eyes to enjoy the urgency of Nathan's hot mouth on his neck, the strong hands on his ass. He remembered the night Nathan questioned him, the sly sensuality of his method, and he wanted Nathan to throw him down and fuck him with the same determination.

Far too many clothes impeded their movements. The high probability that this was a one-shot deal made Sam want to put the brakes on and savor while he could, but ultimately he was too impatient for foreplay.

"Bed?" he offered. Nathan stilled a moment before nodding. He rested his hands on Sam's thighs and squeezed.

The way Nathan followed him closely, pressing his body into Sam's from behind as they walked, gave Sam a secret thrill. His bedroom was dark, but he flipped on a light. He was grateful he'd been more conscientious of his messes lately. Nathan kissed the back of his neck and ran his hands under the front of Sam's shirt, urging it up and over his head. Sam tossed it to the side, turned around to help Nathan with his own, and fumbled with the tiny buttons.

Undressed, Nathan's body was familiar and unfamiliar. His lean swimmer's build had been the object of Sam's appreciation on many occasions, but now that he was fully naked, Sam realized what he'd been missing. His cock was long and thick and best of all, uncut. It stood proudly out from his body, the swollen glans pushing back the ring of foreskin. A bead of precome clung to the slit—evidence of long-standing arousal—and Sam dropped to his knees to take it into his mouth. He wondered how many people had done this to Nathan before, and he wanted to make it good. He wanted to be the best.

Nathan tasted musky and sweet. The smell of his arousal mingled with the soap of his shower. His thighs clenched as Sam worked him over. Sam stared up through his lashes in the way he knew drove most men wild. He made the shaft wet, tickling the sensitive underside with his tongue, and then licked the taut frenulum and pressed down into the slit. He paid equal attention to the pendulous balls between Nathan's thighs, nosing the tightened sack and sucking first one, then the other, into his mouth. The rasp of hair over his tongue contrasted with the firm, wrinkly skin. Nathan obviously loved it. He grunted in protest when Sam abandoned his sack—but then moaned when Sam teased the tip of his cock with his open lips and let the head slip inside his mouth. Nathan twisted his fingers in Sam's hair, tugging gently. In response, Sam nudged Nathan's foreskin back with his tongue.

Once Nathan was gasping, Sam took pity on him and let the whole length inside. He did his best to control his gag reflex and allow Nathan to control his thrusts. His eyes blurred as the shaft hit the back of his throat, but he kept them open and watched Nathan watching him. The intense pressure of his gaze and the forceful slide of his cock made Sam's painfully hard dick throb, still confined in his jeans. He palmed himself to relieve the pressure, but the ache only increased. It didn't matter, though, not when Nathan was petting him, fucking his throat, and telling him how good it was—how good he was.

All too soon, though, Nathan pulled out, leaving Sam on his knees. He was vaguely aware of a sound like a whimper, and realized, embarrassed, it had come from him. The cock he'd been sucking bobbed—angry, red, and wet—mere inches away.

"I want to see you," Nathan said, drawing him up to his feet. Sam swayed for a moment as he regained his balance. The crouched position had left his legs asleep. He shook them to get the blood circulating as he kicked off his jeans and boxer briefs.

Nathan ran his hands over Sam's chest and pulled him toward the bed. The question in his eyes made Sam remember Nathan was relatively new to gay sex and that he was used to being in charge. He didn't know how much of a Dom Nathan was, or whether he expected Sam to be submissive. An unnamable excitement shivered through him at the idea.

Of course, that brought back the fear that Nathan had spent the last couple of weeks in the company of other men and women. Sam tried to push the thought out of his mind. After all, back at the bar, Nathan had said he'd been tested since his undercover work at the club, and there was no reason to think all of his cases required sex. He'd never been the jealous type and wasn't about to start now.

"Hey," Nathan said, bringing his hand to Sam's face. "Where'd you go?"

"Sorry. I'm here. I was only thinking."

"Should I get ready to put my pants back on?"

"Absolutely not." Sam kissed Nathan again, this time controlling the action, getting his semi back up to full mast. He let Nathan roll them over so Nathan was on top, and they finally made full contact. Skin to skin was always great, but this time it felt like electric wiring connected them in all the right places. Nathan's chest hair rasped against his, and Sam grabbed two handfuls of his firm, flexing ass. A few more minutes of this and Sam was going to blow his load, but the friction wasn't quite right. He reached for the slick he kept in his bedside table and Nathan got the message—he squeezed lube onto his hand and coated both of their cocks with it.

"Why don't you tell me what you were thinking about?"

"I don't think you want to know." Besides, with Nathan's fist wrapped around their cocks, jerking them together, who had time for talking?

"I do. And I know already. You were thinking about what I told you about the sex club. You were wondering if I wanted to do those things with you."

"Not bad, detective." He didn't mention his jealousy or his worry Nathan hadn't been completely honest about his work.

"God, you're gorgeous. What do you want?"

"I, ah—" Sam's eyes rolled back in his head as Nathan squeezed the tip of his cock. It was the most excruciatingly slow hand job of his life. "I don't know…."

"You can do better than that."

"I want you to make me come."

"Oh, I will." Nathan's hot mouth on his nipple made Sam cry out. Nathan grazed it lightly with his teeth and then gave Sam a wet and filthy kiss. "How am I supposed to resist you when you look at me like that?"

Again, the pace slowed. Sam forced himself to keep his eyes open. Nathan was enjoying this. His dark eyes glittered with excitement.

"It was this, wasn't it? Having someone under your control. That's what you want." Sam almost gasped the words.

Nathan didn't answer. He rubbed his thumb in maddening circles over Sam's slit.

"And that's what you liked, what you got addicted to." It was more of a statement than a question. Nathan didn't seem to disapprove, though. He kept his pace steady. Sam felt the orgasm begin to build deep in his belly. "Is that where you've been the last couple of weeks?"

Nathan's hand stilled, leaving Sam on the precipice. His balls ached with the need to come. "I shouldn't have asked. What you do for work is your own business."

"No," Nathan's voice was calm, betraying nothing. "It's all right. You worried about me sleeping with other people? Were you jealous, Sam?"

"Fuck." Sam tried, and failed, to keep his hips from moving. His grip on Nathan tightened. It began again, the slow teasing. Precome made his cock even more slick. Sam's balls drew up, and he bit his lip to hold back a groan. He was sure if Nathan stopped again he'd lose his mind.

Nathan's breathing had become labored, though, and Sam could tell his will was faltering. "I shouldn't like that you were jealous, but I do. God help me." He kissed Sam again, hard, and his stroke quickened purposefully, hurtling them both toward climax. It broke over Sam first, shattering him from the inside out. His stomach clenched as he shot, hot and wet, over Nathan's fist and their stomachs. Nathan let out a quiet moan and followed soon after, still working them together even as Sam's cock softened and grew sensitive.

Nathan flopped onto his back and stared at the ceiling. Their arms were still loosely entwined, and Sam hesitated before getting up to grab a towel from the bathroom. He handed it to Nathan and then remembered how unpleasant it was to wipe off with a towel covered in someone else's cold come. Nathan didn't seem to mind, though. He wiped himself efficiently and tossed the towel over the side of the bed.

Now would come the awkward post-orgasm parting—the real reason Sam made it a point never to invite someone over to his apartment in the first place.

Instead of making a move, though, Nathan drew the blanket up and over his waist. He seemed intent on trading awkward leaving for awkward… cuddling? When Sam didn't get back in bed right away, Nathan sat back up. "Do you want me to go?"

"No," Sam admitted. "I just hadn't planned for this."

Nathan gave him a wry smile. "Neither had I. But the thought of going back to my house doesn't sound appealing."

Of course. His first Thanksgiving without Emma.

"Haven't you found an apartment yet?"

"I've looked at a couple, but neither felt right. I'm not sure what I want, actually. I don't want to be there anymore, but I can't quite... let it go."

And didn't that say it all.

It was funny, or perhaps sad and awful, that Sam hadn't thought about Emma until then. Everything had seemed so natural, so—he almost cringed to think it—right. But the reality was back, and with it the fact Nathan was still a man grieving over his dead spouse.

He wanted to slide close and wrap his legs and arms around Nathan like a human squid. Maybe wait until their erections decided they wanted to play together again. But reality made him scoot a little farther away so he could resist the urge.

"Are you sure you're okay with me staying?" Nathan asked. Sam nodded, though he'd turned out the light when he'd gotten back into bed, and he doubted Nathan could see him. He lay on his side facing the room, feeling unsettled.

"Sam, are you awake?" Nathan whispered sometime later.

"Yeah." Sam rolled onto his back. "What's up?"

"Before, when you were asking me about what I'd done, I was worried you might have found it strange."

"Strange? Nah. I've been around the block a few times, Nathan. You're gonna have to work a little harder to shock me." He didn't need to add he'd found it incredibly arousing, not after how he'd responded to the slight tease.

The bed shifted, bringing the heat of Nathan's body closer. Sam smiled and relaxed into his embrace, instantly conscious of the fact that they were still naked. His cock stirred, and Nathan's prodded against his ass, but both of them were too tired to do anything about it. Anyway, it felt pretty good to sleep.

Chapter 13

SAM GASPED awake with his heart pounding in his throat. He ran a
hand over his face and sighed, even as the dream he'd been having
dissipated and left his head in a tired fog. Nathan lay next to him, his
deep, even breath blowing warm through Sam's hair. Sam could barely
make out the arm snug around him, only that it was heavy and a little
too hot.

He was surprised Nathan had turned out to be a cuddler. Sam had
always preferred sleeping on his own side of the bed when he chose to
sleep with anyone at all. He'd always been too conscious of irritating
the other person with his inevitable tosses and turns to fall asleep. And
he liked his space.

This wasn't too bad, though. He hadn't disturbed Nathan with his
nightmare.

The next time Sam woke up, light had begun to stake its preliminary
claim on the room. He groaned and turned over, shielding his eyes, and
came chest-to-chest with Nathan, who was very much awake. His
morning erection prodded Sam between the legs, and Sam's responded
eagerly.

"Good morning."

"Morning," Sam replied. He reached down between them, took
Nathan in hand, and explored the hard length of him with his palm.
Nathan groaned and buried his head against Sam's neck. He teased and
nipped Sam's throat as Sam stroked him, but the angle made it difficult
to get a rhythm going.

"I want to fuck you," Nathan said. Sam wanted the same thing, but he was already late for work.

"Grab the lube." Sam gestured to the side table.

Sam positioned himself as the little spoon and slicked Nathan's cock so it could slip easily against his crack. He pushed back a couple of times to give Nathan the idea, and then let him take over while Sam beat himself off. He loved the way Nathan grabbed his ass to make it tighter, and the surprised, pleased sounds he made. Nathan's cock slid under Sam's balls and Sam squeezed his thighs to trap it there, reveling in its width and hardness. He imagined it sliding inside his ass, how the stretch would feel, and that was it. He sped up his hand and came heedlessly all over the covers.

Nathan stilled as Sam came, and then he swiftly moved until he was straddling Sam's chest, finishing himself off while Sam watched him. Sam was surprised at how intimate it felt. Maybe it was the fact that jerking off was normally such a private act. Doing it in front of someone else took a sort of courage and even trust. He liked the way Nathan held himself at the base of his cock, his fingers lost in the thick nest of dark curls, while his other hand moved efficiently, up, around the head, and back down. When Nathan whispered he was close, Sam decided he'd been a bystander long enough. He took the tip of Nathan's cock into his mouth and swallowed his spunk as he came. Then he continued sucking him through the aftershocks, applying just enough pressure to make Nathan shiver and curl his toes.

Nathan watched him with a wrecked expression.

"What?"

"You seem to enjoy that." The sated lust in Nathan's eyes created a swirl of arousal and tenderness in Sam's belly.

"Are you kidding? Of course I do. You mean you don't?" Sam licked his lips, and Nathan tracked the movement.

"I don't… not like it, I guess."

Sam rolled his eyes. "Then there are still a few things you need to learn about gay sex, despite your *training*. One of them is worshiping cock." Nathan chuckled and leaned down to press a kiss against Sam's temple. They lay together for another few minutes until Sam remembered himself.

"Shit," he said. "I'm going to be late if I don't get going." The clock read quarter to eight already, and it would take at least half an hour for him to reach the site, even if he skipped a shower. He would much rather stay in bed. Nathan looked gorgeous sprawled out with his prick softening on his thigh.

Nathan touched Sam's arm. "How long do you have?"

"Not long enough for another round, if that's what you're thinking."

"It would be nice, but no. Are you going to tell me about what you've been up to while I've been away?"

Sam sighed and scrunched his forehead. Nathan didn't seem angry, but that would probably change when he presented his theory. "Are you gonna be pissed at me?"

"I guess that depends."

"Okay, well. I've been going back over my notes on the Feldman case, and I'm wondering if Feldman's death was murder after all. The autopsy gave drowning as the cause of death, but what if someone made him take the pills? Someone who would immediately benefit from his death."

"Who?"

"Isn't it obvious? Mayor White." Over the past few days, he'd wondered why it had taken him so long to follow up on his original suspicion.

"You think the mayor had Feldman killed?"

"It makes a perfect kind of sense. I mean, Feldman made a big splash downtown, doing more than the mayor has ever done to help clean up the city, but he had a firm, anti-gentrification stance. He even contributed to White's opponent's campaign during the last election. He was a problem. So White stages the murder to look like a suicide, and when Emma finds out, he gets someone to kill her too. And then, to top it all off, White comes up with this 'Streets Clean' plan in honor of Feldman to make himself look good. It's sick, when you think about it." Nathan raised an eyebrow, and Sam took it as a sign to go on. "I'm thinking someone in the PD is in on it. Maybe Rich Petersen. I saw him at the bar the other night, and he was squirmy. And of course, there's Patricia Feldman's suicide. It has to be linked. Maybe someone threatened her kids and she killed herself as an act of desperation, to protect them by sacrificing herself."

Nathan had that look on his face, the one Sam had decided must have been part of his basic training. Completely unreadable. He seemed to be taking in everything Sam said and weighing it in the back of his mind, and there was no telling whether he was angry or pleased. Sam hoped for the latter, not least because he'd enjoyed their night together and wanted to do it again. Nathan being angry with him would most certainly interfere with those plans.

"Well? What do you think?" Sam wanted to touch Nathan for some reassurance he hadn't fucked things up between them. "Are you going to say anything?"

Nathan sat up, wrapping the covers around his waist. He certainly didn't look happy. "I'm trying to decide whether to level with you."

"You don't trust me. I'm sorry. I—" Sam's gut twisted. Nothing he could say would make up for the fact he'd gone back on his word to Nathan and poked his nose where it didn't belong.

"This isn't about trust. There's a lot at stake here, beyond your safety. You're not trained for this, Sam. I know you want to help, and you're curious and smart, and frankly you've come up with some interesting theories, but you're going to have to leave this to the professionals."

Sam bit the inside of his lip. "So you're not angry?"

"Oh, believe me. I want to be. Worrying about what you've been up to these past couple of weeks has only made my life more difficult."

"So where were you, anyway?"

Nathan smirked. "I wasn't at a sex club. That case is finished."

"Oh, sure. I mean, I don't care."

"You're not a very good liar." Nathan stretched his legs and stood. He bent over to retrieve his briefs from the floor and pulled them up over his fabulous ass. Then he leaned down and whispered in Sam's ear. "We both know you were jealous."

"So that's how it's going to be, huh? Holding things I said when you had my dick in your hand against me?" He'd intended the words to sound indignant. They didn't.

"What if I told you I was jealous too, thinking about who you might be fucking while I was away?"

Somehow they'd gotten very off topic. Sam didn't mind. Heat flared in his groin at the words, and his obvious erection stood up, poking the sheets. God, it had been a long time since he'd been ready to go again so soon after coming. Maybe because most of the time he was drunk, and last night and this morning, he hadn't been.

"I wasn't. I mean, I didn't," he said, not sure why the confession made him feel so raw. Nathan's eyes tracked down to the tent he was making.

"I wish I could stay here all day and take care of that for you."

"I have to work. And you're distracting me on purpose, aren't you?"

Nathan had the decency to look guilty.

"And here I was, thinking I was irresistible." Sam got up and dragged the bed sheet along with him.

Nathan yanked it away and gathered Sam close. "You are. You have no idea." Their bodies pressed together, and Sam could feel Nathan's erection against his stomach. He had no choice but to wrap his arms around Nathan in response and kiss the salty skin of his neck. He smelled like Sam's bed.

"But you're still not going to tell me where you were."

"You never stop, do you? It's almost like you want me to get irritated." Nathan's voice was slightly annoyed, but his eyes betrayed amusement. He kissed Sam once, softly, and then backed away. "Listen. I would tell you if I could, but it's not an option at this point. Can you please try to understand?"

Sam nodded, but it didn't mean he was going to stop being concerned. "Can't you even give me a hint?"

"All I can say is that there's been a break in the case. I'm working with some people from my team, but the best thing you can do right now is stay out of it, Sam. This time for real. The more you know, the more likely you'll become a target yourself. I shouldn't have come here, but I wanted to see you."

Sam grabbed a pair of clean boxer briefs from the dresser next to his bed, hiding his smile. "I'll be fine."

Strong arms wrapped around his waist. "You will if I have anything to say about it."

Until now, Sam hadn't given himself permission to think about what might happen after this. He had no idea what Nathan wanted or even what he wanted for himself. Not so long ago, Nathan told him, in no uncertain terms, that nothing could happen between them. But Nathan was human, after all. It made perfect sense that he'd break down in a moment of weakness. Sex was one thing, but emotions were another. Sam refused to delude himself into hoping it might mean something more. However, he was greedy, and if he could only have this for a little while, he'd make the most of it.

But time kept ticking, and Sam had to leave for work. He leaned into Nathan's embrace for a moment before regretfully pulling away.

They dressed in comfortable silence, yet each layer of clothing seemed to add distance to the easy intimacy of the morning. Once Nathan had donned his leather coat and stood by the front door, Sam could hardly believe that only minutes before they'd been unable to keep their hands off each other. Now he couldn't imagine giving Nathan a casual kiss or hug good-bye. He seemed so perfect and untouchable, dressed for the chilly November morning.

"We probably shouldn't do this again," Nathan said. Sam felt the blood drain from his face, replaced by ice.

"Yeah, probably not," he agreed.

"It's too dangerous."

Yeah. Sam knew all about those kinds of excuses. He nodded, wanting to give Nathan the easy out. But instead of leaving straightaway, Nathan pulled a small, black handgun out of the inner pocket of his leather jacket. He held it out to Sam by the barrel.

"Do you know how to use one of these?"

Sam's mouth almost dropped open. He'd been to the range with his father as a teenager, but he'd never enjoyed shooting like the other boys seemed to. Something about the unyielding metal under his fingers and the harsh kickback of the gun after release unsettled him. Still, he went, and he never told his father he didn't like it.

"I don't want it."

"Take it, please."

"I'll wind up shooting myself in the foot."

"It'll make me feel better if I know you have some means of protection."

"Yeah, well it won't make me feel better. Hey, I've lived in this neighborhood for years and I haven't gotten shot once yet." He didn't bother to add he had *nearly* been shot twice—once during a mugging and once when he'd been on the street during a gang drive-by.

"Sam—"

"I'm not taking the gun, Nathan, and that's final. Okay?"

Nathan's frown deepened, and before Sam knew what was happening, he found himself pressed against the front door, caught between it and Nathan's body. Nathan tucked the gun into his own back pocket, and a frisson of fear and desire tingled up Sam's spine. It wasn't the first time Sam had ever seen Nathan act like an FBI agent, but it had been a while.

"You have no idea how much I want to make you obey."

Sam's cock started to fill. "You couldn't."

Nathan kissed him hard, tangling his hands in Sam's hair and holding him fast. His tongue slid, hot and lush, into Sam's mouth. The next time they broke apart, Sam gasped for breath. He'd pretty much decided being late for work would be worth it if he could get Nathan to fuck him. Just once. The thought it might never happen hollowed his insides with want.

"Take the damn gun."

"No." The word came out as a whimper—maybe a little less effective than he'd intended. But he didn't want a gun or the responsibility that came with it. "You told me yourself I'm not trained for this sort of thing."

Nathan released Sam, and he sagged back against the door.

"All right. Have it your way."

Sam couldn't be positive, but he thought he detected *this time* as a barely concealed subtext. Or maybe not. Wishful thinking wouldn't get him anywhere.

"Buy a can of pepper spray, then. And whatever you do, stay the hell away from the police."

"Okay, okay. *Master*."

He'd meant it as a joke, but Nathan didn't seem inclined to laugh. His eyes widened into a startled, almost innocent expression. And then they narrowed.

"Watch what you say," he said. "Or you might get what you ask for."

Chapter 14

SAM'S HANDS trembled on the steering wheel as he drove, a delayed reaction to everything that had happened at his apartment over the course of the morning.

The gun made everything real. Until then he'd been operating under the assumption that he was untouchable, but Nathan's intent to furnish him with a weapon proved the legitimacy of the danger. He worried his meddling had damaged whatever plan Nathan had in the works. And he finally realized how out of his depth he was. He kept checking his rearview mirror, skeptical of the car following him until it headed in a different direction.

Then there was Nathan's sexually charged threat or promise— Sam didn't know which—and his own reaction, which had been undoubtedly interested. He had no idea how the man had been able to get under his skin in such a short period of time and how he seemed to know the right buttons to push. Sam had purposefully goaded him too, knowing how Nathan might respond. He'd said Nathan couldn't get him to obey, but that had only been a half truth. Sam wasn't a submissive person by nature, but in the last twenty-four hours he'd begun to see a part of himself he'd never known existed.

He turned up the radio to drown out his thoughts, but they got louder too.

He made it to work in time to find the crew standing around drinking coffee to warm up. Sam cut the engine and slid out of the cab. He helped himself to a cup and a donut and half listened while the others shot the shit, belatedly realizing the breakfast was a kind of impromptu celebration. Juan's wife was expecting a baby, and given her age, the guys seemed to think this meant Juan possessed supersperm.

Yuri noticed something was up right away. He didn't ask about it, though, until lunch break. "What's the matter with you today? You're quiet. It's freaking me out a little."

"It's nothing," Sam said. "How are things in lovers' land?"

"Pretty awesome, actually. And don't think I didn't notice you trying to change the subject."

"You know all my tricks."

"You have a limited repertoire."

Sam thumped his hand over his heart. "Ouch, that really hurts."

"So seriously, you're jittery as hell. What's going on with you?"

"Nathan came back last night." He glanced around to ensure the other guys were out of earshot.

"So please tell me you finally fucked?"

"The guy's wife just died, Yuri."

"That good, huh?"

"May the fuck be with you." Sam smiled in spite of himself, remembering.

"I'll take that as a hell yes." Apparently getting laid regularly was making Yuri into something of a self-satisfied shit. Now Sam understood how his friends had suffered all these years. He sobered instantly, though, when the rest of the morning came flooding back—including Nathan's suggestion they shouldn't see each other again. There wouldn't be a repeat for a long time, if ever.

Yuri took the opportunity to launch into a story about Michael, and Sam tried his best to muster enthusiasm for his friend. At least one of them had a reason to smile.

The next day was more of the same, and the next. Sam slowly started relaxing again, not bothering to look over his shoulder every two seconds, slipping back into the rhythm of his life. November drifted uneventfully into December. Sam started thinking about the inevitable Christmas parties and merrymaking, wondering how he could get out of it again for another year. His grandparents wanted him to visit for a week, but buying a plane ticket to Florida was out of the question, and they didn't have the money to front the expense. And in one month, he'd be out of money for Tim.

In Sam's life, shit liked to pile up all at once. Rachel sent him an enigmatic, yet characteristically emphatic, text message as he was leaving for work.

Dude. Call me right the fuck now.

Got 2 work. Later?

Right. The fuck. Now.

Rolling his eyes, he hit send. She picked up instantly. "Where are you right now?"

"Heading out the door, why?"

"Because you need to turn on the TV. It's all over the news. Nathan has been arrested for murder."

SAM STARED at the television, his stomach bottoming out at the scene of Nathan being led up the steps of the station with his head held high. Sam could make out two of the cops—McCormick and Petersen. Each man held one of Nathan's arms, gripping him tightly right above the elbows. Petersen had a particularly smug look on his face, and if Sam could have lunged through the TV and taken him by the flabby throat, he would have. Nearby Chief Sheldon watched the proceedings with a stern expression.

Sam got the surreal feeling he was watching a movie, but there was no off switch on this flick. His knees buckled.

The headline *Husband Of Murdered Cop Charged With Murder* flashed on the screen, and not only on the local news. Sam flipped to CNN and saw Nathan's handsome profile there too. He didn't look indignant or angry, just resigned, and Sam remembered what the chief had told him weeks before.

The man is dangerous.

"What the hell is going on, Nathan?" he whispered as the remnants of his hastily eaten breakfast threatened to rise.

"Sam? Are you okay?" Rachel's concerned voice broke through his racing thoughts. He'd almost forgotten he was on the phone with her.

"He didn't do it."

"Do you want me to come over? I'm sure Yuri will understand if you don't go in today."

"No, Rach. You don't know what I know. And I know Nathan didn't do this."

"Well, why would they arrest him now, if he didn't do it? They must have new evidence. Sorry, baby. I hate to say it and I don't want it to be true. Okay?" He could hardly hear her over the rage boiling his brain. This was a setup, plain and simple, and he was going to get to the bottom of it.

"You're not going to do anything stupid, are you?"

"I'm going down to the station. Call Yuri and tell him for me, will you?"

"Do you think it will do any good? Sam, stay home. I'll come over, and we'll talk it through. If Nathan is innocent, you're not going to help the situation by storming down there with your panties in a bunch—"

"I'll talk to you later." He flipped the TV off and went to pocket his phone, then thought better of it and silenced it first. If he knew Rachel, she'd be relentless until he agreed to sit tight, and he had no interest in sitting tight, not even after Nathan's warnings. This arrest changed things. All bets were off.

The station swarmed with reporters from all over the state. The pressroom, which wasn't large to begin with, was filled to capacity—claustrophobic with a lack of oxygen and fresh air. There wasn't a vacant seat to spare, so Sam hovered near the back of the room, keeping an eye on the front desk in case someone he knew appeared. It seemed unlikely Sheldon would make a statement so soon. Sam saw a couple colleagues from the *Gazette*, though he didn't suppose he could call them colleagues anymore. He hadn't been asked to write anything for the paper since the fluff piece on the mayor's plan. They gave him cursory nods, and he told himself he had as much right to be there as anyone else. He still had his blog.

His blog. Yeah, maybe it had become a joke, but he made a silent vow to get back into it, once all this blew over. He imagined the sort of exposé he could do if Nathan would allow it. People had a right to know what kind of crap the Stonebridge PD had been selling the past few years. Instead of cleaning up the streets, they were charging innocent people with crimes they didn't commit.

After an hour or so, Chief Sheldon entered the room and approached the podium to disperse the crowd. He used a certain grandfatherly firmness and promised details would be released as they became available. He couldn't discuss an open investigation. A few tenacious stragglers remained behind, shouting questions at Sheldon as he disappeared through the door at the front of the room. Sam hung back too, and slipped out of the pressroom to approach the officer on duty.

"I'm here to see Nathan Walker."

"I'm sorry, but if you hadn't heard, Walker is being detained." If the guy thought sarcasm would deter Sam, he was wrong. And obviously new.

"I'll wait."

"You're gonna be waiting a long time, pal. No visitors for Walker. I'm under strict orders."

"Then I'd like to see Chief Sheldon."

The guy wrinkled his forehead and said in a slow voice, like Sam was simple, "I'm sorry, but the chief is busy, so I'd suggest you move along." He punctuated it with a long-suffering look.

"That's all right, Phelps, I'll take care of Sam."

Sam turned to find Sheldon behind him. "I want to see Nathan," Sam said.

Sheldon shook his head. "I'm afraid that's impossible."

"What is he, in solitary confinement? I'm not gonna try and bust him out, but I have a few things I need to tell him."

"Maybe we can arrange something tomorrow, once he gets transferred to county. But if I were you, son, I'd walk out the door and never look back." He raised one of his remarkable eyebrows. "Remember when I told you Walker was dangerous? I was hoping the message might have sunk in, but apparently not."

Sam shook his head. As close as Sheldon had been with his father, it didn't make him infallible. This was a mistake, a huge one, and Sam refused to leave until he saw reason. "You're wrong about Nathan. He didn't kill Emma, and I have the evidence to prove it."

He was bluffing, but the chief didn't know that. He didn't seem very convinced, though. "Sam, with the kind of evidence we have against Walker, no jury in their right mind is going to let him off the hook." He crossed his arms. "Come to my office, though, and let me hear what you have to say. Strictly off the record."

Sam followed Sheldon with a lump in his throat. He wanted to hear the evidence against Nathan, but at the same time, he didn't know what he'd do if there really *was* evidence. No, he told himself, slowing his pulse through deep breathing. All of this was part of Nathan's plan, the one he'd been working on and couldn't tell Sam about. He'd obviously intended to get arrested. Sam just had to find out why.

As they walked down the linoleum-floored hallway toward the staff offices, Sam remembered his last visit. He hoped this time the outcome would be different.

The chief's office was the nicest of them all, midway between the front of the station and the squad room. It still retained an old-school feel. Article clippings, some of them yellowing, decorated the wall behind his chair—most of them highlighting the PD's successes. Sam almost snorted a laugh when he noticed one of his own.

"What do you really know about Nathan Walker, son?" Sheldon asked once he closed the door behind them and sat down at his desk. He shuffled some papers absently. "Did you know he was FBI?"

Sam straightened up and looked Sheldon in the eye. "He's never lied to me about anything."

"Oh? I'll bet you didn't know he was suspended from duty after Emma's murder."

"What are you talking about?"

"You can ask him, Sam, but it seems your *friend* was with another man the night his wife was killed. His partner was a double agent. Turns out this man had connections to a child prostitution ring, and Nathan helped him escape prosecution. Next time you see him, ask

141

him about Luan. He must be back home in sunny Brazil by now, free as a bird."

The enigmatic new partner. The sub to Nathan's Dom. When Nathan told him about the case, he never mentioned the fate of the man who'd gone undercover with him—only that he'd been chosen in the first place because of his connections in the community. He'd never even mentioned his name. Could this Luan have been in on it the whole time? Nathan had been so distraught about the job, about the kids who'd been used and exploited. He never would have helped any of the sick bastards who ran the place. Sam dug his fingers into his thighs, reminding himself he didn't know the whole story.

"That's not true."

"The FBI seems to think so. Did Nathan tell you about the double indemnity clause in Emma's life insurance policy?"

"Lots of cops have those clauses. It's run of the mill in a dangerous job."

"Hmm, but when the policy is changed only a month before a murder, things start to get suspicious." In spite of himself, Sam's gut swam with unease. Nathan had never mentioned a life insurance policy at all.

"Nathan has plenty of money."

"His *family* has plenty of money. What if he suddenly decided he wanted to take off with a male lover, a lover who was wanted for conspiracy and child endangerment and abuse? What if he decided he wanted to get rid of the wife holding him back, now that he realized his twisted desires? He'd be disinherited." Sheldon's expression was grim.

"How do you know all this?"

"Emma told me some things before she died. She was uneasy about the state of her marriage, and she confided in me. The poor kid." Sheldon shook his head. "Afterwards, I checked out the story with Walker's boss, and it gave us our case."

"Why are you telling me all this?" Sam could barely breathe. He needed fresh air. Sheldon's story sounded like the truth, but it warred with the emotion in his gut, the deep-seated belief the man he'd slept with, the man he'd cared for, was innocent.

Sheldon gave him a slight smile. "You know why. When your dad died, I promised myself I'd look out for you. Walker's going down like the Titanic, and the only way to save yourself is to swim free of the undertow."

"But you said yourself he was out of town on the day of the murder. With Luan, or whoever. How could he have done it?" Sam grasped desperately at this line of reasoning in the hopes of unsettling Sheldon's narrative.

There was a small tape recorder on Sheldon's desk. Sam recognized it from the night he'd been brought in for questioning after Emma's murder. Sheldon pressed *play* and then leaned back, bracing his head with his hands.

The first voice was Sheldon's, soft and coaxing. "When did you first hear from Nathan Walker?"

"I got a call from him about eight months ago. He had heard about what I owed my bookie and he wanted to meet me." Sam squinted at the recorder, trying to recognize the second voice, but unable to place it. Whoever it was sounded male, perhaps eastern European.

"So you met with him. Is this the man?" The sound of paper being slid across a smooth surface.

"Yes, that is him."

"And what did you talk about when you met in person?"

"He told me he would pay my debts if I helped him out with his problem."

"Oh? What sort of problem?" Sheldon's voice stayed neutral.

"His wife. He wanted her taken care of."

"What did you think he meant by 'taken care of'?"

"Killed," the man whispered.

"Are you sure? That's a pretty serious accusation." Sheldon again.

"Yes, killed."

"And did you agree?"

The other man's voice cracked. He sounded like he was crying. "I owed so much money. They were going to hurt my young son, my

143

wife…. We are poor. I saw it as a way out. And he told me, if I did not do it, then he would make sure my family suffered even more."

"So, Nathan Walker hired you to kill his wife?"

"Yes. He had a plan. If I showed up and said I was hurt, that I had an accident? His wife would let me inside. But no guns, he said." A pause. "He wanted to make sure she did not scream."

The words hit Sam like a sledgehammer. His skin went cold and clammy all over. If Sheldon hadn't stopped the recorder when he did, Sam might have been sick on the desk. His eyes watered.

"Heard enough, Sam?" For the first time ever, Sheldon seemed unaccountably cruel, the edge to his voice hard.

"Yeah, I've heard enough."

"Now, I know Walker has you thinking somehow it's the police who are involved in this murder. It's the last ditch attempt of a desperate man who knows he's been cornered. Emma was killed by a husband who wanted her out of the way, not by anyone else."

It was too much to process—how Nathan had come to him asking about what Emma had told him the day of the murder. His virtual interrogation. At the time Sam had seen it as the noble attempt of a man trying to avenge his wife's wrongful death, but now he could see it in another, much more sinister light. He'd made it a seduction, played it so well, and exploited Sam's feelings in the process. Maybe he'd never been interested at all. He only wanted information. And he got it. Sam had fallen hook, line, and sinker.

Sheldon seemed to know where his mind had drifted. "You were the last one to see her that day. If anyone had information about Emma that might be used against him, it was you, Sam. No wonder he wanted to keep you close, get you on his side. Son," Sheldon's voice grew gentle. "Is there any other evidence you remember now, that you didn't tell me before?"

Other evidence that seemed to point to an insider in the PD—the wiped hard drive, for one, and Emma's missing cell phone, for another—could have been masterminded by Nathan. Sam did indeed feel as though he were being pulled under by a tide, swept adrift from land and the story he'd clung to for so long.

Sheldon cracked his knuckles. "I told you before. Nathan Walker thinks he's above the law. He's a master manipulator, Sam. It's no wonder you were taken in. Just be thankful you managed to get away in one piece, all right?"

All of those times Nathan had told him to stay out of it for his own safety, and more recently, to stay away from the police. Was this the reason? Because he knew the growing evidence in the case against him and wanted to make sure Sam never heard about it?

Or had Nathan been right all along, and genuine. And was Sheldon now playing Sam like he'd so persuasively argued Nathan had?

If the Feldman cases were connected to Emma's death, and police corruption was as pervasive as Nathan seemed to suggest, Nathan would be the perfect fall guy. He'd be convicted of murder, while the responsible parties went free.

Still, they had an actual confession by a man who'd claimed to have killed Emma under duress. He'd not only confirmed Nathan's identity, he'd described Nathan in a cold, callous way. Sheldon was right. No jury in their right minds would let him walk.

"Now," Sheldon said, standing. "I'll see if Walker is done with his lawyer. If you'd still like to see him. I'm sure you have a lot of things on your mind."

The challenge was there in his voice. He wanted Sam to say "no," afraid of what he might hear from Nathan, afraid of having Sheldon's evidence confirmed first-hand.

Sam blinked. "Yes. I would, actually."

Sheldon shrugged and beckoned Sam to follow him toward the inner sanctum of the station, where he was told to wait outside a second set of metal detectors. Sam forced his mind blank. Once he spoke with Nathan, everything would make sense. It had to.

A few minutes later, another officer wearing plain clothes left the holding area and nodded to him. "Are you Sam Flynn?" she asked.

"Yeah. I'm waiting to see Nathan Walker."

"I'm sorry, but Mr. Walker has refused all visitors." She smiled at him, apologetic. "The chief wanted me to let you know."

Sam returned her smile, amping up the charm. "But he'll want to see me. Trust me."

"Actually, he mentioned you, specifically. I'm sorry."

"I don't understand. Did he give a message?"

She shook her head. "No. No message besides he doesn't want to see you."

"I don't believe it."

"Sorry, but that's what he told me. I'm going to have to ask you to leave."

The gray winter sky mirrored Sam's mood as he left the station. He thrust his hands in his pockets and walked toward his truck, feet heavy as lead, like they didn't want to believe what he had heard either.

For some reason, Nathan hadn't wanted to see him. The doubt Sheldon had planted grew and blossomed into a cancerous weed, wrapping itself around Sam's internal organs and squeezing—hard. All it would have taken from Nathan was one word, one glance, and Sam would have known to keep his mouth shut and his head down. That this was all part of the plan. The fact that he'd denied Sam's visit could only mean there was some truth to what Sheldon had said. And why would Sheldon lie?

But try as Sam might, he couldn't reconcile the Nathan he knew with this stranger Sheldon and his anonymous witness described. The man who offered comfort when Sam had needed it most was not an evil, twisted person who would hire a hit man to take out his own wife—the woman he'd vowed to love and cherish. It didn't make any sense.

Yet he couldn't forget what Sheldon had told him. Nathan's refusal to see Sam spoke loudly. And Nathan had even admitted that things between himself and Emma hadn't been good. He'd wanted a divorce.

And Sam needed a drink.

Chapter 15

"SAM, I think it's better if you come over. It'll be fun."

"I don't feel up to it, Rach."

"But it's not a holiday party. It's a party that happens to be taking place during the holidays. We won't sing any songs this time, I promise." The previous year, Sam had been subjected to a mishmash of Christmas and Chanukah favorites. He'd had the dreidel song stuck in his head for weeks. "Come on. I haven't seen you for almost two weeks."

Sam sighed. Outside, snow had begun to fall, the large flakes turning the pavement below into a slushy, brown mess. Though it had been cold, the city sidewalks and streets were kept salty enough to melt the snow unless a large storm blew through. Tonight the forecast promised at least twelve inches.

"I've got to go see Tim."

"What about after that? We're not eating until eight. And I'm making the brisket you like, the one with the tomato sauce."

A quick glance at the time gave him at least two hours left for visiting with Tim. Then he'd have to come back to his empty apartment. Brisket did sound more appealing than another lonely frozen dinner. His mouth watered.

"Fine. But if the roads get bad, I'm crashing at your place."

"That's cool. We've got the sleeper sofa. See you in a few hours, then?"

"All right." The "we" didn't escape Sam's attention. Alex had pretty much moved into Rachel's apartment.

Sam pulled on his winter boots and coat, then searched around for his gloves and found only one. He'd have to get a new pair before Monday, and he groaned at the thought of fighting his way through mobs of Christmas shoppers at the mall. If there was a worse way to spend a Saturday, he didn't want to know about it.

The parking lot at Shady Brook was packed. During the holidays patients who hardly had a visitor the whole year suddenly had friends and family coming out of the woodwork. Guilty consciences got guiltier in December. Sam knew from personal experience.

The on-duty nurse told him Lisa had gone on vacation for the holidays, but Tim was doing fine. As was the orchid he'd brought Lisa, Sam noticed. It had bloomed again—its perfect white petals evidence it was flourishing under her care. The new nurse didn't mention anything about the arrangements they'd have to make after the holidays for Tim's transfer. Sam had gone there the week before to check the place out. If he'd thought Shady Brook sterile and depressing at times, it looked like Disneyland compared to the state-run facility. He'd left with a lump in his throat, his fears confirmed. It was a place people went to die.

He didn't want to think about that.

Helen's son and his wife were visiting with their baby, who'd gotten big enough to sit up on her own. She giggled and cooed and pulled on her grandmother's blanket while her parents spoke in hushed tones. They greeted Sam kindly and offered him some cookies they'd brought along for show. As if Helen could eat them. People did stupid things when they were sad. That was another thing Sam knew about.

"Heya, Timbo," Sam said, sitting down in his chair. "How you doing today, bud?"

It didn't matter if he didn't get a response back. He ate one of the cookies in silence. A few minutes later, once Helen's family had left, Sam leaned forward and took Tim's hand.

"I need to talk to you. I could use some advice, okay?"

He hadn't been able to talk to Yuri or Rachel about what Sheldon had told him. Apparently the evidence had been enough to keep Nathan in jail without bail, pending trial. Every day that passed only confirmed Nathan's guilt. Sam couldn't imagine the FBI leaving an agent to languish in county jail if he were innocent.

Nathan had refused to see him a second time and a third. Sam didn't bother going again, after that.

"I don't know what I should do, or why I even care. If he did it, he's a sick sonofabitch," Sam said after he'd finished the whole story. Tim stared vacantly at the ceiling. "I don't know what to think, anymore. I mean, maybe Emma *was* talking about Nathan that day. She must have been, right?"

The sound of a cart wheeling down the corridor distracted Sam for a moment. A nurse looked in and gave him a smile. "Visiting hours are almost over, dear."

"I know. Just another minute."

"Better get home before the storm picks up. They're saying it's going to be a bad one."

"I will."

After she'd gone, Sam turned back to Tim. "And who is this guy who says he killed Emma? It doesn't seem like Nathan to be so sloppy, you know? To threaten someone? He would have no guarantee the guy wouldn't talk. It doesn't make any sense."

In Sam's mind, Tim nodded in agreement.

"Maybe someone *else* threatened him? Hmm. That's an interesting thought. Maybe he made the confession under duress. But why?"

In his mind Tim frowned thoughtfully and shrugged.

"I worry I'm trying to justify all of the evidence because I don't want him to be guilty. I really…. I like him. I liked him, or whoever I thought he was. Jesus."

A weary numbness seeped into Sam's bones. Going over and over the details had tired him out. Now that he'd unloaded on his brother—even though he got no response—a weight had been lifted.

"Thanks for listening, Timmy." He patted Tim's lax hand and then released it. "I love you."

The snow had picked up by the time he got back to his truck, but he still had an hour to kill before dinner at Rachel's. He turned on the engine and started to drive without any destination in mind.

Driving in the snow always brought a certain, strange calm. Flakes swirled and danced in his headlights as they got the best of the salt and sand and swathed the road in white. Except for the occasional service vehicle, the roads were deserted. Everyone else was home preparing for the Nor'easter.

The numbness didn't dissipate, only increased the longer he drove. The rhythmic swish of the wiper blades and the splash of the tires through thickening slush interrupted the silence, creating an almost musical cadence. It had been snowing the night of the accident. Peaceful. Sam wondered if his father's death had been peaceful too. They said he was killed on impact. One minute, he was driving through the quiet falling snow, and the next the car had hit an icy patch, tumbled off the road, and exploded against a tree in a shower of glass and metal. Maybe he hadn't even felt anything, only known a moment of surprise—a twist of panic in his gut and then nothing at all.

But after the car rolled and expelled them, Sam's mother and Tim hadn't been so lucky. No quick release for them. His mom had lingered on for a few days, until her internal injuries finally claimed her. The doctors could place a vena cava filter to stop the blood clots, but they couldn't stop the swelling in her brain. She'd still looked beautiful, though. When Sam arrived at the hospital the next day, he'd almost believed for a moment that his family had played an elaborate, horrible joke on him.

The drowsiness settled on his shoulders like a warm mantle as the long road stretched before him. Only occasional headlights punctuated the dark. Sam floored the gas pedal and wondered how fast he could go. His father had been driving fast, too.

At some point he realized he was crying. That was strange. The speedometer had passed sixty, and if he needed to slam on the brakes for any reason, he was probably toast.

And then what would happen to Tim?

He started to ease up then, and his truck slowed, bringing him back to himself. His heart thumped loudly and he exhaled, then breathed deeply and took account of his surroundings. He'd driven far out without knowing it, but the road he'd turned onto was familiar. It was Nathan's. He kept driving. The last he'd heard, Nathan's agent had listed the property for sale, but Sam had no idea whether the house had been purchased yet. A partially obscured realty sign still marked the property boundary at the base of the long driveway. Murder probably made the place a hard sell for most people.

Sam turned up the driveway and parked in view of the house. The snow and darkness did little to improve the scene. The place looked desolate and abandoned with its darkened windows. Not at all like the familiar house and land he'd gotten to know over the past few years. What the hell was he doing out here?

But before he turned around to head back into town, he noticed something on the ground, illuminated by his headlights. He stared hard and thought he made out footprints in the snow. Fresh, from the look of them.

His pulse accelerated. Maybe Nathan had been released? But no. Sam would have heard something. More likely, Nathan had asked a neighbor to collect his mail or check on the house in his absence. Sam killed the engine and headlights anyway and zipped his coat.

Small bits of ice mixed with the flakes and pinged on the ground like tiny insects hitting a car windshield. Sam knelt down and noticed the footprints were larger than his own, but only slightly, and made by heavy-duty boots. He pressed his palm into one, and the cold snow bit his skin. Difficult as it was to see in the darkness, they appeared to originate from the seldom-used road that ran parallel to the house—the old orchard road that led from the barn to the groves beyond and then looped around the property to connect with the main road about a mile away. Soon the snow and ice would obliterate all traces.

A harsh gust whipped sleet against his face. Something about the scene unsettled him, and then he realized what it was. There was only one set of footprints. Whoever they belonged to had either gone back another way, or still lurked somewhere nearby.

Adrenaline spiked in Sam's veins. He approached the front door cautiously, aware whoever was inside the house would have noticed his arrival minutes before. For once, he wished he'd taken the damn gun when Nathan offered it instead of stubbornly refusing.

Sam thought he saw an arc of light flash beyond the curtains in the living room, but it disappeared as soon as he registered it. Maybe the electricity had gone out. Or maybe, as seemed increasingly likely, someone had broken into Nathan's house. The perp returning to the scene of the crime?

He found the door slightly ajar, with the key stuck in the lock. Jesus. Had Nathan escaped from jail? Sam pushed the door open and peered inside, only to be met by silence and the darkness of the front hall. A chill that had nothing to do with the cold winter wind made goose bumps break out on his skin. He had the uncanny feeling he was being watched.

His flight instinct clashed with curiosity and suspicion. He paused on the threshold of the house, unsure whether to go or stay. Ultimately, though, there was never any choice, not when he could be on the verge of a discovery that might shed light on the crazy developments of the past few months. He clenched his freezing hands into fists and stepped inside.

The feeling of unease increased, making the tiny hairs stand up on the back of his neck. He strained to hear anything beyond the wind and snow and his own hammering heart. And then Rich Petersen stepped out of the shadows.

"What the hell are you doing here?" Sam demanded, the words leaving his mouth before he had time to think about what business Rich Petersen might have in Nathan's home. At night. In a snowstorm. Dressed in black clothes.

"I should be asking you the same thing. This is a crime scene."

Petersen crossed his arms, and his stance assumed a kind of genuine formidability that Sam never suspected his old school rival possessed.

"Not anymore it's not, so why are you at Nathan's house?"

"Police business."

"In the dark? Hmm." Sam flipped the hall switch, and the house flooded with comforting light. "There. That's better. Now you can see what you're doing. I always find it helpful to work with the lights on."

"You think you're so smart, don't you?"

"I'm smart enough to know you don't have a warrant."

"Of course I have a warrant."

"Let's see it, then."

Petersen's fleshy mouth tightened into a line. He glanced over Sam's shoulder into the night beyond. "I don't have to show you

152

anything. This isn't even your house." Sam didn't doubt Petersen wanted him to think he had a legitimate reason for being here, yet everything about the circumstances seemed suspicious.

Sam grinned. "I know. And it's definitely not *your* house, unless you bought it from Nathan?"

"Shut up, Flynn."

Maybe it would have ended like that. Sam, after all, didn't have anything besides his misgivings to go on. But in the next moment, another set of footsteps thumped up the stairs and Petersen's eyes widened with surprise.

Sam spun around to come face-to-face with a figure in the doorway, a man he'd never seen before in his life. He was older than Sam, maybe around forty, and tall, with a deep divot in his square chin. He carried a gun in one black-gloved hand.

"Richard, what are you doing with the lights on?" he asked, only then seeming to register they weren't alone. He blinked at Sam. "Who is this?"

Sam's brain whirred from third gear to fourth. The voice was familiar. The accent, the intonation. He'd heard it before, and recently, but where?

Sheldon's office. The nausea came on strong as a Pavlovian response. Oh shit, this was the guy, the hit man who'd confessed to killing Emma. Sam tried to keep his expression neutral, a difficult task since the guy apparently liked to wave his Glock for emphasis. The hit man frowned. "Who is this?" he demanded again.

"We've got some company."

"We cannot afford company, you stupid man. Did you find it?"

"Shut up," Petersen said through gritted teeth. The man turned toward Sam, coming close enough for Sam to notice he reeked of cigarettes. His large body suggested a brutish, blunt strength.

"Did you follow us here?" he demanded, ignoring Petersen. "Who sent you?"

"No one sent me," Sam said. "I'm here to pick up the mail."

If neither of them knew Sam had heard the taped confession, maybe he had a shot of getting out in one piece. He kept his expression innocent, glancing between the two of them.

"So he does not know," the man said to Petersen.

Petersen rolled his eyes. "He obviously knows something now."

Dread curdled in Sam's stomach as he glanced toward the open door and tried to calculate the likelihood of making a run for it without being shot. The hit man seemed to sense his thoughts. He smiled a deadly smile. "But he's not going anywhere, are you, errand boy?"

That was the last thing Sam heard before everything went black.

He came to sometime later, expecting to be in the trunk of a car, or worse, and was surprised and relieved to find they were still at Nathan's house. His head throbbed with a pulsing ache where the hit man had clocked him. He appeared to be in the dining room, or what was left of it. All the packed boxes had been torn apart, their contents scattered. He could hear the voices of the other men coming from the living room, but he couldn't move his hands or feet. Groggily, he realized he'd been hogtied to a chair.

"Where is it, you idiot?" It was the hit man. "We need to get out of here before we are trapped in this blizzard."

"It has to be here. She said it was."

"Well, how do you know she did not lie to you?"

Sam couldn't tell who they were talking about, but the female pronoun suggested either Emma or Patricia.

"She didn't. I know she didn't. You didn't see her face." Petersen's voice cracked. "She said her husband had a record of everything, and she'd given it to Emma. She said we… we'd all get what was coming to us. She said it was only a matter of time."

So, Patricia, then. Petersen must be talking about the night on the bridge. Sam stayed completely still, afraid if he breathed, he'd miss something.

"How do you know she was not, how do you say, bluffing?" The hit man scoffed. "Stupid woman tries to get under your skin, and then she kill herself. She knows you cannot hurt her at this point. And we all know the little Jew was afraid of his wife. He would not have told her anything." The hit man cackled as if he'd told a hilarious joke.

Petersen seemed less amused. "Nothing else makes any sense. Emma was a good cop, but she had to get her information somewhere.

It has to be here," he said again, and then again, repeating the phrase like a bizarre mantra.

"No. She would have told me during interrogation. Everyone always tells me the truth in the end. Before they beg for mercy." From the twisted cadence of pleasure in his words, the hit man was obviously experienced in methods of torture. Bile rose in Sam's throat, and he blinked back tears of hatred and remorse as he envisioned the scene, even as his mind tried to blot out the images. Emma had been strangled, and likely over an extended period of time. He could almost hear her pleas. "I searched everywhere," said the hit man. "There was nothing."

"And then you killed her."

"I could not leave her alive."

"If something *is* here, and we don't find it, Walker and his people will." Petersen's voice trembled, and Sam despised him even more. He had always been a bully and a coward, but never more so than now, when he was afraid of being caught for his complicity in the worst crime imaginable.

"Do not worry about Walker. He is finished." The hit man was more certain.

Everything from the night after Patricia's death flooded back, especially the look on Petersen's face in the jail. Sam had interpreted his sickness at the time, perhaps benevolently, as distress over what he'd seen on the bridge. But then at the bar, Petersen had flipped when Sam asked if Patricia said anything to him before she jumped. Not because he was actually worried about Sam writing a blog post about it, but because she *had* said something. Something that had scared Petersen enough to make him lose his dinner. Something that had scared him enough to send him out on a stormy night to find whatever it was. Emma's evidence was somewhere in the house. Perhaps.

But if what the hit man said was true, this particular evidence would not only incriminate them, it would help Nathan—maybe even exonerate him. A desperate hope rose in Sam's chest until curses and crashing from the other room derailed his train of thought.

If Sam hadn't been tied to a chair and in fear for his life, he might have laughed. He'd always known Petersen was an idiot, but the hit man, twisted and murderous as he was, had proven himself just as bumbling. They were quite the pair, with hardly enough brains between them to realize they'd given away key evidence in close vicinity of a witness. As far as they were concerned, Sam wouldn't be a problem for long. But still. Sam had no idea how they'd explain away the disaster they'd made of Nathan's house.

"The chief will have my head for this," said Petersen mournfully. "I'm as good as dead."

"He is not the only one you should worry about, friend. We had a sweet deal going here until you had to ruin everything."

"Me? It's not my fault!"

They began bickering like an old married couple, but Sam couldn't make out any more accusations in the rising cadence of their angry words. Besides, he'd heard what he needed to.

Sheldon had been involved all along. The confession he had played Sam must have been a fabrication. The hit man was a willing murderer, not a helpless victim of Nathan's manipulation. And Emma had been killed because she had evidence about Feldman's death, evidence linking the men in this house—and likely Sheldon—to the crime.

The man who'd looked out for him, who'd known and loved his father…. How could that be possible?

Sam blinked back angry tears as he struggled against the ropes incapacitating his hands. He only succeeded in cutting his wrists with the sharp, strong nylon. His ankles were crossed and tied to the back of the chair, and the contraption looped around his wrists so he couldn't move his feet without pulling on his hands. The more he moved, the tighter it seemed to get, cutting off the circulation until it didn't even hurt anymore. Finally he gave up and relaxed against his bonds, panting.

More crashing came from the other room, and an impotent rage bubbled in Sam's throat. They were destroying Nathan's things. Emma's things.

"We need to get the hell out of here," the hit man said. "This is not doing any good."

"What are we going to do about *him*?" Petersen asked in a harsh whisper.

"We kill him, of course."

"But his truck. He could have told anyone he was coming. They'll be looking for him."

"I will take care of it. No one will come until after the storm. And by then... well, it is very possible that he had an accident driving in the snow, yes?"

Sam's heart stopped. They were going to kill him and make it look like a car accident, but they were too dumb to recognize the irony.

Heavy footsteps heading in the direction of the dining room only seconds later gave him little time to react. Pretending to be unconscious wouldn't make any difference at this point, but his head kept lolling to the side anyway. He was so sleepy.

"Wake up." Petersen smacked him across the face. Sam groaned as blood filled his mouth. He spat and blinked at the figures towering over him. "It's time to go."

Chapter 16

"GO WHERE?" Sam's tongue felt heavy, thick in his mouth. "I was just starting to get comfortable."

Another smack, this one right under his eye. Burning pain blossomed and radiated out from the point of impact, and Sam saw stars.

"You keep your smart mouth shut." Sam grimaced as Petersen cut the bonds around his ankles. The hit man pointed his gun in Sam's direction, and Sam had the distinct impression he might have peed his pants. Neither made any move to untie his hands, though, and his arms remained trapped behind his back.

"Stand up," the hit man demanded.

"I can't."

With a brutal shove to his shoulder, Sam lurched out of the chair, only stopped from face-planting by Petersen, who grabbed him by the back of his jacket. Sam stumbled to regain his balance, even as his mind scrambled for something—anything.

"Walk."

"Wait a second. I know where the evidence is." Sam started to sweat under the weight of his coat and the glare of the two men. It was a last-ditch attempt, but even so, he had to take the risk. He had nothing to lose.

The hit man scowled. "What do you mean, you know?"

"I was the last one to talk to Emma. She told me she'd hidden it in the house… in the attic."

The hit man looked to Petersen. "Is that true?"

"It's true he was the last one to talk to her."

"There is nothing in the attic," the hit man said. "I looked myself."

Sam shook his head. "Because Nathan packed everything up. She said she'd hidden it in… an antique clock." Yeah, pulled that one out of his ass.

The hit man didn't seem convinced. "Why would you not come look for it sooner?"

"Because I was scared. I thought I'd be killed."

It seemed feasible enough. Maybe. Sam hoped the two of them were desperate enough to believe.

Petersen looked at him with disgust. "That night at the bar when you came and talked to me, I should have known you were up to something, asking me what the Feldman bitch said. You and Emma, always so buddy-buddy. I should have killed you when I had the chance."

Sam tried not to show his fear. He wouldn't give Petersen the satisfaction. How he resisted spitting in the man's face, he had no idea. "If you kill me now, you'll never find it. I'm the only one who knows."

The hit man seemed to be losing his patience. "I think you are only saying this to us because you're going to try something funny, like escaping. Yes? You find this clock, we'll let you die quickly. Not like your friend, Emma. She did not like to cooperate, you see, so I took my time."

If Sam had use of his hands, he probably would have done something stupid, like lunge at the guy. "Who hired you?"

A smirk. "You think I am a stupid man?"

Sam's vision swam and his gorge rose again. It all made such twisted sense. This scumbag had murdered Emma. When Petersen and McCormick found her, they had the chance to clean up or destroy any relevant evidence. Maybe they even helped. No wonder it had been such an open and shut investigation, a case of home burglary gone wrong—until Nathan started poking around, making himself a target in the process. Unless Sam had it all wrong and Nathan really was involved. Maybe they'd all been working together until Sheldon decided Nathan should take the fall.

"I can't help you with my hands tied," Sam said, injecting a bit of real desperation into his voice. He didn't need to act scared shitless. "Let me go, and I'll find it, I swear."

Petersen and the hit man exchanged a glance and seemed to agree. The next thing Sam knew, he'd been cut free. Feeling gradually started to return to his hands and feet with pinpricking needles. Wincing, he massaged his wrists where the flesh had been rubbed raw.

Now the hit man spoke up. His accent seemed to get thicker the angrier he got. "Remember what I said. No funny business."

Sam knew he was living on borrowed time, but at least he had reason to hope Nathan was innocent after all. It shouldn't have been comforting, but it was.

The hit man pushed him forward. Sam stumbled, aware of the gun pointed straight at his back as he entered the chaotic living room. The assholes had upended all of the boxes Nathan had packed, strewing their contents everywhere—household items, clothes, pictures with broken frames. Sam tried to look purposeful. He nudged a broken vase with his foot before kneeling down. The movement made him dizzy. Behind him, Petersen and the hit man argued with each other, making it impossible to concentrate.

He had no idea what time it was. Rachel would worry if he was late for dinner, but he wasn't sure she would call the police. God, he hoped not. His only chance of escape was to distract them long enough to head for the door… and then what? From the sound of the wind howling, the snowstorm had only worsened along with the shitstorm in the house.

Sam remembered his truck was in the driveway, and the other two had likely parked on the back orchard road and come on foot. If he could get to his truck and start it without getting shot, he'd probably be okay. But that was a big "if." His only hope lay in distraction.

"You don't know where nothing is," said the hit man to Sam. Another blow shattered his concentration and sent him crashing to the floor. Something wet and warm ran down the side of his face. "We were stupid to listen to you. Richard, get him up."

Sam clung to the stapler he'd found in a dismembered box of office items. He tried to think, but his head was throbbing, turning his brain to marshmallow.

And that's when he noticed the orchids.

All of them had been ripped out of their pots. They lay scattered throughout the other debris, their fibrous roots exposed and torn. The porous soil darkened the carpet. He picked up one broken stem and tried to focus on it. Emma's beloved plants had been completely ruined, and for nothing.

Or had they?

The orchid he'd given to Lisa, Emma's favorite. It was a complete long shot, but could that orchid have a hidden secret?

Don't overwater the soil.

The hit man's eyes were keen. He nudged Sam with his boot.

"You have seen something? What is it?"

"Nothing."

Another strike, this time to his temple. Blood pounded in Sam's ears, and pain bloomed and clouded his thoughts, blotting out everything else. He dropped the plant. His vision swam, and his shoulder protested in agony as the hit man yanked him to his feet. Sam dropped the stapler when Petersen twisted his hands back behind him and tied them again. The barrel of the gun dug into his spine. He closed his eyes and waited for whatever pain would come next. He hoped against hope death would be swift and that someone would take care of his brother.

"Shit." Petersen cursed. Sam's eyes flew open at the word. "Get down."

Sam thought he might be hallucinating. Lights beyond the house appeared first, and then he heard men yelling. Someone flipped him unceremoniously onto his back and onto his bound wrists. His wounds screamed in protest. He tried to push himself upright but only managed to flip onto his belly and wriggle like an inchworm away from the fray. He couldn't lift his head. The air got cold as the storm burst into the room.

There were men in SWAT gear, and Sam dimly recognized one of them. Or he thought he did. His head hurt.

More yelling. Guns fired and someone fell down next to him. There was a ragged hole in the guy's skull, and blood and brain matter spattered out of the oozing wound and onto the carpet. Rich Petersen was dead.

Sam vomited before he lost consciousness.

Someone touched his head, right near the place where it hurt. It didn't feel good, but he liked it anyway. The touch was nice. Gentle. He opened his eyes.

"Jesus, Sam." It was Nathan. "Thank God you're alive."

"Nathan?" He tried to make his mouth say something else but the words didn't come. Nathan wore a dark blue jacket with the words "FBI" written across the chest in big white letters. He had on a woolen winter hat. Behind him, people were moving and doing things, but Sam didn't care. He blinked slowly. The vision didn't go away. Nathan was here and not in jail. He had Sam's head in his lap, and he looked worried.

"Can you hear me?"

Sam nodded, but it hurt.

"You're okay, but you have a nasty laceration to the scalp, which is why it's bleeding so much. I'm pretty sure you have a concussion too, which is why it's so hard to keep your eyes open. I'm going to have to ask you to stay awake, okay? No matter how much you might want to sleep. Can you do that for me?" Sam nodded again. His feet were cold as icicles.

"Okay. We're going to go to the hospital and get you stitched up." Nathan smiled, but it didn't reach his eyes. His hands were covered with blood.

"Nathan—" Sam started. Petersen's body had been concealed with a sheet. A large puddle of blood spread underneath it and across the floor.

"Shh. We'll talk later, once you're all taken care of, okay? It's going to be fine. I promise."

"Nathan, the plant. Listen." He tried to think of the word he needed to say.

A frown turned down the corners of Nathan's mouth. He spoke in hushed tones to another man wearing an FBI jacket. "It's worse than I thought. He's not making any sense."

The other man peered down at Sam with a serious face. "Let's get him on a stretcher."

"The orchid," Sam finally managed. That was the word. He smiled. "Lisa's orchid."

Chapter 17

THE DOCTOR who stitched Sam's head made him drink a little carton of orange juice. He didn't particularly like orange juice, but he did it anyway, hoping they'd let him go home if he cooperated. His stomach protested at the juice. He'd been sick several times since his arrival at St. Mary's, an effect of the concussion, the doctor said.

Nathan had disappeared after helping to load him on the stretcher. Sam wanted to ask where he was, but he still wasn't sure which strangers he could trust.

"You're going to have to stay here tonight for observation." The doctor, who looked startlingly like an older Shaquille O'Neil, flipped through Sam's chart. "We'll get you transferred to a quieter room."

"I don't want to stay here." Hospitals weren't really his thing.

"With this storm, no one's going anywhere. And it's only a precautionary measure. Tomorrow morning you can go home, as long as you promise to rest up for the next few days. You should be fine."

The doctor called a nurse, who brought a wheelchair and helped Sam into it, though he insisted he could walk.

"You've got some pretty worried friends out in the waiting room," the nurse told him. "Once we've got you all situated, we'll send them up."

Sam could only imagine. Rachel would be furious with him for driving to Nathan's in the first place. He hated to think he'd ruined her dinner. And Yuri would give him shit for poking his nose where it didn't belong. Sam smiled. He'd been so close to never seeing his friends again, he was almost looking forward to being yelled at.

They didn't yell at him, though. Yuri and Rachel hovered like nervous hens while their significant others lurked in the background, as if afraid to intrude by coming too close. Rachel sat on the edge of the bed, watching him with wide eyes, and brushed his face with the back of her hand. Sam tried to pretend he wasn't disappointed not to see Nathan.

"That bad, huh?" Sam asked her.

"You have a helluva shiner. Two, actually."

Sam touched the gauze bandage wrapped around the top of his head. Yuri frowned. "Does it hurt?"

"They numbed it to stitch it up, so not really. I think it probably will, though."

"You scared the shit out of us, Sammy." Yuri had to be worried if he was using cutesy nicknames. Sam chuckled. His brain seemed a little less foggy.

"What's so funny?" Rachel looked from Sam to Yuri.

"I was thinking this would have been a great Halloween costume. I feel partially mummified."

"Yeah. Well, maybe you can put a beard on and be a badass Santa," Michael offered from the other side of the room. "Scare the crap out of some little kids."

Sam smiled at Yuri. "You know, I like him. He gets to stay."

They talked about the dinner he'd missed—Rachel's famous brisket and Alex's latkes—before Sam finally managed to turn the topic back to the events of the night.

"So, how did you know I was here?"

Rachel and Yuri exchanged a glance, and Sam saw a whole conversation pass between them—they'd obviously agreed not to broach any serious subjects with him until they decided he could handle it. Sam groaned.

"I'm fine, you guys, seriously. I'm not used to being pistol-whipped, that's all. So, what happened I don't know about?"

"Sam, this can wait until—"

"No. I want to know."

Yuri finally relented. "You were late for dinner. So, when you didn't answer your cell, we called Shady Brook, and they said you'd left a couple hours before. I figured you went back to your place, but you still didn't answer. The snow was coming down at that point, so we started to get worried." His tone said they'd been concerned about more than Sam driving in the storm. His state of mind the past couple of weeks hadn't been exactly cheerful.

Rachel spoke next. "And then Alex had the idea that maybe you'd gone to see Nathan, so we called the county jail to ask, and they told us Nathan had been released. They weren't going to tell me any more, but you know me." Sam nodded. He definitely did. "I demanded to know where he'd gone. They told me to call the police department, so I did. Nathan was there."

Sam's eyebrows shot up. "What?"

"I still don't know all the details. Nathan was worried—he was worried about you—and he was talking really fast. It seems the FBI had some sort of surveillance on his house, and he said you were with Rich Petersen and some other guy, the guy who killed Emma. He insisted he was going to get you out. But with the storm, well, I could tell he was worried he wouldn't get there in time."

Yuri cleared his throat. "He told Rachel he'd call her, and he did about an hour later. That's when he asked us to meet you here."

A dull ache started to throb at the base of Sam's skull. The unexpected news of Nathan's release and his role in Sam's subsequent rescue didn't seem real.

"Where is he now?" Even in a room full of his best friends, he wanted Nathan nearby. It had been so long since they'd seen each other.

Another shared glance. "I don't know," Rachel said. "He was here for a second when they first brought you in, but he didn't stay. I figure he probably had some things to take care of down at the station."

Rachel kept looking at Yuri, obviously holding something back. "What?" Sam asked.

Yuri spoke reluctantly. "Petersen is dead and they arrested the other guy, Hoffman or something. And, I'm sorry to tell you, Sam, but it looks like Chief Sheldon was involved. He's been arrested too."

Sam blinked as the words sank in. Sheldon's involvement had become apparent back at Nathan's house, but he hadn't wanted to believe it. Hearing a trusted friend confirm it to be true was even worse.

"I just don't understand." His voice sounded dull in his ears.

"I know, baby," Rachel said. "But I'm sure Nathan will be able to fill you in when he comes back. Rest for now, okay? You must be exhausted."

"We could all use some sleep." Alex massaged Rachel's shoulders.

Rather than chance the drive home in the blizzard, Sam's friends decided to camp out in the hospital room until the snow let up or someone kicked them out. The nurses didn't seem to mind, and no one bothered them. Sam was glad for the company, save for the way Rachel or Yuri kept waking him every hour on the hour to keep tabs on the concussion. He didn't sleep deeply. Every time he dozed off, he saw the blood-soaked carpet and Petersen's oozing brains. He dreamed that Sheldon stood over him with a gun and scolded him for sticking his nose where it didn't belong. And Sam woke with a start, heart pounding, at the sound of his desolate laugh.

The cold gray dawn began to stake its claim on the room. Alex and Rachel were curled up together on the other bed, and Michael was slumped asleep in a chair. Yuri, however, was awake, and he looked like he hadn't slept all night.

"Hey," Sam said, his voice gravelly.

"Hey."

"Thanks for staying."

"It's no big deal." Yuri stood and patted his arm.

None of the others stirred. Sam kept his voice low. "I know I haven't always been the best friend, and I'm sorry. I'm sorry for being selfish and treating you like shit."

"Damn. They must have hit your head pretty hard after all."

"Shut up. I'm trying to be serious. It's not just a cliché, you know. That whole life-or-death thing makes you think. And I'm grateful you're my friend."

"We're family, Sam. You know that."

It was true, after all. Some people were born with family, and some people found family along the way. He didn't deserve Yuri's loyalty, but maybe now that he had a second chance, he could try to earn it.

"Aww, boys," Rachel said, whispering over Alex's sleeping head. "You're so precious, I want to puke."

"Don't give me any ideas," Sam groaned.

Soon after, everyone else started to stir, and grumblings of hunger arose in the room. It looked like the storm had ended, leaving Stonebridge under a nearly two-foot blanket of white. Yuri and Rachel promised to dig out the car and come back for Sam once the doctors approved his release. Rachel kissed him on the cheek. "We'll be back for you later."

"Where's my truck?"

"They told us it's still at Nathan's, probably buried under the snow. We'll have to get it another day."

"Well, then, I'll get a cab. It's fine."

"Absolutely not." Rachel frowned. "Cabs aren't even running. I think you should come and stay with me and Alex for a couple of days."

"I could take him home," another familiar voice added. Rachel stepped to the side, and Sam saw Nathan standing in the doorway, still wearing his FBI gear. So it hadn't been a dream. He gave Sam a tentative smile, and Sam's heart skipped a beat. "I mean, if you want. I don't mind."

"Yeah," Sam said, smiling helplessly back. "Sounds good."

Rachel put her hands on her hips. "Perfect." She leaned down and whispered in Sam's ear. "Damn, he's fine." But before she could embarrass Sam further, Yuri grabbed her around the waist and dragged her toward the door.

"We'll talk to you later, okay, Sam?"

Sam rolled his eyes at them. "Yeah, yeah."

"We want to hear everything," Rachel said.

"Well, maybe not *everything*," Michael added.

Once they were alone, sounds of laughter fading down the hall, Nathan approached Sam's bed. "You have some pretty great friends there."

"Yeah. I'm lucky like that." Sam couldn't stop staring, but he didn't feel self-conscious since Nathan seemed to be doing exactly the same, taking in everything from head to foot.

"How are you feeling?" Nathan's eyebrows knit together.

"My head hurts worse than a hangover after a week-long bender, but given the circumstances, not bad. Better than the other guy. Did you find it?"

Nathan nodded and regarded Sam with something like wonder. "We found a plastic bag with a flash drive in the potting soil, just like you said. I can't believe it was there this whole time and I had no idea."

"Emma was sneaky."

"She was brilliant."

Sam struggled to sit up. He felt strange talking to Nathan from the business end of a hospital bed.

"So what was on it?"

"Everything I hoped. But I can't get into it right now. I'm actually expected back down at the station in a few."

"They told me Sheldon's been arrested."

"He has. Yes." Nathan's face didn't give anything away. "I know you cared for him. I'm sorry."

"He was my father's friend." Sam waited for the anger, hurt, and betrayal to kick in, but he only felt numb. He wanted to sleep for a thousand years, preferably in the same bed as Nathan. He wondered if that was still a possibility, or if what Nathan said before still held though the danger had passed.

"Sam, I—"

Someone knocked lightly on the open door. The same doctor Sam had seen the night before poked his head in. "I'd like to give the patient a quick examination before he's released." Sam nearly groaned aloud in frustration at being interrupted.

Nathan swept his hand through his hair. "Should I go outside?"

"It'll only take a minute."

The doctor examined Sam's pupils and checked his reaction time, then wrote some notes on his chart. He smiled. "Looks good. Your concussion was severe, so no drinking or driving for a few days, especially not together. Rest up and don't run any marathons. Okay?"

Sam nodded. The doctor left and Sam got dressed, keeping the scrub shirt he'd been given and discarding his old one, which was covered in blood. Nathan came back into the room.

"Did that doctor—" he gestured toward the door.

"Exactly like Shaq, am I right?"

Nathan chuckled and nodded. "They're signing your release form." He approached the bed and squeezed Sam's shoulder affectionately.

Sam looked up at him. "What were you gonna say before we were interrupted?"

"Let's get you home first, okay? You need to get cleaned up. We'll talk later."

"But you've got to tell me—"

"Yes. I promise. And Sam, I'm sorry I couldn't get there sooner. With this goddamn snow, it's a miracle we got there in time. I don't know what I would have done if we hadn't."

Another knock—this time an orderly with a wheelchair—stopped the conversation. He guided the offending vehicle to the side of the bed and parked it, then gestured like Vanna White.

"Your ride."

"I can walk myself." Sam scowled.

"That's probably true, but this is hospital policy. Giddyup." The orderly patted the seat—he'd heard it all before.

Sam let himself be wheeled to the parking lot where Nathan's car waited. He did feel wobbly enough on the icy pavement not to protest when Nathan helped him into the passenger's seat. He could buckle his own seatbelt, though, thank you very much.

The entire city still seemed to be asleep, or waiting for the thaw. Even with Nathan's powerful engine and winter tires, his car skidded out of the hospital lot and onto the snow-covered road. Sam could hardly remember the last time they'd gotten so much snow. Plows were up and running, clearing the main streets, and Sam thought about all the business he and Yuri would miss out on if he couldn't work.

Nathan's car smelled like cold leather and cinnamon. The high-tech dashboard panel had more gadgets than the Batmobile.

Sam's stomach growled.

"Hungry?"

"I could eat. I don't have any food at my place, though."

"Let's get some breakfast to take home."

BREAKFAST TURNED out to be the only cleared-out drive-through, which was fine by Sam. He was starving. He'd wolfed down one breakfast burrito and was starting on his second by the time they made it back to his apartment.

Four flights of stairs had never seemed so daunting.

"We can rest if you need to," Nathan said.

"I'm... I'm fine." Sam didn't want to let on how much his head hurt. It would only add to Nathan's guilt about not getting to him soon enough.

Even so, Nathan kept one hand on Sam's waist as they ascended the stairs, as though he were afraid Sam would decide to faint and take a header back down. Sam liked it enough not to complain.

"One of these days, we'll climb the stairs and not have to lean on each other for help," Sam said, before blushing at his presumption. Only yesterday he'd wondered if Nathan's attraction had been an act to escape a murder charge. But Nathan only laughed.

Sam's apartment was slightly less of a shithole than usual. He'd actually cleaned during the past week. Depression did strange things to a guy. Nathan switched on the lights, turned on the heat, and then removed his FBI jacket and bulletproof vest.

"Here. You go change and lie down, and I'll bring you something to drink."

"Great. I'll take a double whiskey."

"Water, Sam, or juice." Nathan didn't sound amused.

"I know. I know. I'm joking."

Changing did sound like a good idea, though. Sam kicked off his shoes and retreated to his room, which was fucking freezing. He shivered as he discarded his dirty jeans and the scrub shirt. They'd washed his head and the wounds on his arms, but the rest of him felt grimy from being in the same room with a dead Rich Petersen. He brushed his teeth and then used a warm, wet towel to sponge himself off, not wanting to get his bandages wet in the shower. After he felt reasonably clean, he dressed in sweats and climbed into bed under his thick winter quilt—another gift from Grandma, courtesy of the Florida move. Kitchen sounds drifted into the bedroom from beyond.

A few minutes later, Sam accepted a steaming cup of sugary tea from Nathan, who watched expectantly as he sipped. "Careful. It's hot."

"I didn't even know I had tea," Sam said.

"You do," Nathan said. "But the packaging was a little old. I hope it's still okay."

"It's great." Sam didn't give a crap about the tea or anything else. Not when Nathan was finally here instead of in jail—or worse. Here, and doing the most adorable boyfriend things ever. He sipped again for emphasis and then set the mug down on the side table, putting that ridiculous thought out of his mind. He was already in danger of believing this meant more than it did.

Nathan stood with his hands in his pockets, looking like he didn't know whether to stay or go. His uncharacteristic awkwardness made Sam's stomach drop.

"I hate to leave you alone like this, but I've asked Yuri and Rachel to come over. There's a lot of paperwork that can't wait."

"Oh." Sam's disappointment must have been visible. Nathan's features softened.

"I was planning on coming back later, if you want me to."

"Yeah." Sam almost croaked out the word. He wanted Nathan to touch him, but he simply nodded and said good-bye before disappearing out the door.

Sam spent the day drifting in and out of sleep. Yuri and Rachel did come by as promised. They piled onto his bed with him and watched a couple of Sam's favorite eighties comedies, even though neither of them particularly cared for the genre.

"You're missing out on work," Sam told Yuri.

"Some things are more important than work."

"Yeah, like Tom Cruise's booty." Rachel raised an eyebrow as the man in question shimmied onto the screen clad in nothing but a button-down shirt and tighty-whities. "You know, this movie ain't half bad."

"The bottom half," Sam remarked, his eyes flicking from ass to window, where it was already growing dark. Most of the city was without power after the storm, which had dumped almost twenty-six inches of snow on Stonebridge in record time. Residents would spend the next couple of days digging themselves out, and parking downtown had become a nightmare. Schools would be closed the following day, leading into an extended Christmas holiday.

Christmas. Huh. Sam waited for the familiar pain and realized he'd stopped dreading the anniversary, though it was only a couple of days away. Maybe something had gone screwy in his head after all.

"We should get some Chinese for dinner," Rachel proposed. "Or pizza."

"Extra cheese?" Yuri asked hopefully.

Another arrival put their dinner plans on hold.

Sam hadn't let himself think about Nathan all day. He knew whatever conversation they'd have, once they finally *had* a conversation, would answer his questions. He worried it would be the end.

But Nathan came back as promised, tired but smiling. He chatted with Rachel and Yuri, who made their excuses while aiming some knowing glances in Sam's direction.

"Hey, I still need dinner." Sam shouted at them as they retreated into the living room, probably to talk about him. "You guys are jerks." It was only a performance, a half-hearted protest. He wanted to be left alone with Nathan.

"I brought sandwiches," Nathan said, once they'd gone. "I didn't know what you'd like, so I got a couple different kinds."

A couple different kinds turned out to be five. Sam chose a meatball sub and ate half of it before his curiosity got the better of him. He wasn't very hungry anyway.

Nathan sat on a chair next to his bed. He insisted Sam stay put in his room instead of going to the couch to eat like a normal human.

"Thanks for the sandwich."

Nathan eyed the half-eaten sub on Sam's lap.

"I'm full." And tired. Sam tried to stifle a yawn, but Nathan's hawk eyes saw everything. He stood up.

"You should probably get some sleep."

"Are you leaving?"

"Do you want me to go?" The hesitance in Nathan's voice made Sam's stomach squirm. He decided on honesty.

"No."

"I thought you might, after everything." Nathan ran his hand through his hair.

"You forget I don't even know what 'everything' is. The last I knew, you were in jail, arrested for murder, and wouldn't speak to me." Sam realized he was close to pouting.

"I know. I hoped you'd understand. It was the only way I could think of to keep you out of it."

"By blowing me off." He didn't add "by making me think you were a murderer," though the thought was probably visible on his face. Nathan's rejection had hurt, badly.

"I'm sorry."

"You should have told me."

"I think this should wait till morning, Sam. I don't know about you, but I'm beat."

Sam crossed his arms and took a deep breath. His pulse quickened. "Okay, well? Are you going to stand there staring, or are you going to come to bed?"

It was more demand than suggestion. Nathan gave him a wry smile before untying his boots.

They arranged themselves as comfortably as possible with Sam's bandaged head to consider. The stitches would dissolve themselves as the wound healed, the doctor had said, but they'd needed to shave the area to do the stitching. Sam figured he looked pretty frightening, but Nathan didn't seem to mind. He pulled Sam close, and Sam rested the unhurt side of his head on Nathan's chest. He drifted off to sleep almost instantly, listening to the steady rhythm of Nathan's heart.

THE NEXT morning Sam awoke alone. His head throbbed, but the pain was nothing compared to his hurt over Nathan taking off again… until he heard the sound of the shower running. Sam slid off the bed and adjusted his morning wood in his sweats. Apparently concussions didn't have much effect on his libido.

Nathan's blurred form through the shower curtain made Sam smile. He thought about climbing in after him but then remembered his bandages—the dressings on both his wrists and his head would need changing, and it didn't promise to be a sexy business.

He didn't know if Nathan would mind him in the bathroom, so he gave himself a reason. Luckily his bathroom cabinet held the needed gauze and antiseptic. Sam swiped the mirror with his arm to remove the fog.

It was the first time he'd gotten a look at himself, and besides the two shiners, a bruised and swollen cheek, and a slight cut on his lip, it wasn't as bad as he'd feared. The bandage on his head started to moisten in the humid air, so Sam started to unravel it. The wound was clean and sewn tight and didn't seem like it would have trouble healing. His wrists had been rubbed raw too, and the flesh cut, but they had already started to scab over.

"What the hell." Nathan gave a violent flail from inside the shower and then poked his head out. He looked kind of adorable with his hair plastered against his face, especially with the added indignation. "This shower is possessed."

Sam smirked back at him. "I see you've met my upstairs neighbor." He held his breath and tried not to stare as Nathan pulled back the shower curtain and stepped onto Sam's newly purchased bathmat. The erection that had subsided during his self-examination sprang into action at the sight. Sam had no idea how Nathan stayed in shape during winter with swimming as his major fitness regimen. Maybe he belonged to one of those fancy fitness clubs with an indoor pool.

Nathan dried his lean, muscular body with efficient swipes of the towel and then wrapped it around his waist. He didn't comment on Sam's unannounced presence, but he frowned when he noticed his ham-handed attempt to rebandage himself.

"Let me help you with that." Sam gave up the gauze, put the lid down on the toilet to sit, and let Nathan take over. "So, where do I start?"

Sam looked at his hands. The left wrist looked worse than the right, and he held it up. "Maybe this one?"

"You know that's not what I mean."

Sam cleared his throat. "I need to know the truth. You didn't have any part in this, right?" He flushed and avoided Nathan's gaze.

"Of course not." Even-toned. Not upset. "Not even a little."

"Sheldon had a confession from that guy. It sounded so—"

"I know how it sounded. I've heard it. It was very persuasive."

Air rushed into Sam's lungs, flooding him with relief. Guilt, however, wasn't far behind. "I'm sorry."

"Don't be. I'm good at my job. I would have been insulted if you didn't doubt me a little."

That placated Sam for the moment, but he wasn't entirely ready to let the matter rest. "Okay. Well, maybe you can tell me what was on the damn flash drive. I can't believe there was a flash drive."

"Neither can I, to be honest. Emma must have gotten a kick out of hiding it. *She* was the Bond fan, of the two of us."

"Is that why she married you?"

"Probably." Nathan seemed lost for a moment, and Sam regretted the joke. But then Nathan refocused on his task. "So, do you remember the night I called you over to talk, and we looked at the computer?"

Sam did, indeed. It had been the night Nathan first admitted his attraction—the one he said he'd never act on. "Yeah."

"You told me you'd talked to Emma about Patricia Feldman down at the station, and it gave me an idea. So I called Patricia the next day. At first, she wanted nothing to do with me. She said she was sorry about Emma, and I could tell she was scared. But finally, after I told her I was an FBI agent and could promise her protection, she agreed to see me."

Nathan moved on to the second wrist, swathing it with careful, practiced motions.

"So you met?"

A nod of assent. "Turns out she had reason to be scared. She was sure her husband hadn't killed himself. She'd met with Emma several times and could tell she didn't buy it either. And when Emma finally got her hands on Feldman's toxicology, it didn't gel with the autopsy results. The pills they found in Feldman's stomach had barely started to dissolve, which meant someone drowned him before they had a chance to do the job. Probably force-fed him the pills as well."

"No wonder Emma was so quiet about those results," Sam muttered, staring down at his hands. He'd been so disappointed at the time.

"Once Patricia finally trusted Emma enough to tell her what she knew, Emma put two and two together." A pregnant pause. "Sheldon knew what the toxicology and autopsy results indicated. He told Emma they were inconclusive and ordered her to drop the case. Of course, she couldn't." Nathan closed his eyes for a moment.

In spite of the warm, close quarters, Sam shuddered. He couldn't believe they were talking about the same man who'd brought him Christmas presents as a child. "But I don't understand. What did Patricia know? Was she withholding evidence?"

"She was trying to protect her kids. Seems her husband was in a boatload of trouble with the mob and had evidence to incriminate members of the PD as well."

Sam grimaced, half from the pain in his head, half in commiseration for poor Patricia Feldman. He was also more than a little pleased his own guess had been so close to the mark. "She must have been scared out of her mind."

"She was."

A droplet of water beaded down Nathan's lightly haired chest and onto his firm stomach before disappearing into the treasure trail below. Sam watched it, distracted by the overwhelming urge to put his hands on Nathan's waist and pull him close to lick the trace it left behind.

Nathan paused to rip the gauze and tape Sam's hand before he spoke again. "Patricia felt guilty about Emma's death. When I asked why, she told me she'd given Emma all of the info about her husband's involvement with the Voronkovs and the police. It was a million-dollar, drug-money-laundering scheme. The drugs came into Stonebridge port, and the Voronkovs paid the cops to look the other way. Then Mark Feldman filtered the money through his foundation and gave the dirty cops an additional cut on top. And that's where Chief Sheldon came in. He was working directly with Bernhardt Hoff to bring the drugs into the city and benefitting quite handsomely from it all."

"Bernhardt Hoff? Was he the one who made the confession?"

"Yes. And he killed Emma." Nathan swallowed deeply and glanced away from Sam's concerned gaze. "He did this to you too."

Sam's fist clenched with outrage. He wanted to punch something, but without a productive outlet for his anger, he could only sit and listen—and be thankful the perps were finally behind bars. "Meanwhile, the cops are arresting dime-bag dealers left and right to make it look like they're doing something to solve the drug problem."

"Exactly. Addressing the symptom and not the cause."

"Because the cause is paying the bills." Sam shook his head. "I thought the Voronkovs were mainly in New York?" He'd done some research on the new Russian crime elite for an article the previous year and knew the Feds were having a difficult time getting charges to stick, mainly because the bosses seemed to keep their hands clean while delegating the dirty work to a coterie of very dedicated and skilled henchmen, like Hoff.

Nathan seemed to pick up the thread of his unspoken thoughts. "From what we've gathered in our questioning so far, Hoff's job was to extend operations north. He's not a stool pigeon, though, and he's not naming names. It's our hope we can… persuade him."

Sam's head ached. From what he'd seen, the man had been incredibly cocky and self-assured about his own prowess. The callous way he'd spoken about Emma's murder had turned Sam's stomach. He seemed like the kind of guy whose loyalty could be bought for a price, but ultimately only cared about himself. "I wonder how a guy like Mark Feldman gets involved in something like this."

"Money. Power. You can't underestimate how seductive those things can be. But apparently Mark decided he wanted out. He was going to cut all ties and go clean. Sheldon and the Voronkovs couldn't have that, not with everything he knew."

"So they killed him."

"Actually, Petersen did."

"What?" Sam's eyebrows shot up.

"He botched it pretty badly—he didn't wait long enough for the pills to dissolve, which is what tipped Emma off in the first place. The way I see it, he's lucky he's dead."

"I'll say. At least the bullet was quick." Sam had hated the guy, but he didn't like to imagine what Hoff might have done to him if he got the order.

Nathan bit his full bottom lip as he considered Sam's head, turning it gently to the left, then the right. "This doesn't look half bad."

"So I'm not Frankenstein's monster?"

"I'm going to put a little antibiotic ointment on. Hold still."

Sam did as he was told while Nathan uncapped a tiny squeeze tube of petroleum-like stuff and smeared it on the wound. The touch was efficient but kind and conjured up a vision of Nathan dressed in hospital blues. He would make a damn fine doctor, Sam thought, cracking a smile.

"What's so funny?" Nathan asked.

Not wanting to lose track of the conversation, Sam shook his head and let the fantasy go. "Nothing. So, how did Patricia find out about Mark? Did she know all along?"

"She said no, and I'm inclined to believe her. A few days before he died, Mark gave her a flash drive full of conversations and bank reports. He told her to pass it on to someone she trusted if something ever happened to him. Of course, at the time, she had no idea what he was talking about. But after his death, she checked out the contents, which put her in jeopardy."

"Jesus. Couldn't he have given it to his lawyer?"

"A guy like Feldman? He obviously thought they would never have the balls to kill him. And his image was very important to him."

Sam scoffed. "Typical. So, after they offed him, Patricia gave Emma the drive."

Nathan paused a moment in his work to adjust his towel, which had fallen dangerously low on his hips. "She was worried about what would happen to her kids when the Voronkovs and Sheldon figured out she knew too much. And that's where I came in. We needed irrefutable evidence about their involvement. Even though we had Patricia's firsthand testimony, that drive was the only tangible proof. Sheldon kept himself very clean."

Sam thought of the chief's grandfatherly demeanor. Nothing more than a façade to hide a profiteer who'd lied and left his city to languish at the hands of the mob. The betrayal hit him hard. He closed his eyes. "Shit."

"I'm sorry, Sam. I wish this were a nicer story."

Sam shook his head. "It's all right. Go on."

"So I proposed something crazy." Nathan crossed his arms over his chest and inspected his handiwork.

"Wait a minute," Sam whispered. "Patricia's not dead, is she?"

Nathan gave him a brilliant smile. "Not even a little bit."

"You staged the whole thing? How?" Sam thought about the frigid winter waters of Long Island Sound, the bone-crushing drop from the Baptist Street Bridge.

"We had a boat waiting under the bridge and a team of elite divers in the water. We knew we'd have at least ten minutes before the Coast Guard arrived to search for the body."

"Still, that's a long drop."

"She knew the risks, and she was willing to take the chance. She had some bruising, but no major injuries. And now she's safe with her kids in witness protection." Nathan had begun to look positively gleeful. "Those bastards thought they were home free."

"Except Patricia scared the bejesus out of Petersen with whatever she said before she jumped."

"Staged. I figured if we could catch somebody back at my house looking for the evidence, it would make our case watertight. But first we needed to make sure Patricia was safe. We also had some guys decoding the Feldman Foundation books in case we never found the drive. Mark Feldman was a smart guy, and the illegal transactions were buried deeply. We needed to buy some time."

"So you let them charge you." Sam didn't even try to hide the resentment in his voice. Nathan's arrest had hit him hard. Still, he vowed to let the matter go—for now.

"Sheldon had no idea Patricia was still alive. He thought they could pin Emma's murder on me, so we let him. And in fact, we even fed him information to increase his confidence—confidence makes people careless."

Sam grimaced. "The chief told me the FBI had put you on probation after the sex ring case. He said you helped one of the perps to escape to Brazil. Your partner." He paused, not sure whether he should go on. "Sheldon said he was your lover."

"Luan."

Nathan said the name a little too wistfully for Sam's liking. He grit his teeth. "Yes."

"It's true he went home to Brazil after the case finished. But no, he wasn't involved, and I wasn't ever on probation." Nathan touched Sam's chin, urging him to look up. His dark eyes tracked over Sam's face, then locked with his. They seemed more honest and open than ever before.

"Were you lovers?" Sam asked, his throat dry. He wanted Nathan to keep touching him, to bend down and kiss him.

This was the question Nathan had, so far, evaded. He dropped his hand and let Sam go. "Only once."

"Sheldon said you wanted to run off with him," Sam said, aware his pushing might lead somewhere he didn't like, but pursuing it all the same. He needed to know what was real, even while he hated the jealousy in his voice.

Nathan shook his head. "Not true, but we let him believe it. I'm sure Sheldon thought he had me skewered."

"He said something else about an insurance policy—a double indemnity clause." It had been one of the most convincing aspects of Sheldon's accusation, rounding off an already sinister motive with a shiny, selfish polish.

"That *is* true. But he probably didn't know we'd both decided to get one, to be on the safe side."

"He might have left that out," Sam said sheepishly.

Nathan rubbed Sam's arm. Either the concussion or the conversation had made Sam a little nauseous.

"Let's get you back into bed," Nathan said.

Sam followed Nathan into his bedroom. He couldn't stop thinking about the night at the station, after Nathan's arrest. All of the things Sheldon told him had seemed so plausible, but now he saw the conversation for what it was—an attempt to find out what Sam knew. Sheldon wouldn't have hesitated to kill Sam if he'd shown the least bit of knowledge about what had really happened. All of that bullshit about wanting to keep Sam out of trouble. Yeah, Sheldon had wanted that, all right. Wanted to make sure Sam believed Nathan was a cold-blooded killer so he wouldn't try to help. Little did Sheldon know he was the one being set up, and Sam bought right into it, because he trusted the guy.

Nathan sat on the bed next to Sam and smoothed the covers. "Are you okay?"

"I can't get over the fact that I believed him. A part of me did, at least. He said he cared about me, but he didn't. He didn't give a shit."

The silence stretched out for a moment, and Sam wondered what was going on behind Nathan's dark eyes. Even after all of this, he remained an enigma.

"I don't know if that's true. I think one of the reasons you're still alive is because he cared enough to warn you away."

"Don't stand up for him. What he did—"

"I'm not trying to," Nathan interjected. "I only mean that motivations aren't always black and white, even in bad people. That's what makes them so hard to understand."

Sam frowned. "He didn't give a shit, and I fell for it."

"Okay." Nathan stroked Sam's bare arm, and the touch sent a distracting shiver up his spine. "But why wouldn't you have? He used your trust. And it was for the best, really. It kept you safe. Well, it would have."

Maybe. Sam wasn't so sure. He understood why Nathan had needed to keep quiet about Patricia, but nothing had been worse than thinking a man he'd grown to care for had been responsible for murder. It never would have happened if he'd really known Nathan at all.

"Sam, you look pale. Maybe you should take a nap."

Sam shook his head. He didn't want to think anymore, but his brain kept circling like a car on a racetrack. "So, did you ever find out what Emma said to Sheldon?"

Nathan sighed raggedly. "She confronted him about the undigested pills. That's when he sent Hoff and Petersen to find out what else she knew. He's admitted as much."

Another thought made Sam's heart lurch. "Shit. Nathan. I was asking her about the toxicology. I asked her to talk to Sheldon about Feldman. What if I—"

"No." Nathan silenced him with a firm tone. "Emma was a cop, Sam, and she wanted to be a detective. She was following her own lead. And Sheldon was like a father to her."

The words punched Sam right in the gut. So this was it, the final proof Emma had been talking about Sheldon on her last day—not Nathan and not herself. She'd been trying to decide what to do with the evidence that her boss and mentor was a crook and complicit in murder. Maybe she knew she was living on borrowed time. Sam could only imagine what Nathan must feel, taking care of Sam even as he dealt with his own grief.

"She never let on Patricia told her anything," Sam said. The memory was still fresh enough to be frightening.

"What?" Nathan's eyebrows drew together, and the question hung in the air.

"I overheard the two of them talking when I was tied up—Hoff and Petersen. Hoff said he was convinced Emma didn't have any evidence. She protected Patricia even though it meant...." He couldn't complete the thought. His throat was dry. She'd protected him as well. "And all the time, it was hidden right under their noses."

Nathan's eyes glistened. "I think she figured no one would ever think to look. No one except you." For a moment he looked as lost as the first time Sam had gone to his house and found him in the backyard, drinking himself into oblivion.

"She was a hero. You know," Nathan said, rubbing Sam's arm absently. "I don't think she thought Sheldon would hurt her. That's the worst part. If we'd been on better terms, if she'd only told me—"

Impulsively, Sam took Nathan's hand and brought it to his lips. He kissed Nathan's open palm and nuzzled against it, breathing in the clean scent. Nathan watched him without speaking. When Sam held his hand, he didn't pull away.

"We can't change what happened," Sam said. "You've done good things too, Nathan. Patricia is alive and so are her kids. Where is she, by the way?" Sam hoped the question would distract Nathan from the guilt trip he was about to take himself on, though Sam knew he'd probably never get over it. Not entirely.

"All set up in a safe house with the kids. She'll be there until the trial, and then they'll get new identities for witness protection. That's where I was, by the way, those weeks I was gone."

"Oh." So, not at a sex club screwing anonymous men. Not with Luan either. Sam had a lot more questions about how they'd managed it, but they could wait for later. Drowsiness had started to pull him under, and he wasn't sure he wanted to resist anymore. He hoped Nathan would stay.

"Just think. I might never have found the flash drive if it weren't for you. I was too involved to think clearly."

"So are you saying you're glad I'm a nosy fuck?"

"Not glad, not since you could have gotten yourself killed. But grateful. Emma can finally rest in peace."

"And so can you," Sam said, though he had a feeling it wouldn't be so easy.

Nathan leaned down and kissed him. It wasn't passionate, but it wasn't chaste. It was a kiss full of promise, soft and sweet.

Chapter 18

NATHAN MADE it his duty to ensure Sam followed doctor's orders. The next few days passed with more bed rest than Sam had seen since he came down with chicken pox as a teenager. Nathan took care of the food—mostly takeout and a botched attempt at soup—and drove Sam crazy making sure he didn't overexert himself.

"He did my laundry," Sam complained to Yuri and Rachel on one of their visits. "My fucking laundry. You know, dirty clothes I wore on my body? He washed them." Neither of his friends seemed to find this problematic. Rachel rolled her eyes.

"Well, someone has to do it, and you can't exactly run down to the basement in your condition."

"I'm fine. I can walk down a few flights of stairs."

"Be quiet and let him take care of you."

"As long as your underwear didn't have skid marks, I don't see what the problem is," Yuri chimed in. "I wish someone would do my laundry."

They were both assholes. "I want you out of my room."

"Aw, baby." Rachel patted his head. "Get some sleep and be a good boy."

"I hate you."

In spite of Sam's protests, Nathan was nothing if not persistent, and Sam eventually felt his resistance crumble. It was only a few days, simply as a precaution. And anyway, some of the things Nathan did were pretty nice.

He didn't express any interest in sex. They slept together in the same bed every night, but it never went further than a cuddle, despite the erections involved. Sam's frustration was reaching epic proportions. He never had a moment alone to jack off, except in the shower—and he'd never been a fan of using conditioner as lube. Plus, who wanted to masturbate when there was a hot man around?

He couldn't decide if Nathan's reticence came from worry over Sam's health or another matter entirely. But enough was enough.

On the fourth day of their arrangement, Sam tested the waters by rubbing his ass back against Nathan's morning wood. Nathan, half asleep, arms wrapped around Sam, groaned encouragingly. So Sam did it again.

His own dick was harder than a rock, and Nathan's felt amazing sliding right against the ridge of Sam's ass. He moved Nathan's hand from where it rested on his chest down to his aching cock, and Nathan gripped him through his boxer briefs, then fished his erection out through the opening. Skin on skin, finally. Sam tilted his head back to find Nathan's mouth, careful of his injured scalp.

The kiss grew hot and heavy fast, and Nathan started a satisfying rhythm, jacking Sam's cock under the covers. Sam didn't want to come like that, but his dick didn't seem to care. His hips surged forward, thrusting into Nathan's hand.

Sam broke off the kiss. "Can you please just fuck me already?"

"Your injuries—"

"Are fine. I'm fine. And even though this is nice, I want you to fuck me."

Nathan twisted his hand around the tip of Sam's cock and rubbed the sensitive, wet head as if to prove a point. And then he did it again— and again. The intense sensation made Sam's eyes roll back in his head. "Is this nice?" Nathan whispered.

"I don't even—ah—"

It was certainly different from the way he jacked himself, usually quick and to the point, no muss, no fuss. Nathan, Sam realized, got off on controlling his partner's pleasure. The cock poking into Sam's ass from behind certainly betrayed Nathan's eagerness.

This domestic bliss could only last so long, though. Sam was going to get Nathan to fuck him, or die trying. In fact, he almost had.

He chuckled to himself.

"What's so funny?" Nathan said hoarsely.

"You don't want to know." Using the willpower of a thousand men, Sam rolled away to ferret through his sex drawer. Nathan peered over his shoulder.

"That's… big," he said when he noticed the longest and thickest of Sam's dildos, bought on a lark in the Village. He'd never even dared use it.

"You wanna try it out?"

"Maybe another day."

"Your loss." Sam shut the drawer and threw the packets he'd found on the bed, trying for casual even as his mind screamed *another day. Another day.*

"Strawberry?" Nathan asked, picking up one of the condoms.

Sam grinned. "Sometime life needs a little flavor."

"I'm allergic to strawberries."

"Seriously?" Sam couldn't tell if he was teasing or not.

"Yeah, though I doubt any actual strawberries were used in the making of this condom."

"Okay, so no to strawberry." He tossed that condom on the floor and picked up a regular, along with his bottle of lube. "How do you want to do this?"

Nathan didn't answer as he lay back on the bed, his cock resting lush and hard on his belly. He reached down and squeezed the base, and Sam knew it wouldn't take much for him to lose his resolve. Sam shucked off his own briefs, squeezed a dollop of lube onto his fingers, and got onto all fours.

"Well, if you're not going to fuck me, looks like I'm going to have to fuck myself."

It had been a while since he'd bottomed—his adventure in New York with the anniversary couple was the last time—and he couldn't recall ever wanting another man inside him so badly. He slipped two fingers inside his hole, hamming it up a little for show. Something made him want to tease Nathan the way Nathan had teased him during their first encounter. From the look on Nathan's face, it was working. Nathan watched him with dark, impatient eyes.

"Jesus, Sam."

"Feels good," Sam said, angling for the spot inside that made his cock leak onto the sheets below. He circled his hips and felt his balls start to tighten.

Nathan stroked his erection slowly as his eyes tracked every one of Sam's movements. Sam's mouth watered. Each movement of Nathan's hand unveiled the velvety, wet head of his cock. It wouldn't be so bad to swallow down Nathan's erection and finish him off, but Sam recognized his victory for what it was.

There were his stitches to consider, so he climbed astride Nathan's thighs and took a moment to lean down and lick Nathan's cock, savoring the drop of salty-slick precome beading at the tip.

Nathan's breath hitched, and his legs tensed beneath Sam as he kept his urge to thrust at bay. Sam hoped the bruises from his injuries had started to fade. He hadn't looked in the mirror after the first day. He grabbed the condom. "All right?"

"Fuck, yes."

Sam smiled and then scooted up for better aim. The first push burned in a satisfying, not-quite-painful way. Sam paused with half of Nathan's cock inside him, waiting for the stretch to abate before he sank down. Impaled on Nathan for the first time, he took a moment to appreciate the beauty of the man on his bed. The hollows under his eyes told tales of sleepless nights, but his cheeks were flushed, and his eyes glowed like coal candles. He gripped Sam's thighs and thrust up to seat himself even deeper, and Sam bit his lip as the last inch entered him, sealing them together.

Nathan seemed to be having a difficult time staying still. Sam could sympathize. Nothing quite like the first moment of being inside someone, holding back the urge to plunge deep, again and again. He rocked his hips, and Nathan squeezed his ass in encouragement.

"You feel good," Nathan said, starting to move. The anxiety of the past few months dissipated like fog burned off in the morning sun when Sam looked at Nathan's face. Tenderness and sleepy desire softened his patrician features, but intensity simmered there too. Sam wondered how he could coax it out.

With one hand Nathan pulled Sam down for a kiss and with the other he guided his hips as they built a steady, slow rhythm with their tongues and the rest of their bodies. In spite of the coolness of his apartment, Sam started to sweat, but his muscles rejoiced at the exertion after so many days of rest. He broke off the kiss and leaned back, bracing himself with one arm between Nathan's powerful splayed thighs as Nathan started to drive up into him with more force. Nathan groaned underneath him.

"Yeah. Like that." Nathan pulled him harder onto his cock with each thrust. It felt so good to be filled, that empty part of him. The air crackled with the sounds of their lovemaking, the slap of skin, the mingling noises of pleasure.

Sam wondered if it had ever been like this for Nathan with another man. He imagined having Nathan in his bed on a regular basis. Would he be careful and protective, or would he give into the darker side of his nature Sam had glimpsed only a few times? Both?

Would it become more than sex for Nathan, as it had become more than sex for him?

Sam quickly pushed the thought from his mind. He didn't want to remember and he didn't want to think about the future. He was tired of thinking. Tired of fending for himself, and tired of being strong for his brother. He was tired.

"Hold my wrists, Nathan." They didn't hurt anymore.

"What—"

"I want you to."

Nathan grabbed Sam's hands instead, held them firmly in his grip, and laced their fingers together. He started fucking harder, slamming his hips up and shattering the silence of the room with a quiet moan. Sam couldn't touch himself, and his erection ached in protest, but that only made it hotter. Every feeling intensified—the cock plowing him, the tight grip of Nathan's fingers, the smell and heat of sex. He still wanted more. He wanted to be under Nathan's control, tied up, unable to move. He wanted to feel the thick cock taking him over.

"Fuck me harder," he panted, leaning back in surrender. Nathan gathered him in his arms and kissed his sweaty neck. Sam moaned when Nathan's teeth grazed his Adam's apple. "Harder," he whispered.

Nathan surged up, repositioning them so that Sam was on all fours, then slid back home with one long thrust. It was even better from the new angle. Sam shuddered and let his upper body collapse against the bed. Nathan started fucking him slow and deep, punctuating each thrust with a sexy grunt. Sam closed his eyes and started to float, grounded only by the thick anchor of Nathan's cock. Waves of pleasure rolled over him as his body loosened, letting Nathan even farther inside.

"You have no idea how hot you look with my cock inside you." A finger circled his stretched rim.

"God—"

"Do you like it?"

"Yes. Fuck, yes."

"You want me to touch you?"

Sam whimpered.

Nathan slid deep and held himself there, squeezing Sam's ass. "You think you deserve to come after how you made me worry?"

"Maybe?"

"That's not an acceptable answer." Nathan still didn't move. He pulled Sam back more firmly onto his dick and pressed hot kisses along his spine. Sam wanted to beg, but he couldn't.

"I can wait," Nathan said.

Sam tried to move his hips, but Nathan still held him firmly. "I… need to come."

"But do you deserve it?"

"N-no. But I could. I'll be so good. I promise," Sam panted.

"Ask me nicely, then, and maybe I'll let you come. Say please." Nathan's finger teased Sam's stretched rim again, and the sensation made Sam's toes curl. "I can't hear you."

Something in Sam, the damaged, hardened part that never asked for things from people, said no. Another part of him, new and more fragile, wanted to give in.

"Please. Please. Please," Sam said, louder and louder as Nathan started to fuck him again.

"Good boy." Nathan kissed the back of his neck, and then he started jerking Sam's dick in time with his thrusts. By then, Sam was so close it didn't take more than a few strokes. He shot his load as Nathan continued to fuck him, slamming his hips once, twice more, and then losing rhythm, pulsing deep inside of Sam.

They both collapsed, exhausted. Sam's eyes filled with tears. He blinked them away, not wanting Nathan to see and misinterpret. Nathan held him while their breathing returned to normal.

After some time, the bed shifted as Nathan got up to dispose of the condom. When he returned, he looked troubled. "Why did you ask me to hold your wrists?"

"I dunno." Sam looked at his bandages, which were probably unnecessary by then. "It seemed like fun?"

"Is it because you thought I would like it? Because of what I told you about the club?"

Sam shrugged.

"I'm not a sadist. I don't get off on hurting people."

"I know you don't."

"Do you?"

Still, Nathan hadn't ever been specific about what exactly had gotten him off, had he? Sam knew he was into teasing and control. Maybe from there, he'd jumped to certain conclusions. "I wanted it, okay? I wanted it, because the thought of you being in control turns me on." Sam's face flamed at the confession. "I didn't even think about my wrists being hurt, honestly. You say you're not a sadist. Well, I'm not a masochist. Much." But obviously what Sam had taken as a moment of play, Nathan had read differently. Sam would have to be more aware of what he asked for in the future. He ran his hand down Nathan's chest. "I should have realized, though. I'm sorry."

"It's okay," Nathan said finally, in an unconvincing way.

Sam turned away to search for his boxers.

"I think we need to talk, Sam."

"Do we? It seems like all we do is talk."

"I mean about us."

The rawness in Nathan's voice opened up a pit of nerves in Sam's stomach. He wasn't sure he liked where this was headed.

"I have to leave on a new case in a few days."

Yep. He definitely didn't like where this was headed. "How long will you be gone?"

"Not sure. Could be a month or two, maybe more."

"Ah." A frog lodged in Sam's throat. "What about the trial?"

"They're not going to need my live testimony."

Sam swallowed. The frog got bigger. "All right. Well, have a nice trip." He mustered a smile but couldn't quite meet Nathan's eyes. He'd known all along this wouldn't last. His mental walls, lost during the sex, started to reassemble themselves to prevent any more damage. They'd need to be even taller this time.

"Say something," Nathan said.

"What do you want me to say? That you can't go? It's your job. Whatever this is," he gestured between them. "It was temporary. And maybe it shouldn't have happened in the first place."

"I'd be gone already if I thought you believed that was true." Nathan touched Sam's shoulder.

"What are you getting at?" Sam wanted to pull away, but he couldn't resist the comforting pressure of Nathan's hand. Over the last few days, it had become something precious.

"These past months have been the hardest of my life. I don't think I would have gotten through them if not for you." Ah, so he was grateful and he felt obliged. Perfect.

"Listen, you don't owe me anything—" He started to shrug Nathan off.

"I do, but that's not what this is about. I have feelings for you, Sam, but I need time to figure out what that means. I still—Part of me still loves Emma. I'm not over it, and how fair is that to you?"

"I'm not trying to substitute for your wife." But when he thought back over the past few days, all of Nathan's solicitousness—how much of it had been for Sam and how much of it for the wife Nathan had wronged and lost?

"I know. But these feelings…. How well do we really know each other? We were thrown together under extraordinary circumstances. The worst thing we could do would be to plunge right into something without sorting ourselves out first. That is, if you feel something for me."

Nathan looked suddenly vulnerable, naked, and in need of care. Sam wished he could be the one to draw him out of his darkness. But he also knew he couldn't. "I do have feelings for you, but you're right, we don't know each other well."

"You're not angry?"

Sam shook his head. "I had no idea you were allergic to strawberries. God, we could be back at the hospital right now." They both laughed, appreciating the momentary release of tension. It didn't last long.

"So, what I'm proposing is a short hiatus, while I'm away. No strings attached, no expectations." Nathan reached out and gently touched Sam's face, under his swollen eye. Always assessing for damage.

Sam understood what that meant. He would be free, and so would Nathan. Free to do whatever—or whomever—they wanted. While part of him hated the idea, he knew why it had to be that way. He nodded. "Okay." He kissed Nathan again, slowly.

"When I come back, I'll give you a call."

"Fuck you. When you get back, I'll return the favor."

"Is that a promise?" Nathan's eyes glittered.

"Yes."

"I have a feeling I'm going to miss you."

Sam swallowed the lump in his throat. "I'm going to miss you too."

Chapter 19

SAM STARED at Lisa. She grinned back—an ear-to-ear smile. Her nurse's scrubs were covered with bipedal orange and black cats wearing top hats, and for a moment Sam wondered if he was dreaming.

"What do you mean, the bill has been paid?" Sam asked.

"I mean your brother is all set. His hospital bill has been paid indefinitely. He'll stay here at Shady Brook for as long as you want him here."

It was the week after New Year's. Sam had taken the day off to make sure he'd be there when they moved Tim from Shady Brook to the state facility. But now Lisa said the transfer had been canceled.

"I don't understand."

"Sometimes there's nothing to understand." Lisa patted one of his hands. "Sometimes, it's best just to accept kindness."

"But whose?" Lord knew his grandparents would have already paid if they could afford it. Yuri and Rachel got by, but they didn't make any more money than Sam. And he'd certainly heard enough from the insurance company not to be under any illusion that they'd forgiven the debt.

Lisa's smile spoke volumes. "I'm sorry, sweetie, but I'm not able to disclose that information. Confidentiality reasons."

That left no doubt. Only one other person fit the bill, possessing both the money and the cause. Nathan had left town two weeks before. They hadn't communicated since then, and they didn't plan on it until his return, whenever that would be—a month, two months, even three or four. He'd never given the slightest hint he might have been planning something so ridiculous… and incredibly generous.

Sam didn't know what to say. "It was Nathan Walker, wasn't it?"

She shrugged. "I don't know."

"Oh you. You're in on it."

"A lady never tells."

Sam could have kissed her. He definitely would have kissed Nathan. Even though he knew he shouldn't accept the gift and risk being forever indebted, he couldn't refuse it.

"Why don't you go down and tell Tim the good news?"

The staff had decorated Tim's room for the holidays. A wreath with fake shellacked apples and pinecones hung on the door. Inside, a tiny plastic tree covered with miniature lights graced the table that separated Tim's bed from Helen's… or what had been Helen's, but now waited vacantly for a new patient.

The week before, Helen had woken up.

Sam hadn't been there, but two days later when he came to see Tim, Helen's family had been packing up her things. At first, Sam had feared the worst, but her son had quickly explained what had happened. His mother had moved her right arm, and then made a sound that sounded like his name. Paul.

Now they'd transferred her to another wing of the clinic to start intensive therapy, hoping to stabilize her enough to bring her home within the month. There was a long road to recovery ahead, but Paul was confident his mother would pull through.

Sam had promised to come by and say "hi," but he hadn't gotten up the nerve yet. Maybe soon. Anyway he was happy for Paul and his family, though he wondered how long it would take Tim to get a new roommate and whether he'd be lonely in the meantime.

"Looks like you're staying put after all, bud," Sam said as he sat down. The lights on the tree twinkled. For six years they blinked at him. Six years. "I think Nathan paid your bill. I can't believe it."

Tim stared at the ceiling, but Sam imagined him smiling. His blue, blue eyes seemed clear and trouble-free.

Blue as the sky.

LATER IN the day, Sam met up with his friends at the Star. Yuri and Michael had become one entity. They practically clung to each other like little gay koalas on one side of the table, leaving the other side to Alex and Sam. Rachel was finishing her shift at the bar.

"Muriel is definitely your couple name." Sam crossed his arms and leaned back in his chair, pleased.

"Muriel?" Yuri wrinkled his nose.

"It suits you. And it's a real name. I'm a genius."

Alex nodded in agreement. "It's so cute."

"Thanks for backing me up, Alex," Sam said.

"So what are we, then?" Rachel asked as she joined them at the table and slung her arm around her girlfriend.

Sam gave a thoughtful hum. "Unfortunately for you, Ralex is the only thing that makes any sense."

"Sounds like a planet on *Star Trek*," Michael added. This apparently was not a bad thing. It had recently been brought to the group's attention that Michael was a huge Trekkie—mainly because he said nerdy things about *Star Trek* all the time.

"What about you and Nathan?" Yuri raised his eyebrows. "You're so intent on giving us all stupid couple names."

"There is no me and Nathan."

"That's not what it seems like to me." Rachel punched his arm. "He paid Tim's hospital bills. I mean, who even does that?"

"I think it's romantic," Alex added.

Yuri smiled wryly. "Sneaky and maybe a little weird, but romantic."

The topic of conversation quickly shifted to the night's plans. Sam listened as his friends tried to agree on a movie, a subject that inspired a lot of strong feelings from resident amateur film critics Rachel and Michael.

He sipped his soda and eyed the rest of their beers enviously. Recently, Sam had made a pact with himself to cut out drinking and maybe do some serious writing on his blog again. A New Year's resolution, though Sam didn't believe in those. If, when Nathan came back, they decided to start something, Sam wanted to be in a better place than he'd been. That was all. He took it one day at a time. And he tried not to miss Nathan too much.

It didn't work.

The trial had sped forward and was due to begin the following month. At first, it had seemed like Sheldon might reach a plea bargain and agree to sentencing, but his lawyers must have advised him otherwise. Already a story had begun to take shape in Sam's mind, a story of greed and loss and justice—maybe. With such compelling evidence, Sam couldn't imagine any jury letting Hoff or Sheldon off the hook, but it wouldn't be over until it was over.

Sam had tried to talk to Sheldon the previous week but had been turned away. He'd left the county jail—where Sheldon was being held without bail until the trial started—feeling a mixture of anger, disappointment, and relief.

He might never get the chance to ask Sheldon why he'd chosen money over honor and friendship. But maybe that was okay. Because sometimes greed was just greed, and evil was just evil, and no reason or rationalization could bring back the dead.

"Okay, Sam." Michael's voice interrupted Sam's thoughts. "It's between *Gravity* in 3-D."

Rachel cheered dramatically. She thought Sandra Bullock was hot. "I need to see it before it leaves the theater. Come on, Sam. You're my man."

Michael cleared his throat and continued. "Or, we can go back to my very cozy, comfortable house and watch *Star Trek Into Darkness*. Zachary Quinto and Chris Pine wearing skintight wetsuits, 'nuff said."

Rachel and Alex both made vomiting sounds.

Sam stared at the faces around the table. He was the fifth wheel, as always, and thus the deciding vote. The last thing he wanted was to spend a Saturday night cuddling on the couch with two couples, though. "Sorry, Mike. I'm going to have to go with *Gravity*." An eruption of victorious cheers to his left and heavy sighs and forlorn gazes from across the table. Sam smiled. His friends had been doing a good job of distracting him these past couple of weeks.

He was one lucky bastard.

THE SPRING thaw came later than usual to Stonebridge. March had been a cold and snowy month, but the first week of April warmed the air enough to make any future accumulation unlikely. In spite of the mud and rain, Sam didn't mind this time of year. Work started picking up again, and it was nice to be outside without freezing his ass off.

But this year, he had another reason to anticipate spring.

Sam had heard from Nathan in late February, just a brief e-mail to say that the case was taking much longer than he'd anticipated, and he didn't expect to be back for another month or two.

He'd also said he missed Sam.

Sam e-mailed him back—saying the same and asking about Shady Brook. Nathan hadn't responded. He didn't know what that meant, but figured Nathan wanted to play coy about it. Not mysterious, Sam's ass.

A new family finally bought the Walker house. When they moved in, they asked Manella's if they'd continue landscaping. Sam had to tell them no. It was too strange—too many memories, good and bad. He thanked them and gave them one of their competitors' numbers. He hoped the new family would have better luck in the house than Nathan and Emma had.

On a Sunday morning in late April, Sam rolled out of bed and hit the shower. Then he booted up his computer and sat down at his desk. As a witness for the prosecution, Sam had been advised not to talk about the trial until the verdict came in, and he hadn't. For months, he'd been posting once a week on the social and political issues that always interested him. *Under the Bridge*'s follower count had increased slowly but steadily, as had the responses to his posts, and he had tried to make a point to reply to his readers individually. He'd even gained some new fans. One in particular, Sidney, had written thoughtful responses to every one of Sam's posts. Yuri never failed to tease him about his new Internet friends whenever he got the chance.

The verdict had condemned Sheldon and Hoff to life, and Sam felt he should write something about his own experience of the trial. Other accomplices, including McCormick, had received lesser sentences. Big forthcoming changes in the police department—including a new chief—

meant things were looking up for Stonebridge, but that didn't mean the wounds would heal overnight. Though the trial had taken down one of the members of the Voronkov family, the mob would find another way to get drugs into the city, and people in positions of power would continue to be vulnerable to extortion and greed.

The blank page stared back at him. He always found it hard to begin a post, but this would be the most difficult entry of all. It seemed almost impossible to sum up all that had happened in the past year. It occurred to Sam he shouldn't even try. Maybe people weren't looking for all the answers tied up in a neat little bow, as the *Gazette* had tried to do with its headline announcing the "End of Corruption." Of course, he didn't want to go the opposite route either and forecast nothing but doom and gloom for the city that he loved, despite everything.

He sighed, ran his hand through his hair, and scrolled back through some of the conversations he'd had with Sidney.

S Flynn: So, do you think they got everyone involved? Or is there still some rottenness at the core of the Stonebridge PD?

Sidney: You can never be sure. I think what you're trying to do is important, and I hope it rubs off on your readers. Apathy is what got us here in the first place.

S Flynn: I couldn't agree more.

Sidney: I'm glad we agree. :)

Sam smiled. Rereading the exchange made him wonder if Sidney was flirting with him. The emoticon seemed to suggest it. He immediately felt guilty for the thought, but every passing day made his brief time with Nathan seem more and more like a dream. Since Nathan had left town, Sam had gotten reacquainted with the toys in his drawer. He needed some real sex, and soon.

Was he actually waiting for the guy?

He wondered if Nathan had moved on and was too afraid to tell him. After all, they'd agreed no strings. No guarantees.

He closed his browser window.

SAM STARED at the wall of liquor and beer in front of him. His mouth watered and his fingers itched. It wouldn't be so bad, would it, to buy one bottle? He could ration the contents and have only one drink a day.

His heart started to pound. Just one.

A nice bottle of Jack Daniel's would do the trick. As Sam reached to grab it, his phone buzzed in his back pocket. Hand shaking, he fished it out and brought it to his ear, turning away from the booze.

"Sam?"

Nathan's voice shot through Sam's body like an arrow. Trembling from surprise, he started to make his way toward the door, empty-handed.

"Nathan?"

"Hi, yeah. It's me. I got back into town yesterday."

"I'm glad you called. You stopped me from doing something stupid."

"What's wrong?" The immediate concern in Nathan's voice made Sam's eyes burn. He rubbed them with his fist and let the cool spring evening turn his steps toward home.

"Nothing. And everything. I... it's good to hear your voice." He didn't even care if the confession made him vulnerable. He needed Nathan to know.

"It's good to hear yours. How have you been?"

"I've been pretty okay. You said you're back, but where?"

"I'm at my new place. Fifty-five Lexington."

The news brought Sam up short. The location was only about a half mile from Sam's apartment, in a slightly nicer neighborhood. "Oh, cool."

"I thought you might like to come over and see it, if you weren't busy. So we can catch up. You know, whenever you're free."

"I'm free right now."

Sam hung up the phone and cut through the park in front of the Anglican church, lengthening his stride. He passed a couple of mothers playing with their kids on the swings, and a dog sniffing at an overturned trashcan. In the distance, a police siren squealed its alarm, and the air filled with the smell of spring-blossoming trees. Sam kicked an empty soda can out of his path and resisted the urge to yell like a crazy person. The blood pounded through his veins. He imagined this was what it would feel like to awaken after months of sleep.

Somehow Sam had expected Nathan to choose a fancy place, but this block wasn't much different from his own, save the smoothly paved road and newer sidewalk. The old turn-of-the-century brick façade of number fifty-five needed refurbishment, but the inside lobby looked spacious and clean. Sam pressed the button next to Nathan's name and unlatched the buzzing door. His palms were sweaty by the time he made it to the fifth floor, though Nathan's building, unlike his, had a working elevator.

Nathan was standing in the hallway when the doors opened. A hesitant, almost shy smile spread across his face when he saw Sam. "Hi."

"Hi." Sam let his eyes linger over the tight tee that showed off muscles he remembered clenching under his fingers as they fucked. Nathan's hair was shorter than Sam remembered, and a bit of scruff on his square jaw completed the picture to make one fine specimen.

They stood awkwardly in the hallway for another second before Nathan strode forward and kissed Sam, his mouth hungry and searching. Sam wrapped his arms around Nathan and held on, kissing back with the force of months of sexual frustration. His dick didn't care about talking or sorting out emotions, not at all.

"God, look at you," Nathan said when they pulled apart. "You look amazing." He ran his hands up and down Sam's arms.

"I've been doing some weights with Yuri." Sam flushed. He hadn't been scrawny before, but he'd put on more muscle. Not partying every night definitely helped.

Nathan squeezed his shoulders. "So, this is what I've been missing all these months."

"How was the case?"

"Tiring. But good. It went well, actually."

"You probably can't tell me anything about it." Sam had spent a lot of time tossing and turning at night, but he wasn't sure he wanted to know the details after all.

Nathan must have heard the reticence in his voice. "I can. But I'd rather look at you."

"Maybe inside?" Sam was waiting for one of Nathan's neighbors to catch them in the hallway.

Nathan nodded. His apartment was medium sized for the area, and Sam noticed a few fixtures from the old house. Most of the furniture was new and smaller, to accommodate the tighter space. But it did retain a certain "Nathan" aesthetic—dark and masculine, tasteful. He smiled when he noticed Nathan had kept the large flat screen after all. In deference to him? Nathan watched him with a thoughtful expression on his face. "You like it?"

"It's great." Sam shrugged out of his denim jacket.

"Can I get you something? A drink?"

Again that wanting, hollow feeling. Sam closed his eyes and shook his head. "No. I'm actually on the wagon. That's where I was when you called. At the liquor store." When Nathan saw how damaged Sam still was, he wouldn't want to rekindle anything. But he had to know the truth.

But instead of the uncomfortable silence Sam expected, Nathan pulled him into a tight hug. "Do you want to talk about it?"

"Yeah, but not right now. I'd rather look at you," Sam answered, echoing Nathan's words. He stepped back and got an impressive eyeful. A hint of black poked out from the sleeve of Nathan's tee. Sam pulled at it to unveil a tattooed string of ragged orchids. They twisted in deformed pain up Nathan's shoulder, until the last and most fragile burst from the chaos, delicate and perfect. "This is new."

"Yeah, I got it a couple of months ago. What do you think?"

Sam swallowed and traced his finger over the black lines that decorated Nathan's warm skin. "I think it says a lot."

"I needed to do something. It's still hard."

"I know." And Sam did. Probably more than anyone. "Did you pay Tim's bill?"

"If I admit it, will you let it be?"

"I promise I'll pay you back if it's the last thing I do."

Nathan frowned. "That's absolutely out of the question. You can leave right now if you want to, never see me again, and the order still stands."

"But—"

"I didn't do it for you, Sam. I did it for your brother."

How could Sam argue with that? He nodded and curled his fingers around the back of Nathan's neck, urging his head down. The kiss lingered and built heat until both of them wanted more and their erections strained through layers of denim.

"So this is happening, then?" Sam asked as Nathan pulled up his shirt and bent down, pressing kisses against his abdomen, sucking his nipple into a peak.

"This is happening." More kisses, more items of clothing shed. Somehow they managed to make it into the bedroom and onto the bed without taking their hands off each other. Every touch fanned the flames.

"Aren't you going to ask me about what's been going on around here?" Sam asked through a gasp.

"I've been keeping up. Let's say I have a very knowledgeable source." Nathan knelt between his legs, eyes appreciatively scanning Sam's erection. He looked like he might want to.... Oh God, yes. Sam's back arched off the bed as Nathan took him into his mouth.

The thought hit Sam through the haze of his lust. He almost laughed at himself for not realizing it before.

"Wait a minute." He ran his fingers through Nathan's short hair. "*Sidney*? What the—"

A grin, and then Nathan resumed his task, slurping up Sam's shaft and licking around the head. All of these months, Sam had thought Nathan was incommunicado, but they'd been talking to each other almost every day. And Sidney really was a hot dude. Huh.

"Not mysterious—ah—my ass."

Nathan held Sam's cock at the base and kissed the slit. Sam thought he might explode, and it hadn't even been more than a minute. He'd fallen out of practice, and he both did and didn't want to know if the same was true for Nathan.

Then again Nathan was here with him. Did any of that matter?

"So, you *are* Sidney, right?"

Nathan smiled, giving the impression of a large, predatory cat. "Guilty as charged."

"But why *Sidney*?"

"It's my middle name. Horrible, isn't it?" Nathan tapped Sam's erection against his lips.

"You prick. Why didn't you tell me?"

"Because it was my idea to put some space between us, and I guess I found it harder than I expected." His expression grew serious. He slid up from his kneeling position to lie next to Sam. "I missed you."

"I missed you too." So much. But Sam couldn't say those words, not yet. "You must not have been too lonely, though. Working." He winced at his obviousness.

Nathan didn't miss a beat. He touched Sam's face. "It was a sweatshop case. I'm sorry. I should have told you. You must have been—"

Relief made Sam lightheaded. He laughed and cut Nathan off with a kiss. "It's just, before you left, you said no strings."

"I didn't want you to feel an obligation to me. But let me assure you, the only thing I've been fucking the last few months is my hand, thinking of you."

Unable to hold back his grin at those words, Sam kissed Nathan again, this time with tongue. When they finally broke apart, both of them panting, Nathan rolled them over so he was on top. "So, it looks like maybe we both want to start something. See where it goes?"

"If you can deal with a grumpy, stubborn orphan who likes to drink too much, sure."

"As long as you can deal with a so-called 'mysterious' widower who wants to do unspeakable things to you."

Sam's cock throbbed against Nathan's thigh. "I don't think that's going to be a problem."

"Good."

"Strap in, baby," Sam joked. "It's gonna be a hell of a ride."

And Sam was very, very excited to get on.

MAGGIE KAVANAGH works full time and steals moments to write; you can find her in the wee morning hours typing away on her laptop with a steaming cup of coffee in her living room. Her passions include travelling, eating great food, and writing stories about flawed, human characters finding love. She lives in California.

Contact details:
Twitter: @maggie_kavanagh
Facebook: https://www.facebook.com/maggie.kavanagh.33

Taking Flight

By Maggie Kavanagh

When Hunter decides he wants more from his relationship with Jake, the couple finds themselves at a crossroads. Never home for more than a few weeks at a time, Jake has been running from the pain of a rocky childhood ever since high school, when he first enlisted in the army. The thing is, he always comes back to Hunter's bed. It's not the kind of commitment Hunter wants, but it's the kind he's settled for—that and a dead-end job at the local bookstore in the small Southern town where he grew up. When Jake reveals his plans to make a full-time career in the army, Hunter wonders if he's putting his life on hold for a relationship that will never happen. He needs to say something now before he loses Jake. However, if Jake can't conquer his demons, Hunter's asking for more is sure to drive him away.

http://www.dreamspinnerpress.com

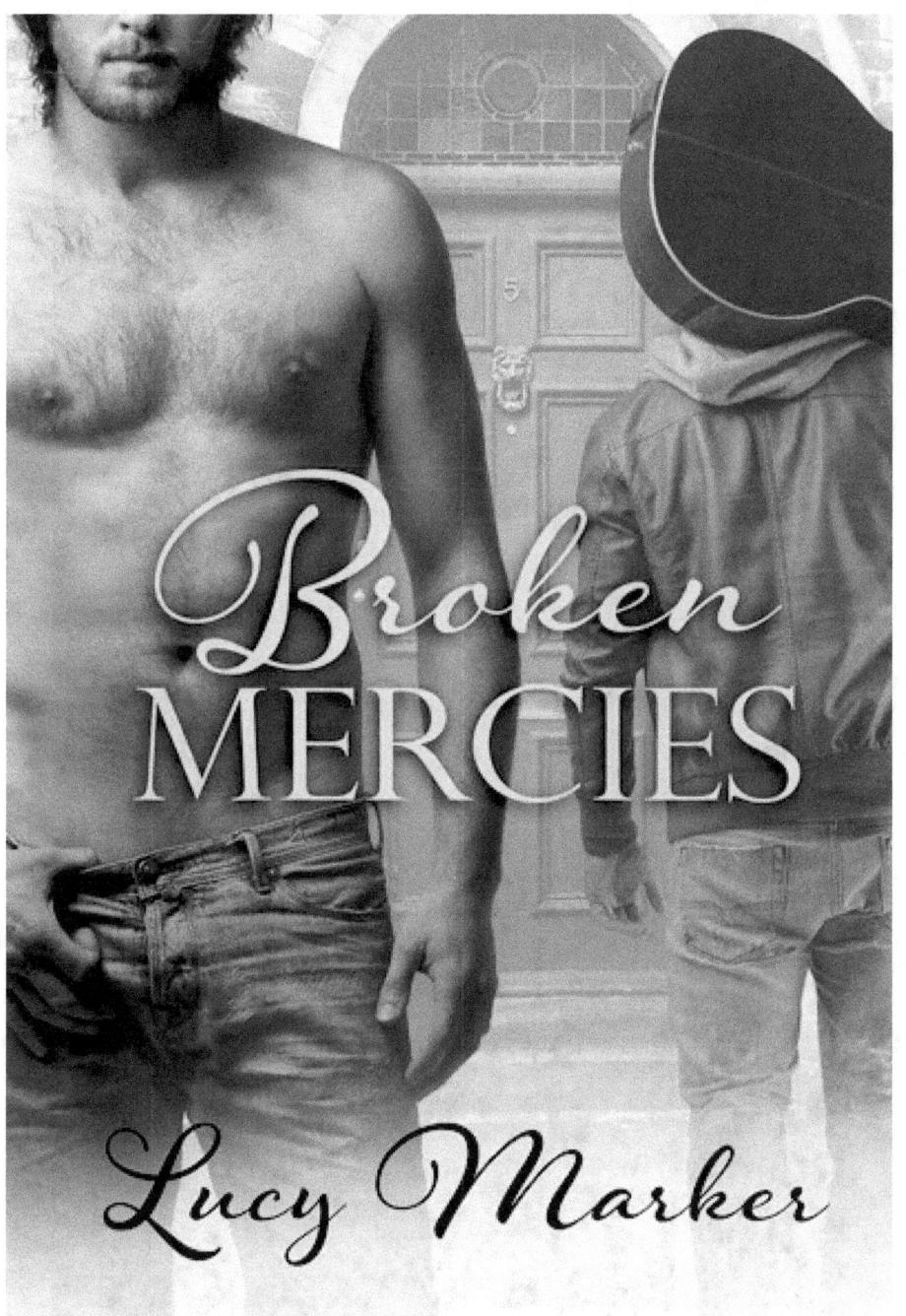

Broken
MERCIES

Lucy Marker

http://www.dreamspinnerpress.com

www.ingramcontent.com/pod-product-compliance
Lightning Source LLC
Chambersburg PA
CBHW070119260626
47160CB00004B/1539